SO-BYJ-867

– ROAD TO –
PARADISE

**Also by Max Allan Collins
in Large Print:**

The War of the Worlds Murder
Daylight
Majic Man
Chicago Confidential
Road to Purgatory

with Barbara Collins:

Bombshell

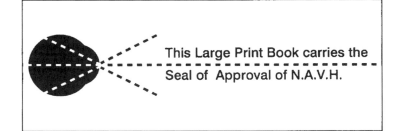

This Large Print Book carries the
Seal of Approval of N.A.V.H.

47.6.11

TT7812

– ROAD TO –

PARADISE

MAX ALLAN
COLLINS

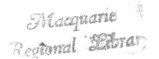
Macquarie
Regional Library

Thorndike Press • Waterville, Maine

Copyright © 2005 by Max Allan Collins.

All rights reserved.

This book is a work of fiction. References to real people, events, establishments, organizations, or locales are intended only to provide a sense of authenticity, and are used fictitiously. All other characters, and all incidents and dialogue, are drawn from the author's imagination and are not to be construed as real.

Published in 2006 by arrangement with William Morrow, an imprint of HarperCollins Publishers.

Thorndike Press® Large Print Mystery.

The tree indicium is a trademark of Thorndike Press.

The text of this Large Print edition is unabridged. Other aspects of the book may vary from the original edition.

Set in 16 pt. Plantin.

Printed in the United States on permanent paper.

Library of Congress Cataloging-in-Publication Data

Collins, Max Allan.
    Road to paradise / by Max Allan Collins.
      p. cm. — (Thorndike Press large print mystery)
    ISBN 0-7862-8320-3 (lg. print : hc : alk. paper)
    1. Mafia — Fiction. 2. Arizona — Fiction.
  3. Chicago (Ill.) — Fiction. 4. Witnesses — Protection — Fiction. 5. Murder victims' families — Fiction.
  6. Criminals — Crimes against — Fiction. 7. Large type books. I. Title. II. Series: Thorndike Press large print mystery series.
  PS3553.O4753R628 2006
  813'.54—dc22   2005031422

FOR

RICHARD PIERS RAYNER —

whose pictures
paved the road

National Association for Visually Handicapped
-------------------------- *serving the partially seeing*

As the Founder/CEO of NAVH, the only national health agency solely devoted to those who, although not totally blind, have an eye disease which could lead to serious visual impairment, I am pleased to recognize Thorndike Press* as one of the leading publishers in the large print field.

Founded in 1954 in San Francisco to prepare large print textbooks for partially seeing children, NAVH became the pioneer and standard setting agency in the preparation of large type.

Today, those publishers who meet our standards carry the prestigious "Seal of Approval" indicating high quality large print. We are delighted that Thorndike Press is one of the publishers whose titles meet these standards. We are also pleased to recognize the significant contribution Thorndike Press is making in this important and growing field.

Lorraine H. Marchi, L.H.D.
Founder/CEO
NAVH

* Thorndike Press encompasses the following imprints: Thorndike, Wheeler, Walker and Large Print Press.

You're born,
you're gonna have trouble,
you're gonna die.

— W. R. BURNETT,
on what we know about life

Seven out of ten times,
when we hit a guy,
we're wrong —
but the other three guys we hit,
we make up for it.

— SAM GIANCANA

The river flows into the ocean,
and turns into waves,
surging and receding,
without end.
Our lives are like the waves.
We live, we die, we are reborn.

— KAZUO KOIKE

PROLOGUE

A FAMILY MAN

April 1973

At nine-forty-five on a bright and beautiful Saturday morning, Sam DeStefano had less than half an hour before meeting his violent death.

In his tan brick ranch-style house in a suburban upper-middle-class enclave of Oak Park, Illinois, this harmless-looking grandfatherly individual of sixty-four — slim, five feet eleven, wearing large black-rimmed glasses — had no foreshadowing of his imminent demise.

In fact, he was involved in some mundane spring cleaning in his garage, at the behest of his wife, Anita (who was spending the morning with her mother), straightening and sorting and, at the moment, using a new stiff broom to break up and sweep out the caked mud dragged in by their two vehicles over the winter.

His hair a gray, unruly mass, Sam certainly appeared innocuous enough, though his features — close-set eyes, lump of a nose and lipless slash of mouth centered in a cleft-chin oval — were suggestive of a man who might have been formidable in his day. The only thing vaguely eccentric was his dark-blue silk pajamas; he also wore beat-up Hush Puppy shoes, and a lighter blue windbreaker with VILLA VENICE in white script on its back, advertising a nightclub that had been closed for better than a decade.

Like many American males, he had a small workbench and a wall of tools on pegboard; and a gas lawn mower and empty boxes and shelves here and there holding the various small dead kitchen appliances and other obsolete household articles that are typically consigned to the periphery of a garage.

The cement floor took some considerable sweeping, dirt and fragments of cardboard and paper and other detritus catching and sliding on a pair of small automotive oil spills. DeStefano swept with patience and deliberation, creating a modest but growing pile beyond the open garage door out onto the driveway.

His wife had one of their two Cadillac Coupe de Villes — her pink '73 with the white vinyl roof — while his black Caddy (last year's model), he'd loaned to his nephew Little Sam for a hot date Friday night. Little Sam, whose real name was

Antonio (his late brother Angelo's boy), was twenty-two and just starting out in life, and his own wheels were pathetic — a little gray Rambler. Even if you could maneuver some broad into the backseat of an embarrassment like that, what would you do for room?

Right now the Rambler was parked out front of the corner house. Soon Little Sam would be able to afford his own better ride — now that his uncle had put him out on the street as a collector.

Sam surveyed the clean cement floor, pleased with himself, then moved to the workbench and leaned way down, to work the broom under there and get at the hidden grime. Quite a bit of filth emerged, which was a little surprising, since Sam had no particular interest in do-it-yourselfing, and this workbench was seldom used.

On the other hand, in the soundproofed room in the basement of the ranch-style, could be found Sam's *real* workshop. On one wall was a wooden cabinet in which Sam's tools were stored, various exotic instruments of torture, including such oldies but goodies as thumb-screws, blow torches and butcher knives, as well as assorted hammers and mallets, and Sam's specialty, an array of ice picks of various lengths and thicknesses, all honed to razor sharpness. Oh, and razors. . . .

A counter on the opposite wall had a vice, of a perfect size for squeezing the human skull, and in the center of the glorified cubicle, a wooden chair with straps for head, arms and feet — not unlike an electric chair — was bolted to the floor. Not much larger than a fruit cellar, the room could only accommodate one guest at a time, plus up to three interrogators, in comfort. For the interrogators, anyway.

Men had talked, been punished, even died, in the basement workshop. The recording studio-style soundproofing meant that neither his family and certainly not the neighbors had ever been aware of the operas of agony sung in this small chamber.

Of course, within his own circles, Sam made no secret out of his delight in applying suffering to those who deserved it. Not that he was a sadist, far from it — he just believed in discipline (in others). Nobody who ever sat in that chair hadn't put his own goddamn ass down there by his own goddamn doing.

Since the early '60s, Sam DeStefano had been a major player in the Chicago mob. Strangely, he was not officially a member of the Outfit, had never become a "made" man, though certainly not out of an unwillingness to kill for the Mafia (he had); Sam just didn't like taking orders, preferred being an independent. They'd offered him literally trunks of money to come aboard, but he'd told them he didn't have any interest in their little Howdy Doody clubhouse games with the blood oath and all that silly ceremonial horseshit.

"You wanna bring your toughest so-called killer around here," Sam had told Tony Accardo, the man holding the top chair for Paul Ricca (in stir at the time, on that movie-union rap), "I'll go toe to toe, head to head, belly to belly, gun to gun with the cocksucker. Bring him around!"

Decades later, the challenge remained unmet.

Accardo and Ricca respected Sam, who had single-handedly turned loansharking from a smalltime fringe operation into an organized business from which the Outfit made millions every year. Of all the loan sharks in the city, Sam DeStefano was the only one allowed by the Outfit to work anywhere, with only a modest tax; because, after all, any other loan shark in any jurisdiction was just riding on the skids Sam had long ago greased.

They called him "Mad Sam" — not to his face — but that was a designation he treasured, even cultivated. In his business, being feared was key — and you only built fear, which was after all the sincerest form of respect, by doing "crazy" things.

And from day one, back in the '30s, he'd had to show these city boys he had the moxie. He wasn't one of these lowlife slum *goombahs* like Giancana and Alderiso and the other kids in their gang, the 42s. Those toughies had boosted cars when they were in grade school, while Sam was growing up civilized in southern Illinois in a nice middle-class family. The DeStefanos didn't even move to the West Side of Chicago till Sam was in his teens.

He'd had catching up to do. Convictions for rape, assault with a deadly weapon, extortion, bank robbery and (during the war) counterfeiting ration stamps followed in short order, as did various stretches in stir. But all that prison time had its advantages: at Leavenworth he'd hooked up with — and provided muscle for — two incarcerated Chicago big boys, Paul Ricca and Louis Campagna.

The black Caddy pulled in the drive, his nephew behind the wheel. Sam was standing just outside the garage now, adding to the pile of sweepings, and held up a friendly palm for the boy to stop the vehicle at the driveway's mouth. Little Sam hopped out, grinning.

Not that anything about Little Sam *was* little — the boy stood a good six feet . . . a towering size for a DeStefano . . . and had the build of a running back, which he'd been in high school. Sammy's grades hadn't been collegeworthy, though, and anyway the kid had always wanted to go into the family business.

He was a handsome number, looking quite a bit like Dean Martin before the nose bob, with dark curly hair unfortunately kept in that long, almost girlish manner of the day. Little Sam wore a black leather jacket — not the motorcycle kind — and a rust-color sweater, blue jeans and sneakers. Nice, clean-cut kid.

Holding the keys out to his uncle, the boy approached and said, "Thanks, Unk — what a ride!"

Sam reached up and rubbed the kid's head. "You talkin' about the front seat or the back?"

"Both!"

Sam shook a scolding finger. "I better not find any used rubbers down in them seats. . . ."

Little Sam flashed his winning grin. "Who *uses* 'em?"

Sam patted the boy on the cheek, once, a mock slap. "Guys who don't want their wang turnin' black and droppin' off, is who — don't be a *babbo!*"

The kid laughed, and rocked on his heels. He had his hands in his jacket pockets. Something was troubling the boy — his uncle knew this, sensitive in his way.

"What's eating you, Sammy? Work problems?"

Swallowing, his nephew nodded. "You see right through me. . . . Can we talk about it? I could use your counsel, Unk."

"Sure, sure." The older man gestured toward the clean garage. "Step into my office."

Uncle and nephew sat on a couple of stools by the workbench. Sammy leaned on an elbow, looking like a kid with a headache — a kid about to cry.

"Spit it out," Sam said.

The young man shrugged, shook his head; but his eyes wouldn't meet his uncle's. "It's this work. I don't know, Unk. I just don't know."

"Know what?"

"Know if I'm cut out for it." A long sigh came up. "You know, I thought I was

18

tough, but I . . . I was never a bully or anything. In school?"

"I know. You're a good boy. Proud of you. Your Aunt Anita is proud of ya, too."

Little Sam smiled and there was fondness in it. "I know. And that means a lot to me . . . but what I mean is, any fight I was in, I never picked it. I just stood up for myself."

"Didn't take no shit."

"Didn't take no shit, Unk, is right. But this juice collectin' . . . I don't know how to tell ya this, but . . ."

"Aw, kid, you don't feel sorry for these *deadbeats,* do you?"

Hanging his head in shame, the boy nodded. "Kinda. I mean . . . I feel like I'm, I dunno, pickin' on somebody who ain't even my own size."

Sam felt a wave of disappointment wash over him, but he touched the boy's arm and said, "Kid, kid . . . you gotta shake that off. These are sick fucks."

"I know, I know . . ."

"Degenerate gamblers mostly, and burglars and thieves who don't got the sense not to go blow their dough as easy as it come."

The boy swallowed, shaking his head. "Unk, some of these guys are civilians . . . just businessmen, who got their asses over-extended, and now can't go to a bank or a credit union or —"

"Nobody put a gun to 'em and made 'em borrow money from us, son. *Nobody.*"

The boy shivered. "I broke a guy's arm the other day and I just went outside in the alley and puked."

". . . Anybody see you?"

"No. No."

"Good. Good." Sam leaned in, resting an arm on the workbench. He gestured with artistic fingers. "You can't feel nothing for them. That kind of . . . mental toughness, it's all we have to offer."

Little Sammy looked up, his brow tight. "I don't get you, Unk. Mental . . . ?"

"What I mean is, how do we get six bucks back on every five we loan? Fear. They don't fear us, they can rob us blind. Lemme tell you a parable."

The boy blinked. "Like in church?"

"Not exactly." Sam shifted on the stool. "The cops come to a guy, let's say he's me. And they say, Sam, we think you killed them two guys, them burglars that turned up in the trunk of a car on the South Side. And somebody says to the cops, let's say he's me talking, 'Well, don't you know them guys committed suicide?' And the cops, they kinda blink and look like dumb shits, and they say, 'Sam, they was both shot in the back of the head! How do you commit suicide by getting shot in the back of the head?' And somebody says, let's say maybe it's me, I say, 'They committed suicide when they fucked with Sam DeStefano!' . . . Pretty good parable, huh?"

The boy lifted his eyebrows. "Well, I get the moral, all right."

"What, are ya bothered by the sight of blood?"

"No. . . . I just have trouble seeing these people as something other than . . . people."

Nodding, Sam said, "Oh they *are* people — that's to your advantage. If they was just dumb fuckin' animals, some fox that got in your henhouse, there'd be no reasoning with them, right?"

Little Sammy's eyes narrowed. "Is that what I'm doing when I break an arm or a leg? Reasoning with them?"

Sam shrugged. "You're just keeping our end of the bargain, and encouragin' these deadbeats to keep theirs. It's psychology, see."

"How is knocking heads psychology, Unk?"

Suddenly Sam understood why this kid

couldn't get a college scholarship, despite his football stats. "You heard about me and my ice picks?"

Little Sammy grunted a laugh. "Sure. On the street they say you got more ice picks than Picasso's got paint brushes."

"Yeah, well and I paint pictures that make more sense than that modern art crapola. . . . You know what's good about a ice pick? What's good about a ice pick is that it looks nasty as shit." He held up a fist, with an imaginary ice pick in it and they both looked at it. "Really fuckin' wicked. Nobody likes to see a ice pick in the mitt of a guy he owes money to."

"*That* I understand."

"But the beauty is, a ice pick makes little holes. There's all kinds of scary damn places on the body that you can puncture with a ice pick, and leave a poor bastard in a state of utter terror, and . . ." Sam shrugged. ". . . not really do that much damage."

The boy's eyes were narrowing. "Could you teach me?"

"Sure! I can show you exactly where you can stab a borrower in the belly and none the worse for wear. In the ball sack, if you miss the testicles, for example, that'll get their attention — even the throat has safe spots. Man, the throat, they think they *bought* it! And guess what? They don't never miss a payment, after that."

"Such rough stuff, you never had a slip up?"

"Well . . . we did have one guy die on us. I didn't know he had a bad ticker. It was winter, and so we dragged him out and stuffed him down the sewer. But then when spring came, the sewer got blocked up and the sanitation department yanked out the bastard's body, perfectly preserved in a block of ice, like a damn Mastodon. . . . Funniest thing ever!"

While Sam laughed, the boy said, "Never got traced to you?"

"Naw. We had everybody in our pockets. Not that different now."

Little Sammy was slowly shaking his head, admiration glowing in his eyes. "How did you get so good at this, Unk?"

"Brains and practice. Ah, and I got a kinda knack for this."

"For psychology."

"For psychology! You know Patsy Colleta?"

The boy nodded. "He's one of your best men, isn't he?"

"Yeah, juice collectors don't come better. . . . Anyway, *now* they don't, after I made my point with Patsy."

23

Patsy was a big guy, six two and beefy, and just looking at him made most borrowers pay up.

Sam said, "About ten years ago, I found out Patsy was holding back on my collections — skimming from me, if you can imagine. To the tune of maybe fifty grand?"

The kid whistled. "What did you do, Unk?"

"Well, we took him to the basement of your Uncle Mario's restaurant, and we tied him up and kicked and beat the crap outa him."

"No ice picks?"

"Naw. This was just a lesson I had to teach. Anyway, we did this over a period of three days, then I invited his whole family, his wife and kids and a buncha judges and politicians and cops. The wife was worried that Patsy hadn't been around for a while, afraid somethin' bad befell him. So I tell her, he's been doing work for me, and now I'm gonna say thanks by honorin' him with this big dinner."

Little Sammy began to smile; his expression said he knew this was going to be good. . . .

"Anyway," Sam was saying, "last thing we do with Patsy is chain him up to this hot radiator . . . once again, it's the middle of winter, y'know . . . so he starts whining about how it burns. So me and your Uncle Mario and Chuckie and Gallo, we piss all over the guy."

Little Sammy's expression froze.

"Ah, don't be a pussy, kid! He deserved it. So upstairs I join the dinner party and give a speech about Patsy, only it ain't no jolly-good-fellow spiel. It's me saying that Patsy broke my heart by stealing from me, but that I loved him so much, I decided to forgive him. Right then the fellas drag Patsy up and toss him in the middle of the room, naked, burned, dripping with piss."

Sam started laughing and couldn't stop.

The nephew watched with a strained smile.

Shaking a school-teacherly finger, Sam said, "And do you think any of them people ever pulled anything on me again? Patsy is still with me, and he don't snitch a penny since. *See,* kid? Psychology!"

The boy sighed. "I don't know, Uncle Sam. You're stronger than me. Better . . . mental toughness."

He patted the boy's leg. "You'll get there, Little Sam. You'll get there. You remind people of me, otherwise they wouldn't give you that nickname, right?"

"Right. What about this . . . this trial coming up?"

"Just a nuisance. We're workin' on where the safe house is, where they got Chuckie holed up. We'll take care of that little thing."

Sam DeStefano was out on bail, his old partner Chuckie Grimaldi having flipped on him. What a crock! The murder was what, ten years ago? Old fucking news! The ancient stiff in question was that guy Foreman, a real estate broker who'd also been a collector for Sam, and who had been embezzling from Sam (hadn't Foreman heard about Patsy's party?).

When Sam had confronted Foreman (when was it, 1963?), the bozo had said, "Big deal! So maybe I made some arithmetic mistakes."

"Yeah, well add this up," Sam had said. "You think Action Jackson had it tough? You're gonna think we took that fat bastard out on a picnic, when we're through with your crooked ass."

A few weeks later, Foreman died with a smile on his face — happy that it was over.

Now Chuckie, who'd been in on it, had turned government witness, the disloyal fuck.

"Hey," Sam said, walking his nephew

out, a hand on the young man's shoulder, "in the unlikely event it does go to trial, I'll just give 'em a little of the ol' 'Mad Sam' magic."

"What do you mean, Unk?"

"I'm a sick man. I'll go in on a stretcher and do what I did last time — talk to the judge usin' a bullhorn. I'll go off my nut yakkin' about this being America, how we're livin' in a gestapo country, and I got civil rights just like the coons."

"More psychology, Unk?"

Sam laughed. "Oh yeah. If I don't scare 'em away, I'll get off on temporary insanity."

The boy sighed glumly. "Too bad these federal courts are getting into the game."

"Yeah." Sam shook his head. "Goddamn pity. Here I am, biggest fixer in town, can buy anybody outa anything . . . and I'm havin' to deal with this J. fucking Edgar Hoover, who is a fag, incidentally."

"No!"

"Do you know that fed, that big guy — Roemer?"

"Heard of him."

"He tried to turn me state's witness. Me! I played along, a while, had him out to the house maybe half a dozen times. Rolled out the red carpet. He didn't know, every morning before he come around, I was pissing in his coffee."

"What? Unkie, you are outa sight!"

Sam hit his nephew lightly on the arm, saying, "Don't insult me with that hippie shit, you little hippie shit."

"Unk, you're a caution . . ."

Little Sammy was still laughing when he rolled away in the Rambler, waving to his uncle.

The boy would come around; he would.

Walking slowly back toward the garage, Sam smiled to himself, reflecting on how much he loved this boy, and what plans and hopes and dreams he had for his nickname namesake. His own children were not going into the family business — his son was in college, and the twin girls would grow up and marry well, no doubt, smart little cutie pies that they were — and he liked that his three offspring would be free of this dangerous life.

But he also liked having Little Sammy going down the same road as his uncle. Sam had a special kinship for the young man, and even felt he owed Antonio a debt of sorts. Little Sammy was like having a second chance with Angelo, the brother Sam had lost so many years ago.

Angelo had been a drug addict. This was a shameful thing that embarrassed Sam with the Outfit. So when Giancana expressed concern that Angelo might — due to this weakness — become unreliable, Sam had read between the lines and taken on the responsibility.

After stabbing his brother to death in a car, Sam had taken Angelo to where he could strip him and wash his body with soap and water. To send him to God clean, to cleanse Angelo's very soul. Angelo was found that way, naked and clean and dead, in the trunk of a car.

In the garage, Sam got his broom and dustpan, and soon the mound of dirt in the driveway was transferred to a nearby garbage can. Finally he stood in the midst of the garage, hands on his hips, thinking what a job well done this was, how pleased Anita would be with him. He was doing a sort of pirouette, taking the tidy garage in, when — with his back to the street — he missed seeing the new visitor arrive.

But he heard the footsteps, and whirled, and saw a figure dressed for winter — black stocking mask showing only cold dark eyes, and a black turtleneck, slacks and boots, even a black topcoat, from under which emerged in black gloved hands a double-barreled shotgun.

"You fucker," Sam said, and the visitor

fired once, blowing off Sam's right arm.

Sam did not fall, just did a small dance, like a tightrope walker keeping his footing. He stood there, weaving just a little, looking down at his arm, which lay like a big dead fish, even flopping, twitching a little. Damnedest thing. He heard something, a kind of splashing, spraying sound, and his eyes quickly went to the wall at his right, where he was geysering blood, painting his own Picasso, his workshop area finally as bloody as the other one in the soundproofed room downstairs.

The voice was familiar, but muffled enough under the ski mask to remain unidentifiable.

"You really don't deserve it quick," the visitor said, "but I'm in a hurry."

The second blast opened Sam's chest. He gazed down at the gaping hole in himself and swallowed once and collapsed in a pile too big for any dustpan.

Then Sam DeStefano was gone, and his visitor, too.

No time at all for psychology.

BOOK ONE

CASTLE IN THE AIR

One Week Earlier

1

On the morning of the day his life went to hell, Michael Satariano felt fine.

At fifty, a slender five feet ten, with a face that had remained boyish, his dark brown Beatle-banged hair only lightly touched with gray at the temples, Michael appeared easily ten years younger, and the guess most people made was, "Thirty-five?" Only the deep vertical groove that concentration and worry had carved between his eyebrows gave any hint that life had ever been a burden.

He wore a gray sharkskin suit and a darker gray tie and a very light gray shirt; he did not go in for either the cheesy pastels or Day-Glo colors that so many middle-aged men were affecting in a sad attempt to seem hip. His major concession to fashion was a little sideburn action — that was about it.

And unlike many (most) Outfit guys, Michael had no penchant for jewelry — today he wore pearl cufflinks, gold wedding band on his left hand and single-carat emerald with gold setting on his right. The latter, a present from his wife Pat, was as ostentatious as he got.

His health was perfect, aided and abetted by nonsmoking and light alcohol consumption. His eyesight was fine — in the one eye that war had left him, anyway — and he did not even need glasses for reading, which remained the closest thing to a vice he had: if pulp fiction were pasta, Michael would have been as fat as his food-and-beverage man here at Cal-Neva — give him the company of Louis L'Amour, Mickey Spillane or Ray Bradbury, and he was content.

Neither could gambling be counted among the sins of the man whose official position at the resort/casino was Entertainment Director. Nor did he have a reputation for womanizing — he had been married since 1943 to Patricia Ann, the woman he always introduced as his "childhood sweetheart" — and though working in environs littered with attractive young women (from wait-resses to showgirls, actresses to songbirds), he rarely felt tempted and had not given in. It was said (not entirely accurately) that he'd never missed a Sunday mass since his marriage.

For this reason he had acquired a

mocking nickname — the Saint.

Saint Satariano, the wiseguys called him, particularly the Chicago crowd. Not that his church-going ways were the only thing behind the moniker: for three decades now he had served as the Outfit's respectable front man in various endeavors, the Italian boy who had been the first Congressional Medal of Honor Winner of World War II, the combat soldier whose fame rivaled that of Audie Murphy.

"Saint" had not been his first nickname.

During his months on Bataan in the Philippines, when he was barely out of high school, Michael had earned from the Filipino Scouts a deadly sobriquet: *un Demonio Angelico*. He had killed literally scores of Japanese in those vicious early days of the war, and had lost his left eye saving Major General Jonathan Wainwright from a strafing Zero. The latter event had been prominent in his Medal of Honor citation, but so had an afternoon battle in which he'd taken out an even fifty of the enemy.

General MacArthur himself had helped smuggle the wounded soldier off Bataan, to give stateside morale a boost with the war's first American G.I. hero. But Michael had not lasted long on the P.R. podium and rubber-chicken circuit — he kept asking his audiences to remember his fellow "boys" who had been abandoned by Uncle Sam back on that bloody island.

And so the adopted son of Pasquale and Sophia Satariano was sent back to Chicago a proud son of Italy (few knew that the boy was really Irish), and had been embraced by Al Capone's successor himself, the dapper and intelligent Frank Nitti, as a good example of just how patriotic a dago could be, Mussolini go fuck himself.

What Nitti had not realized was that Michael was fighting another war, a separate war, a personal war.

The young man's real father had been blessed (or perhaps damned) with his own colorful nickname: *the Angel of Death*. Michael Satariano was in long-ago reality Michael O'Sullivan, Jr., son of the infamous enforcer who had railed against the Looney gang of the Tri-Cities and their powerful allies, the Capone mob of Chicago . . .

. . . that same Angel of Death whose face had appeared on *True Detective* magazine covers, and in several movies that had romanticized Mike O'Sullivan, Sr., into a kind of Robin Hood who had traveled the Midwest stealing mob money from banks and giving it to poor farmers and other

Depression unfortunates.

The story went that Mike O'Sullivan had been the top lieutenant of Rock Island's Irish godfather, John Looney, but that (back in '31) O'Sullivan and Looney's homicidal offspring Connor had vied for the old man's chair, which led to an attempt on O'Sullivan's life, that succeeded only in taking out the Angel's wife, Annie, and younger son, Peter.

This tale was true as far as it went, but the power-play aspect was guesswork by second- and third-rate journalists. Michael Satariano knew why and how the Looney feud had really begun: he himself, at the tender age of eleven, had stowed away on one of his father's "missions" (as he and Peter used to romantically put it, day-dreaming that Papa and his gun were doing the bidding of President Hoover).

Instead the boy had stumbled onto a mob killing, witnessing Connor Looney murdering an unarmed man, followed by his own father machine-gunning a clutch of the murdered man's understandably riled compatriots.

So it was that Connor had schemed to wipe out the O'Sullivan family, only to fail miserably, as was Connor's wont.

The two surviving O'Sullivans — Michaels

senior and junior — had become outlaws, moving by car from one small Midwestern town to another, striking out at the Capone Outfit by hitting banks where the gang hid its loot, to pressure the Chicago Boys into giving Connor over to the Angel's righteous vengeance. This went on for six long dangerous months — young Michael himself had killed several times in defense of himself and his father — until finally Capone and his top man Frank Nitti handed Connor Looney on a platter to Michael O'Sullivan.

When Connor finally lay dead in the gutter of a Rock Island street, O'Sullivan struck a peace with the Chicago Outfit; but Capone and Nitti betrayed that pact, dispatching an assassin who indeed cut down O'Sullivan Senior — an assassin Michael himself had then killed . . . despite the pulp-magazine-and-Hollywood-sugarcoating of a child unable to pull the trigger, only to have his dying father bail him out with a bullet.

Eliot Ness — the famous Untouchable, to whom Michael O'Sullivan, Sr., had turned over evidence on Old Man Looney, consigning him to stir — had placed Michael O'Sullivan, Jr., in that orphanage in Downer's Grove. And his new parents, the Satarianos, had never known of his real beginnings, raising him in idyllic smalltown De Kalb, outside of Chicago.

In 1942, when he went to work for the Outfit, Michael Satariano's pedigree had seemed as perfect as his Medal of Honor heroics. In those early days, to put himself in solid, he had committed acts for Frank Nitti not unlike those his father had done for John Looney; but his plans for settling scores had gone awry, when the architect of his father's murder, Al Capone, revealed himself to be a drooling VD-ravaged near-vegetable, beyond any revenge, save for what God might eventually have in store.

And then an unexpected friendship had grown between Michael Satariano and Frank Nitti, that dignified, intelligent CEO of organized crime. As an Outfit soldier who'd killed in the line of duty, Michael had taken the blood oath of *omertà,* and now found himself a member of Chicago's La Cosa Nostra family, whether he liked it or not.

The saving grace had been that damned Medal of Honor, and the fact that Michael Satariano had not a single arrest on his record. Oh, he'd been brought in for questioning a few times, and was known to have associated with certain notorious types; but for a Sicilian "made man" to look so respectable was a not-so-small miracle in the world of the Outfit.

His new godfather had been Paul Ricca, and the white-haired, slender ganglord — the only man in the mob who knew that Satariano was in reality O'Sullivan — had over the years treated him almost like a son, or perhaps grandson. Ricca had protected Michael, and used him wisely and well, in key management positions at Outfit-owned entertainment venues.

Michael had started by booking acts at the Chez Paree, the closest thing to a Vegas showroom in the Windy City, and the Chez also boasted a huge casino, running wide-open with police protection. In the early '60s, when Mr. Kelly's, the Happy Medium, and the Playboy Club heralded a hipper Second City scene, the Chez finally folded, and Michael was dispatched to Vegas, where more traditional show biz still held sway.

As "Entertainment Director" of the Sands, he met all the big stars, and became friendly with that charming manic depressive, Frank Sinatra, and the other Clan members like Sammy Davis and Dino (the term "Rat Pack" was one Sinatra despised). Michael did more than just run the showroom and the lounges, however — he learned the casino business, and rose to second-in-command. Soon the Outfit honchos had big things in mind for Michael.

Then, just as the '60s got into gear, Michael's guardian godfathers, Ricca and Accardo, retired, allowing that crazy whack job Sam "Mooney" Giancana to take the top chair. Even on the periphery, however, the two respected elders held a fair share of power, keeping various fingers in assorted pies, and reining Mooney in.

Still, Michael knew his long period of protection had ended.

Giancana, the unpredictable hoodlum who'd been chauffeur and snarling bodyguard to both the former bosses, had come to power via reckless violence and sheer moneymaking ability — Mooney had, for example, taken over (bloodily) the Negro numbers racket, a great earner for the mob to this day. The level-headed, dignified Frank Nitti must have been spinning in his grave, what with that psycho punk from the Patch's old 42 gang holding the Capone throne.

On the other hand, Giancana had always been friendly if patronizing to Michael, for example when he gave Michael the Entertainment Director position at the Villa

Venice, an elaborate nightclub in the northwestern Chicago boonies. For two months, top talent came in, in particular the Clan of Sinatra, Dino and Sammy Davis . . . none of whom were paid a cent, doing the gig as a favor to Giancana (presumably as a repayment for helping Sinatra's pal Jack Kennedy get to the White House). After the show, guests were taken two blocks by shuttle for fleecing at a Quonset hut with a plush casino interior. Then Giancana — aware that FBI eyes were on him — shuttered the facility, pocketing three mil.

Soon, mysteriously, the handsomely insured Villa Venice facility burned down.

Again, Michael had had nothing to do with the casino end, his role that of a glorified handshaker, not unlike the indignity former heavyweight champ Joe Louis suffered in Vegas, where a casino employed him as a greeter. The Medal of Honor winner with the boyish countenance rated big with the Chicago columnists, guys like Irv Kupcinet and Herb Lyon, and if the Outfit could have been said to have a Golden Boy in the '60s and early '70s, Michael Satariano was it.

And Giancana himself was pleased enough with Michael to offer him a real job, specifically that big promotion he'd been groomed for by Ricca and Accardo: in 1964, Michael Satariano became Entertainment Director (and in reality top boss) here at the Cal-Neva Lodge and Casino at Lake Tahoe.

Pronounced Kal-Neeva, the resort dated back to the '20s, a rustic fishing/gaming retreat built on the California/Nevada state line, which bisected Lake Tahoe south to north, running up the hilly, rocky shoreline and through the hotel's central building (and fireplace and outdoor kidney-shaped swimming pool). Six of its acres were on the California side, eight on the Nevada. Before gambling in Nevada was legalized in 1931, the casino's gaming tables were on wheels, to be rolled across the dark line on the wooden floor to California, should Nevada coppers show, and vice versa. In the years since, food, drink and guests had stayed in California, with the casino all the way over in Nevada . . . across that painted line.

Eight thousand feet above sea level, ringed by the peaks of the High Sierras, accessed by one long winding narrow mountain road, the Cal-Neva — a.k.a. the Castle in the Sky — perched high over the northern tip of the lake, ideally positioned to take in Tahoe's deep, clear azure sunshine-dappled waters, against the surrounding forest's plush dark green. The sprawling lodge itself was a sort of barnwood wigwam castle, with a commanding A-frame stone porch. In addition to a motel-like row of cabins, small wooden bungalows and a few larger chalets on stilts clustered on the slope below the lodge, between granite outcroppings, the pine bluff dropping sharply to Crystal Bay.

The Cal-Neva, like so many Nevada casinos, was owned by a syndicate of investors, which often involved silent partners, including over the years various bootleggers and gangsters (Joe Kennedy, for instance), and thus it was that this magnificently situated rustic resort came to be "owned" largely by a certain Italian-American singer. That the singer's half-share of Cal-Neva represented Chicago investments in general — and Sam Giancana in particular — was a fairly open secret.

But Sinatra and Giancana had been arrogant, even for them, and a series of misadventures culminated in disaster.

A cocktail waitress Sinatra had dallied with was the wife of a local sheriff, who got tough with Frank, and when said sheriff was run off the road and killed a few weeks later, the Nevada Gaming Commission arched an eyebrow. They would soon run out of eyebrows, as a state-wide prostitution ring began operating from the front desk, a guest was murdered on the resort's doorstep, and Sam Giancana himself cavorted openly, even beating up one of the customers.

The latter infraction drew more heat than murders and hookers. Whenever the singing McGuire Sisters played Sinatra's acoustically perfect, seven-hundred-seat Celebrity Showroom, Giancana would shack up with his favorite sister (Phyllis); he would also play golf and dine with Sinatra, even though both knew Mooney was under FBI surveillance.

Giancana was, after all, prominent in the Gaming Commission's "List of Excluded Persons" — colloquially, its Black Book — at the top of the list of criminals forbidden even to set foot on a Nevada casino floor. (That half the joint was in California became Giancana's excuse.) When the commission had the temerity to point this out, Sinatra got so indignant and abusive, he had to surrender his license, and sell out.

Everybody, including the FBI, assumed that when Sinatra left Cal-Neva, so did Giancana; after all, the place closed down upon the Voice's departure, and stayed that way for some months. But the truth was, Giancana still held a considerable interest, and although former Outfit rep Skinny D'Amato had exited when Sinatra did, the Congressional Medal of Honor winner from Chicago had stepped in, to continue looking after Giancana's silent partnership.

Though it had been almost ten years since Sinatra's fall from grace, the singer's presence was still felt at Cal-Neva — the Vegas-like showroom he'd built, the secret system of tunnels and passageways that connected the lodge with select chalets, even the orange, beige and brown color scheme within the lodge. This was not a bad thing for business, and pictures of the famous crooner remained on display in both the Indian Lounge and (as it was now known) the Sinatra Celebrity Showroom.

After parking his pearl-gray Corvette in an almost empty lot on this pleasantly cool April morning, Michael walked across the gravel and then through pine and rock to the edge of the bluff.

To him, this job, in this location, was about as close to paradise as he could hope to find, in the life he'd chosen. Las Vegas was just a neon stain on the desert, a loud metal-and-plastic purgatory; but Tahoe was a heaven of clear sweet mountain air, the vast royal-blue lake sparkling with sunshine set against snow-capped peaks. Birds flashed colorfully as they darted between giant pines, while the stripes of speedboats on the water made abstract patterns, and a seaplane tilted a nonspecific salute against a sky almost as blue as the lake.

Back in '64, Michael and his family had relocated to Crystal Bay (on the California side), whose year-round population was just over 7,000, which took some adjusting for the Satarianos, who had lived in Chicago (or that is, Oak Park) forever. Also, since Cal-Neva was seasonal, open Memorial Day through Labor Day, Michael would periodically help out back at the Sands and at Miami's Fountainbleu, covering vacation time for other casino execs. This had taken him away from his family for several months a year, which he had not relished.

He'd been pushing for years to open Cal-Neva year round; the Lake Tahoe area was rife with winter sports, and only January, February and March — when admittedly the snowfall could be severe, up to thirty feet — were problematic. Tahoe often had warm weather from May to December, and the fall months were the nicest. As of several years ago he'd been allowed to expand his season from May first to the Thanksgiving weekend — but that still left Cal-Neva dark for four months.

They would be opening in less than two weeks, and the maintenance people were inside sprucing up the place. In fact, when he entered the A-frame lobby, the sound of vacuum cleaners echoed through the building's high, open-beam ceilings, as did the clip-clop of his footsteps on the stone floor.

He took a quick walk-through, glancing around, checking the status of the cleaning job, the resort's knotty-pine ambience second-nature to him, the eyes of mounted bear and deer and moose heads staring at him as he passed through chambers whose walls were studded with granite boulders.

The rustic hunting-lodge atmosphere of the facility, from the hanging Native American blankets and art to the Indian Lounge with its massive stone fireplace, had always pleased him. The space-age architecture of Las Vegas was cold, Sin City a windowless world with no clocks and endless noise. At Cal-Neva, even the casino room had gaping windows onto the green of pines and the purple of mountains and the blue of lake and sky, and you always knew whether it was day or night.

At Cal-Neva you could do more than just lose your shirt — you could sit by the warmth of a forty-foot granite fireplace, you could sip cocktails and listen to Frank Sinatra, Jr., in the Indian Lounge (couldn't afford Senior anymore, not that he'd ever set foot here again), you could laugh yourself silly at Martin and Rossi ("Hello dere!") in the Celebrity Showroom, you could swim in pool or lake, ski on snow or water, fish for salmon or trout or mackinaw, or ride horseback on mountain trails.

And you could still lose your shirt.

Michael prided himself on providing his patrons with a memorable getaway, giving them more for the money they left behind. But he had no illusions about the nature of this beast — a casino was the ideal business, wasn't it? A business where the customer was anxious to trade you his money for nothing more than a dream and a drink.

Michael did not lay back, as some managers did; he personally kept track of the count from drop boxes at the gambling tables. He would prowl the casino, a presence who might pop up at any moment. In Vegas he'd learned from the best how to spot every scam, every weakness — from a dealer who lifted his hole card too high (Michael would stroll by and casually whisper, "Nice lookin' ace of spades") — to crapshooters palming loaded dice (he especially watched the little old ladies); from contrived diversions — asking a dealer for a cigarette, conveniently spilled drinks — to dealers with "sub" pockets sewn in their clothes to slide in chips on the sly.

On the other hand, while he was paid to keep the professional cheats and the crooked staffers from stealing, part of Michael's job was to look the other way where Chicago's larceny was concerned. Though Tahoe was preferable to Vegas — that city of endless kickbacks — the ultimate kickback remained.

A casino could be skimmed any number of ways, but the time-honored one was in the count room. Once a month a little man from Chicago would collect a suitcase from the count-room safe, and never the IRS the wiser. Michael's role in this was merely to look the other way, but it made him no less a thief, did it?

As a mob-connected casino manager, he accepted this as a standard business practice, however bad a taste might linger, whatever possible criminal consequence could one day rise up out of his comfortable life and threaten everything he and his family enjoyed.

He had not intended to go down this road.

His father had gone down a similar path, and had hoped his son would not follow. But circumstances had led Michael into the Outfit life, and so the Outfit life was his.

Still, he'd been luckier than many. Than most. His godfather, Paul Ricca, had warned him long ago that going down the more legitimate mob avenues would not preclude him from certain duties.

"You can be in a passive part of our business," the dignified gray-haired patriarch had said, so many years ago, "and still be called upon. With your talents — this will happen. This . . . *will* . . . happen."

For the sake of protecting Michael's ability to serve as a squeaky-clean front man, however, the war hero had been largely protected from the violent side of things.

Now the Outfit, as he had known it — as his father had known it — was entering its twilight years. Capone and Nitti were long gone; the mob's corpulent treasurer Guzik had (not surprisingly) died eating, and even the Outfit's fixer and diplomat, Murray "the Hump" Humphries, had succumbed to a heart attack. Gone, too, for that matter, was gangbuster Eliot Ness — dead at his kitchen table, passed out beside a bottle of whiskey over the galley proofs of *The Untouchables*, the autobiography that made him a posthumous household word.

For many years Ricca and Accardo had ruled quietly from the sidelines, reining in Mooney Giancana's more impulsive tendencies while letting Mooney take the heat. Some considered Giancana a mere straw man, shoved forward by Ricca and Accardo into a prominence they abhorred. Finally, after such ill-advised endeavors as flaunting his presence at Cal-Neva and suing the FBI for harassment, Giancana had been removed from leadership and banished to Mexico, where he'd flourished for some years now, running casinos and gambling boats.

A few months ago, a fatal heart attack had taken Paul Ricca out, and the Capone era seemed finally truly over. Michael had a certain fondness for Ricca, the dignified ganglord who'd protected the Medal of Honor winner for so many years. But Michael had never felt about Ricca in the way he had Frank Nitti; for Nitti there had been a sense of sadness, even a tear or two. The death of Ricca brought only relief, as the last living link to his O'Sullivan past disappeared.

Michael didn't even really know who was in charge these days — Accardo, certainly, alternating between Chicago and Palm Springs, oversaw things. (Michael had worked directly under Accardo for a few years, and their relationship remained friendly and mutually respectful.) Back in Chicago, day-to-day operations were supposedly in the hands of Joey Aiuppa, who with his underboss Jackie Cerone was a throwback to Giancana's 42 gang roughneck style. But their influence was mostly on the streets of Chicago, where they terrorized bookies and juice men who welshed on the street tax.

And Michael had even heard disturbing rumblings that Giancana was contemplating a return stateside, to resume his throne.

As for the children of the Capone-era crew, they had largely pleased their parents by going into legitimate pursuits — stockbrokers, Realtors, attorneys, small-business owners. And so many of the Outfit businesses these days *were* legit — hotels, restaurants, car dealerships, real estate tracts. . . .

In Vegas, the Outfit had sold out to

Howard Hughes, Wall Street and the corporations — Sheraton, MGM and Hilton — though there would always be a place in gaming for experienced guys like Michael. Somebody "connected" like Michael, however, even somebody with as spotless a record as his, usually could only manage a work permit; a gaming license required the kind of rigorous background check — net worth, stock holdings, loans, bank accounts — that would have made the Singing Nun nervous.

That was why, officially, Michael remained Entertainment Director at Cal-Neva, and made only thirty grand per annum. Of course his bonuses took him up to over one hundred grand, but what the Gaming Control Board didn't know wouldn't hurt it.

He would soon be in a position to take an early retirement — fifty-five, he and Pat had agreed to — and all of this would be behind him. He had enjoyed managing the Cal-Neva, was considered a good, tough but fair, nice if somewhat remote, boss; he had restored the resort's reputation and made it a consistent earner. And he had ducked, for decades, the bullet of being asked by the Outfit to do something . . . unpleasant.

Satisfied his cleaning staff was on top of things, Michael entered his office, which did not reflect the rustic nature of the rest of the facility.

This was an executive's inner sanctum — dark woodwork, a large neat mahogany desk with matching wooden file cabinets — whose windows provided a striking view of the lake. The fireplace did retain the rough boulder-like look of the lodge, and above the fireplace — other than a few framed family portraits on the desk — was the only personal touch in the room.

Over the mantel a World War II–vintage Garand rifle rested on two prongs, underneath it a small, simply framed document bearing a watercolor American flag and calligraphic lettering: "To Michael P. Satariano, Corporal United States Army, for saving my life in a strafing attack by a Japanese Zero fight on Bataan March 10, 1942," signed "General Jonathan M. Wainwright."

Once a month Michael cleaned the weapon and polished its stock. Other than his father's .45 — stowed away in a safe-deposit box, with various cash — it was the only gun he owned.

He settled into his swivel chair — black leather, comfortably padded — and flipped open a file of receipts, picking up where he'd left off yesterday. He worked on this, and then typed some correspondence — he had no secretary, and used an Olympia on a stand beside the desk — and after a little over an hour, he took a break to wander out into the lodge and find himself a soft drink.

He stopped for a few minutes to chat with two members of the Mexican cleaning staff in the Indian Lounge, and compliment them on their work — they were waxing the dance floor — then walked into the cocktail lounge, with its colorful stained-glass dome of Austrian crystal. He ducked behind the circular bar and got himself a bottle of Coca-Cola from the small refrigerator tucked beneath. No ice, but the Coke sweated with cold. He did not take a glass with him, just using a bottle opener and helping himself to a Cal-Neva cocktail napkin.

When he returned to his office, he almost dropped the Coke, because seated in the visitor's chair across from Michael's desk was Sam "Mooney" Giancana.

"Nothing for me, thanks," Giancana said.

The diminutive, deeply tanned gangster — looking like a golfer in his straw orange-banded fedora, avocado sportjacket, burnt-orange Polo shirt, and lime slacks — leaned back casually, arms folded, legs crossed, ankle on a knee; his shoes were light-brown tasseled loafers and he wore no socks.

"Make yourself at home," Michael said, and he and his Coke went behind the desk.

"In a way, this still is my home." Giancana's face was an oval with a lumpy nose and a sideways slash of a smile stuck on haphazardly; his eyes lurked behind gray-lensed sunglasses.

"Well, you do still know your way around," Michael said, with a nod toward the fireplace.

Giancana smiled. "I checked myself into Chalet Fifty. For old times' sake. Hope you don't mind."

What this meant was, Giancana had entered the chalet and used the underground passage to come up through the secret doorway that was built into one side of the stone fireplace.

Seated now, Michael said, carefully, "*Is* this your place? I've never been sure how you and the Boys were splitting things up, after you left."

Giancana shrugged. "Accardo gets his piece of my Mexican interests. I still get my piece of Chicago's interests. Nothing's changed — 'cept that hothead Aiuppa is sitting where I should."

Michael managed not to smile; the idea of Giancana considering someone a hothead was . . . amusing.

On the other hand, Michael had never really seen Giancana lose his temper. He'd watched the little gangster stab a fork into a guy's hand once, and slap an occasional underling; but always with a cool calculation that was in its way far more frightening.

"I didn't know you were back in the country," Michael said.

"No one does."

"Not even the feds?"

"I'm not wanted for anything. I left the States of my own free will." He shrugged with one shoulder. "But I don't need to advertise, neither. That's why I slipped over the border, like a goddamn wetback. And I'll slip back over the same way. The family?"

It took a beat for Michael to figure out what Giancana meant.

Then he said, "My family's fine, thanks — Pat's busy with her pet projects and charities. Anna's in high school now. And Mike's over in Vietnam — should be home soon."

Giancana nodded. "Finally the fuck

winding down. Them kids'll all be back 'fore you know it — that's good. You must be proud of the boy."

"I am. But mostly I'll be glad to have him home safe, again. . . . And your girls?"

"Grown up. Two married, one divorced. That's about par." Giancana made a disparaging click in one cheek. "No values, these days."

Michael leaned on an elbow. "Sam — surely you didn't come all this way just to make small talk."

Giancana shrugged with both shoulders this time, then put his hands on his knees. "Seeing you's a big part of it, Saint."

"Really."

"Oh, yeah. See, I've let you sit on the sidelines, all these years, 'cause it's been useful to our thing, having a guy like you, all wrapped up in the flag, fronting for us."

The back of Michael's neck was tingling.

"But, Mike — I ain't never forgot who you are, *what* you are. You're still the guy that shot Frank Abatte in Cal City that time. You're still the guy that single-handed took out that hit team on Al down in Palm Beach. And you're still the guy that nailed those two disloyal prick body-guards that turned on Frank."

Michael leaned back; he twitched a

smile. "Actually, Sam, I'm not."

"Not?"

"That's *not* who I am anymore."

Giancana offered up yet another shrug, gestured with open hands; for Michael's taste, the man was working way too hard to seem casual.

"Who's to say any of us is who we was when we was kids? Used to be, I could hump three, four broads in a night. . . . Maybe them days is behind me, but, Mike . . ."

And Giancana removed his dark glasses, and small beady shark's eyes locked unblinkingly on Michael.

". . . I can *still* get it up."

Michael raised an eyebrow. "Good for you."

Giancana tossed the glasses on Michael's desk; they clunked and slid a little. "First time I really got a good look at you was, hell, when was it, '42? When you came over to the Bella Napoli, to talk to the Waiter."

The Bella Napoli was a restaurant in River Forest, a Chicago suburb; but the "waiter" in question didn't serve food: Giancana was referring to Paul "the Waiter" Ricca.

"I miss him," Michael said, referring to the recent death of his godfather.

"Great loss. Great man. Personally? I always thought it was tragic, you know — prison time depriving him of the chair that was rightfully his. Joe Batters, all due respect, a good man himself, never was no Paul Ricca."

"Joe Batters" was a Tony Accardo nickname that dated back to Capone's day.

"I owe a lot to Paul," Michael said.

"Yeah . . . yeah . . . don't we all. Hate I couldn't make it back for the funeral, but hell — the feds musta been on that one like flies on dogshit."

To this touching sentiment, Michael replied, "They were."

"That time, back at the Bella Napoli? I was impressed with you."

"Were you."

"I was. Really, truly." The little man shifted in his chair; he was "little" literally, but he had a presence, even a charisma, that filled the office. "You stood up to Mad Sam. You didn't cut him no slack."

"Did he deserve any?"

Giancana's laugh was curt. "Hell, no! He was a psycho then, and he's a psycho now. You know them glasses he wears?"

"Sure."

"There's no prescription in 'em. He has *perfect* eyesight. But sometimes he takes 'em off and rubs his eyes and then he sneaks peeks at people, thinking he's catching 'em off-guard. Like we all think just 'cause he wears glasses, he's blind as a bat or something!"

Michael managed a smile. "Really."

Giancana sat forward, his small eyes huge. "Did you know he's a *satanist?*"

"A satanist."

"A full-blown fuckin' no-shit satanist! He told me the people he's hit? Blood sacrifices to the devil! I saw him rolling around on the floor one time, havin' some kinda damn fit, foamin' at the mouth, screamin', 'Show me some mercy, Satan, I'm your servant Satan, command me!' . . . kinda shit."

Michael sipped his Coke, put the bottle back on the cocktail-napkin coaster. "Well, that's fascinating I'm sure, Sam."

" 'The devil made me do it!' " Giancana said, in possibly the worst Flip Wilson impression of all time. He pawed the air. "Hell! The stories I could tell . . ."

"You've convinced me. Mad Sam is nuts."

Giancana leaned so close, he almost climbed onto the desk. "He's more than nuts, Mike. He's dangerous."

"Doesn't that go without saying?"

"I don't just mean 'dangerous' he might

stick an ice pick in your ball sack. I mean 'dangerous' this business with Grimaldi, this trial — *you* know how Sam behaves in court!"

"Likes to defend himself."

"Talk about a fuckin' fool for a client. Layin' on a stretcher in his pajamas, yellin' through a bullhorn. Tellin' the judge he's worse than fuckin' Stalin!"

"So what?"

"So an unpredictable prick like Sam, knowin' the things he knows about all of us? Can you wrap your brain around the *risk?* And if they grant him immunity. . . ."

"What does this have to do with me?"

Giancana leaned back; he was framed against a peaceful background of blue sky and green forest and purple mountain in the picture window behind him. "Sam's the problem. You're the solution."

Michael drew breath in through his nostrils.

"We need somebody to take care of this," Giancana said, and gesturing with open hands again, "who's not one of the, you know, usual suspects. You can walk right up to Sam, he wouldn't think nothing of it; and the cops? Even the feds? You been a saint so long, who the fuck's gonna —"

"No."

Giancana's eyes tightened; his frown reflected confusion more than displeasure. It was as if the word Michael had uttered had been in Swahili.

"You've got a pretty cushy job here, Mike," Giancana said slowly. "You really wanna throw that away?"

"Fire me if you want. I have half a dozen standing offers from legit bosses in Vegas."

Nostrils flared. "Le-*git* bosses . . . ?"

"All due respect, Sam," Michael said, raising a pacifying palm, "that part of my life is behind me."

To a bystander, Giancana's smile might have looked pleasant. "Mike . . . 'no' ain't an option."

"Is this coming from Accardo?"

The oval face flushed. But the voice remained calm: "It's coming from me, Mike. It's coming from this-ain't-a-fucking-topic-of-conversation. We ain't breaking up into fuckin' discussion groups."

Nodding, Michael rocked back in his chair. "You're right. Nothing to discuss. I won't do this for you, Sam. Or for Tony or anybody."

Giancana's eyes were moving side to side, frantically; and yet he managed to glare at Michael, nonetheless.

Michael was saying, "You don't just

waltz into my office, thirty years later, and say suddenly I'm a torpedo again."

Giancana stood.

And pointed a finger.

The finger did not tremble, but his voice did, just a little. "*I'll* tell *you,* thirty years ago. Thirty years ago you took an oath. Thirty years ago —"

Michael shook his head. "I don't care about guns and daggers and burned pictures or any of your Sicilian Boy Scout rituals. I was a fucking kid. Now I'm a grown man with a family and a reputation, and I've made you people a lot of money over the years."

"*You* people! *You* people!"

"Go out the way you came, Sam, and get off this property — you're still in the Black Book, and I have investors to protect. Go and find some *goombah* to do your bidding. I run a business for the Outfit. It starts and ends there."

Giancana's face was tomato red. "You're a man with a family is *right,* Mike —"

Michael stood. He looked Giancana squarely in the eyes. His voice delivered words that were hard and cold and even — no inflection at all.

"Understand this, Momo. I may have put killing for you people behind me . . .

but self-defense I'm fine with. Touch my family, even look at them, and you'll wish you were dealing with Mad Sam, not a 'saint' . . . capeesh?"

Giancana drew in a deep breath.

The little gangster plucked his sunglasses from the desk, put them on, and moved to the fireplace, where he worked a hidden lever on the mantel. The left stony pillar swung out, revealing a dark passage.

"Capeesh," Giancana said quietly, and stepped into the blackness.

The stone door closed behind him, making a scraping sound, like fingernails on a chalkboard.

Michael winced, but that sound had nothing to do with it.

2

Two days ago, Patricia Ann Satariano had celebrated her forty-seventh birthday. Like her husband, she looked young for her age, though (unlike her husband) some minor plastic surgery had aided the effect.

Pat smoked, and that had put vertical lines above her upper lip, and she'd had her eyes done, too (she didn't know any mother of two who could reach her age without showing years around the eyes). As for the smoking, the health concerns hadn't been publicized when she began, and the habit had helped her with various tensions over the years.

So she'd had all of that erased, and a little breast lift, too, two years ago (she had met forty-five with the terror some women experience at fifty) and Pat Satariano remained a reasonable, very recognizable adult version of the astonishingly beautiful Patsy Ann O'Hara, who had been a high school Homecoming Queen in DeKalb, Illinois, back in 1938.

Right now, mowing their lawn on this

crisp spring day in her white tube top and blue short-shorts and white sneakers, she was still wolf-whistle-worthy, a slender, long-legged shapely blue-eyed blonde with shagged hair brushing her shoulders, Carly Simon–style. She'd always kept trim, exercising decades before fitness was "in"; her grooming remained impeccable, and she stayed as fashionable as possible, considering the nearest "big" city was Reno, an hour away. (If it weren't for the I. Magnin shop at Cal-Neva, she would have gone mad in Crystal Bay.)

She and Michael had been high school sweethearts, and she'd gone to college right there in DeKalb, at Northern, while initially Michael worked for his folks, Mama and Papa Satariano, at their spaghetti house. Then her beau had been among the first to enlist — even before Pearl Harbor — and was likewise among the first to return.

He'd come back from Bataan with a glass left eye and the war's first Congressional Medal of Honor.

She knew of the torturous history behind Michael using that heroic distinction to go to work for Frank Nitti; she was aware of his misguided and dangerous attempt to take revenge for the murders of his mother, brother and father. She knew, too, the convoluted circumstances that had led to his remaining among those people.

All these years.

And yet, despite the underlying tensions of who her husband's employers were, their life had been almost placid. Michael's job paid very well, they had a lovely home (a rambling ranch-style in the Country Club subdivision), their children had grown up here in the small, affluent community of Crystal Bay (California), under the bluest sky God had ever whipped up in His celestial kitchen.

For the first ten years or so, the couple had stayed in the Chicago area, Patsy Ann teaching (high school literature) and Michael working for . . . those people. The Satarianos had settled in Oak Park, and she taught at nearby working-class Berwyn; and the first few years — when Michael was assisting Mr. Accardo, mostly out of the Morrison Hotel in the Loop — had been tense. Pat wasn't sure what Michael had done for Mr. Accardo in those days, and never asked.

But after that, Michael strictly worked in legitimate areas for his employers, usually a restaurant or nightclub. Occasionally the Satarianos spent time in Vegas, sometimes as long as several months — vacations, really — and almost always over Christmas, when he'd be filling in at the Sands.

The plan had been for Pat to work for a while, and then they'd start their family. They began seriously trying in the late forties, and for a while it looked like she might be teaching school forever; but Mike Jr. came along in 1951, and Anna, in 1956. Good Catholics though they were, the Satarianos nonetheless decided to hold it at two.

Somehow they'd managed to create little replicas of themselves — young Mike was a quiet, serious boy who loved to read, not an A student but a good one, who excelled at sports, football and baseball, as had his dad. Anna was dark-haired and dark-eyed but otherwise the image of her mom; and like her mom, Anna was popular and a cheerleader and an honor student, obsessed with movies, theater and pop music.

No one ever had better kids.

And moving to Crystal Bay had only been beneficial — even in the suburbs, Chicago had a dark side. Mike — their son was always "Mike," and his father "Michael," to differentiate them around the house — had been old enough, at twelve, to find the uprooting traumatic; but the boy got over it, particularly when the girls ooohed and aaahed over his dark hair and dark eyes. Anna was only in the first grade, so that had been less of a problem.

With no Catholic church in either Crystal Bay or its Nevada neighbor Incline Village, the Satarianos joined St. Theresa's in South Lake Tahoe — though only thirty miles, the journey in this mountainous, twisty territory took easily forty-five minutes. Both kids had complained, every single Sunday, from grade school through high school, about this imposition on their time; but the parents insisted, and Pat had been fairly active in the church, now that she was no longer teaching.

Pat couldn't really say Michael had been a warm father, not in the effusive sense — he showered both kids with gifts, and always had time for them, but he was quiet and sparing with praise. Somehow their daughter had always been closer to her father, and their son to his mother.

A funny split between father and son occurred during grade school, when Mike — ever the sports nut — started obsessively following college and national teams, his room a collage of posters and pennants. Though he'd been a high school star athlete himself, the boy's father had no interest in

either collegiate or professional sports —
to him, they were only games that fueled
gambling, and represented a sort of busman's
holiday.

Michael would say to Pat, "That shit's
just the point spread."

So it had been Pat who sat and watched
TV with her son, and followed the teams,
football and baseball, while Michael accompanied Anna to the movies they both
loved, and theater, and he always made
sure the whole family got ringside seats in
Vegas and at the Cal-Neva for Sinatra and
Darin and Judy Garland and Elvis . . . plus
backstage handshakes and autographs.

Because of his line of work, Michael was
in a position to put Anna in contact with
her dreams, and just last year he had ushered her around Hollywood, introducing
her to top actors and actresses and direc-
tors and producers, getting the full tour of
various Hollywood studios, going on set
during the making of (wouldn't you know
it) *The Godfather*. Acting and singing were
Anna's big ambitions, and her father
clearly intended to pave the way.

Pat appreciated both her daughter's
talent, and her husband's interest in
helping their gifted girl, but Mom was
afraid their little A student might skip col-

lege and go right into show business, which was — let's face it — just a bunch of low-life carnival people (however talented) doing the bidding of garment merchants and gangsters. This particular argument was one of the few recurring ones in a predominantly happy, mutually supportive marriage.

"You're a closet bigot," Michael would say.

"I am not!" These were always fighting words to liberal Pat.

"You say 'carny people,' but you *mean* 'wops' and 'kikes.' "

"I do not!"

"Never forget the world thinks *I'm* one of those wops . . . who happens to have provided a pretty goddamn good life for us, I might add."

"Do you think I don't know that?"

"And what makes you think 'micks' are any better than the other European riffraff! We all washed up on the Ellis Island shore, didn't we?"

This was an argument that always ended with Pat retreating to a brooding silence, which was unusual, because the pattern on just about every other topic was the reverse. Michael seldom got as verbal as he did when this particular button got pushed.

And she understood: deep down, he felt guilty about the life he led; but, as he'd pointed out, the result for his family had been overwhelmingly positive. And he was, after all, a legitimate businessman, despite certain ties. . . .

Now, it should never be said that Michael treated Anna as his "favorite." He backed his son's interests, too — however disinterested Michael might be in professional sports, the father had always been a keen follower of his son's local endeavors in the athletic arena. Even with his demanding, often punishing schedule, Michael had rarely missed a Little League, junior high or high school game — even the intermurals at St. Theresa's.

And high school had found mother and daughter forging a tighter bond — the worries and pressures of the various high school musicals Anna had gone out for called for a maternal touch, since Michael didn't deal with emotions that well, his own or anybody else's. Plus, there had been "boy" issues, which (until lately) they had discussed like two girls at a slumber party.

And, then, along came Vietnam. . . .

Pat and her son had had a major falling out over the Great American Misadventure.

Pat — a lifelong Democrat — stayed active with local, state and even national politics, and during the late '60s actively protested the war. (Michael, also a Democrat, always seemed to agree with her, but never participated in marches and sit-ins — though he did not discourage her.)

She so hated the war, she'd even been conned into voting for Nixon — fucking *Nixon!* — in 1968, because the Democrats had imploded at their convention, and Bobby Kennedy had been murdered, and Tricky Dick at least had a secret "plan," right? Who could have predicted that plan was the secret *bombing* of *Cambodia!*

Back in '70, when young Mike — a graduating senior who had several football scholarship offers — drew a three-digit-number in the draft lottery . . . meaning he would likely *not* be called . . . Pat had been ecstatic. And her husband had taken her into his arms and squeezed her tight, and whispered, "Thank God. Thank God."

But then Mike sat his folks down in the living room, one terrible Saturday morning, and explained that he was enlisting in the army.

"Dad served *his* country," Mike said, "and I want to do the same."

"Are you serious?" Pat said, almost

hysterical. "Why would you risk your life in that senseless, immoral war?"

She obviously was well aware that her son — like so many children — had opposite politics to her own; that he had been president of Incline Village High's Young Republicans Club had not been her proudest moment as a parent. For several years now, Mike had pooh-poohed his mother's "hippie anti-war ravings" in that soft-spoken wry way of his.

When the boy was feeling especially mean, he might even say, "*Aging* hippie. . . ."

But this?

"I think you know that I don't see the war that way," Mike said, in a calm measured manner so like his father. "Presidents of both parties thought it was a good idea. And the spread of communism has to be stopped. . . . I want to serve. Like Dad."

She turned to her husband, who looked pale and shellshocked himself; he and the boy were dressed for golf, in pastels that suddenly struck Pat as blood-drained. "Tell him, Michael! *Tell* him this is a bad idea! Explain that you fought in a *good* war!"

"No such thing," Michael said, quietly.

"Michael! Hitler and the Holocaust, for God's sake! Pearl goddamn *Harbor!* But this, this, this, *this* war . . . it's not *about* anything! Not . . . about . . . *any*-thing!"

"It's Mike's decision," his father said.

"Just about boys *dying!*"

"I want you to be proud of me, Mom. Like Dad is proud of me."

She almost snarled at her son. "He *isn't* proud of you!"

"Actually, I am," Michael said.

She had begun to cry, then; but did not allow either of them to comfort her. Michael was telling Mike that his mother was right, that this war was not the same as World War Two, and he would still be proud of Mike if his son would just take his chances in the lottery like any other good all-American boy, and in the meantime there was that scholarship to Fresno. . . .

But it was too little too late, and that night she had told Michael that she would never forgive him, and she made her husband sleep in his study for a week. Then she forgave him, because they were after all best friends, and still lovers, and she could not face this horror without him. . . .

The terrible thing, the worst thing, was she could never work up even false enthusiasm for her son, for this decision he'd made that was so important to him. Even when she kissed him goodbye at the bus station in Reno, she had sensed resentment in him — in his expression, even in the words "I love you, Mom," though she treasured them no less.

When Michael had been on Bataan, in the early days of the Second World War, Pat had written to him daily, and he never wrote her back once. That had been part of his attempt to distance himself from her — he'd broken up with her, or pretended to, before he left — but she later learned he had read and treasured every page.

Over these last almost three years, she had written her son every week, and she had received only half a dozen very sporadic letters in return. Part of it, she knew, was that Mike just didn't like to write — English and literature, her specialty, had been her son's worst subjects. Words came hard to him, self-expression a chore, and the handful of letters the parents had received were chatty, strained things that spent all their time assuring her he was doing fine, and in no danger.

That was one small solace — his job was some kind of company clerk and he had seen no combat.

I'm perfectly safe, Mom. His handwriting was small and cramped and very neat, and looked no different than it had in junior high, her little boy. *Please don't worry a pretty hair on your head.*

Now, with this horrible stupid goddamn fucking immoral *goddamn fucking* war all but over, Pat allowed herself — finally — to experience hope. Allowed herself to believe that the danger was over, that Nixon suffering all that Watergate heat was leading to the administration finally getting something done about the South Asia mess, and Kissinger had reached a peace agreement in Paris. . . .

Hell, by the end of last year, just *months* ago, almost all the boys were home! Only 25,000 remained — *why did one of them have to be* her *son?*

Michael had soothed her saying, "He has to follow orders, dear — he says in his letters, when his three-year stint is up, he's going to college. What more can we ask?"

Then, a couple of months ago, finally, finally, finally a cease-fire agreement had been signed, and all of the boys were scheduled to be home by the end of this month. She would feel better if they'd had a letter lately from Mike, explaining his situation exactly, letting them know when they could expect him. Knowing her son, he'd probably just show up at the house one of these days, and grin the half-smile he inherited from his father, and say, "Still mad at me, Mom?"

She took a break from her mowing.

She left her mower in the middle of the backyard — the lawn was big, and Michael would gladly have hired someone to do it, but she considered the task part of her exercise-and-fresh-air regimen — and walked around the empty pool (they'd fill it in a month) to go in the glass doors into the kitchen. The interior of the house she redecorated (and sometimes remodeled) about once a decade. Michael humored her in this department, and their home had gone from Country House to Mediterranean to the latest: International.

And of course her husband saw to it that she got nothing but the best — in the living room, Le Corbusier and Mies van der Rohe furniture, their geometric coolness warmed up by an antique throw rug and a tufted wine-leather Chesterfield couch and two armchairs. The whole house was a study in yellow and white, set off by geometric paintings in green and black and red and white. This tranquil setting Pat adored, though Michael (she knew) found it sterile.

Only two rooms had been spared her modernistic touch: Michael's study, and their bedroom; the former was a bookcase-walled shrine to her husband's reading habits — to call his tastes middle-brow would be generous — and the latter a simple ivory-walled chamber with an antique oak four-poster they'd splurged on the first year of their marriage, which had somehow managed to sentimentally weather all of Pat's decorating styles over the years.

At the round kitchen table in the modern white-and-yellow kitchen with its travertine surfaces and floors, she had an iced tea and (you've come a long way, baby) shook a cigarette from her pack of Virginia Slims and lighted up with a Bic.

She had quit the vile habit many times over the years, but with a husband who worked for those employers of his, and a son in Vietnam, she felt she had every reason to risk her own life any way she chose.

Still, she had promised Michael that when Mike came home from Nam, safe and sound, she would indeed quit. Finally. Once and for all.

"Gonna hold you to that," he'd said, shaking a finger, but smiling the half-smile she loved so much.

With the war over and her son safe now,

Pat was in a position to indulge herself in concern over her daughter.

With no real sense of hypocrisy — though the teenage life her daughter was living was a slightly updated version of her own — Pat wished her daughter, a senior at Incline Village High, would not obsess over such unimportant things as getting the lead in the chorus's spring musical (she always did), being chosen Prom Queen (the girl had already been Homecoming Queen) and maintaining her four-point average (Patsy Ann O'Hara had been valedictorian of *her* class, and so what?). Even worse, Pat was certain Anna was getting serious with her boyfriend, Gary Grace.

Sighing smoke, the mother knew she was being a hypocrite. She and Michael had become intimate — *all right,* started screwing in the backseat of the O'Hara family Buick — back in high school. But that had been prom night, and they'd become engaged, and eventually married, and . . .

Pat had not meant to find the birth control pills (actually, she'd been looking for her daughter's diary); but there they were. How had the child managed it, without parental consent? Or could a girl these days get the pill when she was just seventeen, like Anna?

Well, things had changed, the Sexual Revolution and all that, but that didn't make Pat feel any the more comfortable about her high school daughter fucking the Boy Most Likely to Succeed (which he certainly had). And she didn't dare tell Michael, who adored the girl, because he might explode. She knew the world thought Michael was one cool customer, but she had seen him lose his temper, and it wasn't pretty.

For almost a week, Pat had been struggling with this — how to confront Anna? Better still, how to talk to her while taking the "confrontation" aspect out of the equation; but when Anna learned her mother had been snooping in her bedroom, how could it be anything *but* confrontational?

By the time Pat had finished mowing the backyard and started on the front, she had held the conversation with her daughter thirteen times — baker's dozen. It would always start out as a rational, reasonable speech, a kind, understanding motherly discourse, until she was screaming at her daughter in her mind, and her daughter was screaming back. . . .

What was it Anna was saying these days?
Yow.
Yow indeed. . . .

She was leaning on the Lawn Boy when the Chevelle rolled up at the curb. The car was dark green, nondescript, and did not immediately come to mind as anything anyone she knew drove.

Tentatively, she started down the long, gently sloping lawn, to cautiously greet her unknown caller . . .

. . . who stepped from the car to reveal his crisp green Class-A uniform with cap shadowing his face, a slender young soldier about five ten.

Her heart leapt with joy — just as she'd predicted, her son had surprised them, showing up unannounced. Wasn't that *like* him! She was within five feet of him when she realized it wasn't Mike at all, but another young soldier, whose face was serious even for a military man.

And she stumbled to a stop, her brain making the connections quickly, because any mother of a boy in service knew that when a soldier came around who was not her child, the only possible news was . . .

Patricia Ann Satariano said, "Oh God, oh my God," and tripped and fell to the freshly cut grass, and — mercifully — passed out.

When she woke in their darkened bedroom, her mouth was thick with sleep and sedation; somehow she'd gotten into her nightclothes, and she pushed up unsteadily on her elbow.

Michael was sitting on the edge of the bed. The room was dark. The world, outside the windows of the bedroom, was dark. Suddenly it wasn't afternoon anymore.

Then she shook her head and said, "Oh, Michael . . . I just had the worst dream . . . the most terrible dream. . . ."

He clicked on the nightstand lamp, to a subdued setting that nonetheless washed the room in more light than either of them might desire.

"Not a dream," Michael said.

But she already knew that, just looking at him. He was in a white shirt, from work, collar open, no tie, the sleeves rolled up, and his face was pale, his hair askew, and his eyes red.

"Our son . . . our son *can't* be dead," she said. "Oh, Michael, tell me he's not dead!"

"We don't know, Pat. We don't know." He moved next to her and put his arm around her; they half-sat, supported by the headboard of the four-poster. "There is hope. Some hope."

"Some . . . ?"

Michael sighed, swallowed, nodded.

"Mike has been declared missing in action."

And hope did spring within her, desperation-tinged. "So . . . he could be alive?"

"He could. But we have to be honest with ourselves. The odds . . . well, we have to be honest with ourselves."

She didn't want to talk there, and he got her her blue silk robe, and walked her to the kitchen, where he had coffee waiting, and served her up. As they sat — where a lifetime ago she'd had a smoke and contemplated problems about her daughter that seemed so small now — she had several long drinks of coffee, as if hoping the hot liquid might rejuvenate her.

Then she said, "Anna? Does she know?"

He shook his head. "She's still at *Sound of Music* rehearsal. I'll tell her. I'll handle it."

She touched his hand. "How is this possible? Michael, the war is over . . . all the boys are coming home."

He sighed again. "Not all. . . . Not right now, anyway."

"What did they tell you?"

The young soldier had been a staff sergeant from the Reno recruiting office — where in fact Mike had enlisted — and he had carried the unconscious Pat Satariano into the house. Down the street, her friend Trudy had been out in her yard, watering some flowers, and saw Pat collapse and ran over and helped. And had called Michael over at Cal-Neva.

"Mike is officially listed M.I.A.," Michael said. "We've been left a document that details what happened, anyway what's known."

"But Michael . . . the war is *over*. . . . How . . . ?"

"This happened in January."

"And we're being told *now?*"

Michael shrugged and sighed. "Apparently some kind of negotiations were under way, to try to determine if Mike and some other boys had been taken prisoner. To ascertain, at least, that they were alive . . . or . . ."

"No," she said bitterly. "I'll tell you what this is about — goddamnit! This is something secret, isn't it? And they didn't want it getting out! Because of the cease-fire and . . ."

Her anger choked off the words.

Michael said, "Do you want me to tell you about it? Or do you want to read what the staff sergeant left us . . . ?"

She swallowed thickly; she felt numb. She shook her head. "Tell me, Michael. Just tell me."

"Well, putting it simply, Mike's position was attacked by communist forces —

troops and tanks, they were invaded, literally. This was in a place called Tanh Canh Base Camp, Kontum Province . . . South Vietnam. He was in a water tower observation post and got the warning out, saved a lot of lives. Right away they started what are called E & E operations — evacuate and evade — and a group of perhaps fifty men tried to get away from hundreds."

"Is this . . . this where Mike was company clerk?"

Michael hesitated. Then he said, "Darling . . . that's something Mike told you, to put your mind at ease. He's been in combat more or less since he got there."

"Oh God. Oh Jesus. And you *knew?*"

"I knew. Be mad if you like, but he made me promise not to tell you."

She felt her chin quiver, but will power — and the sedative — allowed her to maintain her composure long enough to hear the rest of it.

"Go on," she said. "Go on."

"Helicopters came in to rescue these boys, and Mike was among those staving off the onslaught of enemy troops. I guess he had a . . . a machine gun, and was just facing them as they came."

"Mike and . . . and how many other boys?"

"At the end it was just Mike. They were coming down a hill, the enemy, and he . . . he was going up. That's what he was doing when the last helicopter left."

"They . . . they left him there? Just *left* —"

"They had to get away while they could, and . . ."

"And no one thought he had a chance?"

Michael nodded gravely.

"*Did* he have a chance?"

Michael's eyes tightened. "Yes. With a machine gun? He had a chance, all right. He was using a Thompson."

"A what?"

"It wasn't government issue. These kids use whatever they can get their hands on — it was a tommy gun."

"What . . . like in the old *gangster* pictures?"

"Yes."

"Where would he get such a thing?"

Michael said nothing.

Over the years, another of the rare things they had fought about was Michael's weird insistence that his two children learn how to handle firearms. Since Michael was not a hunter, Pat always thought this was ridiculous. Stupid. Barbaric. And yet, since grade school, both Mike and Anna had been members of the Crystal Bay Gun

Club, with their father — a bonding exercise the mother had never condoned.

She glared at him. "You? *You?* You sent that weapon to him?"

"If he's alive," Michael said, "that's the reason. You can kill a lot of people with a machine gun."

She let out what was only technically a laugh. "Well, I guess you would know."

"Baby . . ."

She got up and poured herself more coffee; she was filled with rage and disgust and grief, but it was all just bubbling, like the coffee pot.

"If he's alive," she said, sitting, "where is he?"

"A camp somewhere."

"A camp somewhere. You make it sound like where we used to send him and Anna in the summer. *Prison* camp, you mean."

"Prison camp. . . . He'd be a P.O.W. But with the war over, the Cong won't be as rough on those kids. We'll make deals, we'll negotiate."

"We?"

"The government."

"What, fucking Nixon?"

"Patsy Ann — don't make this something political."

"Isn't it? Isn't politics killing our kids?

Haven't these bastards killed Mike?"

He shook his head. "We don't know that. We can hope."

"You hope. I think I'll settle for despair. It's easier."

"Something the sergeant said . . ." Michael's voice was strange, strained.

"What?" She looked carefully at her husband. "What?"

"I'm not sure I should tell you."

"What, Michael?"

"They say he's being put up for the Congressional Medal of Honor."

She didn't say it. She didn't have to. *Just like his father. . . .*

"If he gets it, Mike'll be the last Medal of Honor winner of the Vietnam war." Michael laughed. "How about that? Like father like son?"

And Michael collapsed onto the table, weeping, tears streaming over the yellow-and-white daisy design.

She scooched her chair over near him, and patted his back, and soothed him. They would take turns, over the coming days, weeks and months, knowing that if they both succumbed at the same time, they could not bear it.

3

A week passed in a blur of tears, recriminations from Pat, apologies from Michael, anger from Anna, constant phone calls from well-meaning friends, relatives and business associates who put Michael (he protected his wife from these) through the painful procedure of filling them in about Mike and his M.I.A. status.

Pat was doing better, now — she was on Valium, and she clung to a quiet, almost religious belief that Mike was after all only missing, and would be back in the family's bosom when all the P.O.W.s were returned in the aftermath of "that terrible war." She never used the word "Vietnam," or for that matter "war," without preceding it with "that terrible." She had no anger in her voice — perhaps that was the Valium — reflecting an acceptance of the difficulty of life, but despite this seeming fatalism, nowhere in her was there room for the possibility that Mike might be dead.

Michael, however, knew that the odds for their son's survival were poor. He wondered — deep in sleepless nights, particularly — whether it was wrong of him to withhold from his wife the complete truth. He had thought that the eventual news (if it ever came) that Mike had been killed would be better handled by Pat after she had at least adjusted to the M.I.A. status. That the process of letting go of her son would be better if a gradual one. . . .

Now she was so deep in denial, caught up in (what was probably) the illusion, even the delusion, that Mike would certainly return to them ("any day now"), that her husband wondered if he might have done her more harm than good.

Perhaps *only* harm. . . .

That first afternoon — when the young staff sergeant had come around, Pat passing out, Michael rushing home to her side — their physician (and country club friend) Dr. Keenan, who was home just a block away, had hurried over to give Pat a sedative.

And Michael had ushered the young staff sergeant into the living room, where the boy had stood in stiff respect and — with the faintest tremor in his voice — delivered to the father the dreadful news.

"Mr. Satariano, as a representative of the President of the United States and the

United States Army, it is my duty to inform you that your son, Lieutenant Michael P. Satariano, Jr., was declared missing in action after a military action on January 7, 1973, in the Republic of South Vietnam in the defense of the United States of America."

Michael could see the discomfort in the young soldier's face, much as the boy tried to hide it, and as squared away as he was in his crisp uniform, the sergeant was just a boy, a kid . . . like Mike. Even looked a bit like him, even the baby face . . . though Mike's eyes were dark, and the staff sergeant had disquietingly beautiful green ones.

Michael had prepared himself for this moment, although — like his wife — he had thought the war was over, and their son would soon be coming home to them, alive, well, in one piece, and not in a body bag.

Still, he immediately banished his emotions to the background of his consciousness — he had experience controlling his feelings, and his priorities were his wife, his daughter, and finding out as much as he could about Mike's status.

"Did you serve in Vietnam, Sergeant?" Michael asked.

"Yes, sir."

"Please . . . please sit down."

The young sergeant said thank you, took off his cap and sat on the edge of a chair, a geometric painting behind him making him the bull's-eye of a yellow-and-white target.

Michael sat across from the soldier on the couch; he, too, sat on the edge. "How long have you been doing this duty? Making casualty notification calls?"

"This is my first week, sir. My first call."

"Your primary duty is as a recruiter?"

"Yes, sir."

". . . Hard assignment."

"Yes, sir. Mr. Satariano, your wife . . . she mistook me for your son."

"Hell."

"You've been expecting him?"

Michael nodded.

"I'm so sorry, sir. You will be receiving a telegram, with the official notification."

Michael almost smiled. "This seems fairly official."

"Understood, sir."

"Do you have more information you can share?"

A curt nod. "I have a document I'm going to leave, which details the military action."

"Have you gone over it yourself?"

"I have, sir."

"Give it to me in your own words."

The boy did.

Michael said, "Do you know why this took so long? This was months ago — we're supposed to be notified in a matter of hours."

"With a death, sir, you would be. And, in fact, your son has been designated Missing in Action only since yesterday."

"*Yesterday?* Do you know why?"

The boy's eyes tightened and widened, simultaneously. "Sir, I . . ."

"What is it?"

"The document —"

Michael sat forward so far he all but fell off the couch. "What do you know? What did you hear?"

"Sir, please . . ."

Michael stood. He looked down at the boy. "I was in the Pacific war, son. You don't have to pull any punches. I was on Bataan."

"I know. You won the Medal of Honor. I'm . . . frankly, I'm in awe of you, sir. And after you served so honorably, to have to . . ."

"Lose my son? Why, if Mike has been declared M.I.A., do I sense you consider him a K.I.A.?"

The boy's chin jutted. "I can tell you this — you and Lieutenant Satariano may be the first father and son both to have won the Medal of Honor. His heroism is being considered in that light."

"You heard that?"

"I did."

"What else did you hear?"

"I'm really not at liberty to —"

"If my son were sitting where you are, Sergeant, and your father in my place? Mike would tell your dad what he wanted to know."

The boy gave up a tiny smile — suddenly human — and said, "You're some interrogator, Mr. Satariano."

"I'm a sergeant, like you, son. Spill."

The soldier had heard his C.O. talking on the phone to someone in Washington. The reason for the delay in classifying Michael Satariano, Jr., "Missing in Action" had to do with conflicting eyewitness accounts. An investigation and a hearing had finally resulted in Mike's current designation.

"Apparently at least one of the men on that Huey," the sergeant said, "claimed to have seen Lieutenant Satariano raising a handgun to . . . I'm sorry, sir . . . to his own temple as the enemy were about to swarm over him."

Michael, pacing as he listened, stopped.

"Saw this from the Huey? The departing helicopter?"

"Yes, sir."

Michael returned to the couch, and sat, leaning back, shaking his head. "I don't believe that, Sergeant."

"Apparently the army's official decision was to disregard that testimony, as well, sir. The night was dark, the helicopter was stirring up dust —"

"No. I mean, Mike's a good Catholic boy. He would not commit suicide."

"Oh." The boy swallowed and sat forward. "That's another thing, Mr. Satariano. We're supposed to bring a minister along on these calls, but I couldn't round up a priest in Reno, to make the trip. And there aren't any in Crystal Bay, and I do apologize for —"

"Was there any reason, other than saving himself from captivity or torture, that my son might have taken his life?"

"I don't understand, sir."

"I mean, did he have any strategic knowledge — mission orders, current troop numbers, deployment information — that would have endangered his men, should it be tortured out of him?"

The soldier swallowed. "I only heard half of the conversation, Mr. Satariano. It was a phone call, remember, and —"

"Did Mike have any such info?"

Another swallow, and the boy nodded, glumly.

And Michael's certainty that his son would never commit the sin of suicide had slipped away from him; he could well understand this sacrifice — and the hope that judgment on the other side would be tempered by mercy and understanding — coming naturally to his son.

The soldier stood, and though his hat remained in hand, he was rigidly at attention. "Sir, I hope I have not overstepped, sharing this information with you. The document I'm leaving with you contains the pertinent information, and represents the army's, the government's, position on your son's status."

Michael rose, said, "Thank you for your candor," and ushered the boy out the front door.

The sun had gone down, and the subdivision's blue-tinged streetlamps were glowing against a dark night — no moon, the stars doing their best against misty cloud cover.

Michael walked the young man to his car. At the curb, he put a hand on the boy's shoulder. "Rough duty."

The boy had tears in his eyes, and a nervous smile flashed. "Yes, sir. No fun being the angel of . . . Sorry, sir."

"What were you going to say?"

"Nothing, sir."

Michael fixed his eyes with the soldier's. "Sergeant, have I come unglued over what you've told me?"

"No, sir!"

"Do I strike you as an hysterical ninny?"

"Certainly not."

"Then tell me — *what* were you going to say?"

A long swallow later, he said: "That it's . . . no fun being the angel of death. That's what they call it, around the recruiting offices, where we get stuck with the job . . . angels of death, showing up at the doors of the families of soldiers."

"I see."

The boy, possibly responding to a perceived coldness in Michael, blurted, "I didn't mean 'stuck' with the job, just that, well, it's . . ."

Again Michael placed a hand on the young man's shoulder; he squeezed. "I asked you to be frank, and you were. Thank you."

They shook hands, and the soldier drove off.

How could this kid know that the phrase "angel of death" had an odd resonance for Michael? That this had been what his father, the enforcer for the Looney mob, had been called back in the '20s and early '30s, due to the mournful cast of his expression when he dispatched his victims? Violent death, and an angelic acceptance of it, was part of Michael's heritage.

And his son's.

Michael had decided not to share with his wife or daughter what the young staff sergeant told him about the military's own indecision over Mike's "Missing in Action" versus "Killed in Action" designation; and the weight of that had its consequence. He had been strong for Pat and for Anna, and — other than that once, with his wife — did not break down in front of them; he professed a belief in Mike returning to the fold one day, and for the first five days, he'd dealt with the burden in his own way.

He would try to go to sleep, knowing it would not happen; then he would wait for Pat to drop off into her mildly drugged slumber, and repair to his study to read a western or mystery novel, nothing overtly violent — mostly Max Brand or Agatha Christie. If he couldn't get engrossed, he would remove his 16mm projector from the closet, and set it up, and the little silver screen as well, and go to the shelves to select canisters of film from his collection.

He had about thirty movies — *Stagecoach*, various Laurel and Hardy features, Hitchcock's *Lady on a Train*, a couple of the really good Abbott and Costellos, *Swing Time* with Fred and Ginger — the kind of movies he'd seen and loved as a kid. He had never cared for Roy Rogers or Gene Autry, singing cowboys didn't make it for him; but he had several old westerns with Buck Jones and Tom Mix he could watch again and again.

By three in the morning or so, he'd have read a paperback or watched a film to the point of tiredness, and would then take a steaming bath, and lie back and think about his son and weep for perhaps fifteen minutes . . . then finally return to bed and fall to sleep rapidly.

For the last two days, he had followed this same procedure successfully, but the crying had finally stopped. He felt he was getting hold of himself.

Anna, however, could not seem to come out of her funk. And she was mad at him. For the first time in years — first time ever, really — his daughter was clinging to her mother, helping her out in every way possible, cooking meals on her own, even assisting with the dishes (well, putting them into the dishwasher, anyway) and offering to do the laundry (though her mother never took her up on it).

For the first two days, following the news about Mike, Anna had done all her crying, all her hugging, her consoling with her mother. She had barely spoken a word to her father, and avoided eye contact, even to the point of looking away with a jerk.

Finally, last night, he had knocked at her bedroom door, behind which her stereo blared Carole King's *Tapestry*, an album that had been his daughter's favorite for some time, but which Anna had never previously listened to at such Led Zeppelin decibels.

"Yes?" she called noncommitally.

He cracked the door — with a teenage daughter he had long since learned not to barge in — and spoke: "Okay I come in?"

"Yeah."

Carole King, who Michael liked also, was singing "It's Too Late," but the volume made him cringe.

"You mind turning that down a little?" he asked.

Sitting Indian-style on the daisy-patterned bedspread, Anna — in a pink top with puka shell necklace and blue bellbottoms and no shoes, toenails pink also — was leafing through *Rolling Stone*. The furniture was white and modular, and the pale yellow walls were largely obscured by posters of recording artists (Janis Joplin), musical plays (*Hair*) and favorite movies (*Butch Cassidy and the Sundance Kid*); unlike most girls her age, Anna's posters were framed, as they tended to be autographed.

Anna had her mother's apple cheeks and heart-shaped face, but her eyes were big and dark brown, and her hair — which was straight and went endlessly down her back — was an even darker shade, a rich auburn. She wore a blue-and-yellow beaded headband. She often affected heavy eye shadow, but right now she didn't have a trace of make-up, not even lipstick — and yet was stunning.

He pulled a white chair away from a small desk area recessed within a white unit of closets and cupboards decorated with signed eight by tens from their Hollywood trip, and sat near her bedside.

"No homework?" he asked, hands folded in his lap.

She flipped a page of the newspaper-like magazine, not looking at him. "Done."

"Expected you to be poring over your script."

She was Maria in *The Sound of Music*.

"Know it," she said, flipping a page.

"Is it my imagination?"

No eye contact. "Is what your imagination?"

"The deep freeze treatment I'm getting from you."

She shrugged.

"I want you to know I do appreciate what you've done for your mother . . . the support. You've always meant a lot to her, but right now —"

She gave him a long, slow, cold look. "You don't make it as Ward Cleaver, okay, Dad?"

"You'd prefer Archie Bunker?"

She almost smiled, but caught herself, and looked down at a picture of a hippie-ish Jane Fonda at a peace rally. "I'd prefer privacy."

He leaned forward, hands clasped. "What is this about, Annie?"

She shot a glare at him — eye contact, at least. "Please don't call me that. It's a kid name. I am not a kid."

"Anna. What have I done?"

She gave him another sharp look, dark eyes accusing. Suddenly he realized tears were shimmering there. "Don't you know?"

"No, sweetheart. I don't."

Her lip curled. "*You* did this. You encouraged him."

Now he got it.

"You blame me," he said, "for Mike?"

"He worshiped you. All you would have had to say was, don't go. Tell him you'd rather see him in Canada than Vietnam. But he had to prove himself to you, walk in your footsteps. The big hero."

"I never encouraged him. I asked him not to do it."

Nostrils flared. "Don't give me that shit! Once you said you were proud of him for it . . ." She shrugged contemptuously, farted with her lips. ". . . all she wrote."

He moved from the chair to sit on the edge of the bed. "Sweetheart . . . it was his decision."

Her eyes flashed. "Do you believe in that war?"

". . . No."

"That's right. You and Mom both spoke out against it. And everything Mom said has come true — look at those fucking Pentagon Papers!"

"Please don't . . ."

"What, my language offends you?" She leaned forward grinning sarcastically. "Do

I smoke pot? Am I a smelly hippie? A flower child banging every boy at school?"

"Don't . . ."

"I have friends who snort coke, Daddy! And I'm so good, I'm so sweet, I'm such a straight little shit . . . I'm even playing fucking Maria in *Sound of Music*!"

Then her anger curdled into something else, her chin crinkling, and she began to cry.

She held her arms out to him, helplessly, and he took her in his embrace and patted her like the baby she was to him.

She wept for a good minute.

Then she drew away, snuffling, and her father handed her a Kleenex from the box on her nightstand, and she took it, saying, "Oh, Daddy, is Mike ever coming home?"

He couldn't lie to her. "I don't know. . . . I don't know, sweetheart. That's why you have to stay strong for your mother."

She nodded, blew her nose; reached for another tissue and dried her face. ". . . I'm sorry, Daddy. I'm sorry."

"I understand. I really do."

"I guess I . . . I had to take it out on somebody."

He smiled a little, shrugged. "And I was handy."

She smiled a little, too; but it didn't last

long — rage returned: "It's not fair. The war is over — it's fucking *over!*"

He shook his head. "It's never going to be over for us. Especially your mother. So stay close to her. Next year . . . when you're off at college? You'll need to come home more often than you'd probably like."

"If Mike is . . . if he's not ever coming home, if he's . . . if he got killed — will we know?"

"Maybe."

"But . . . maybe not? Maybe we just have to hang in limbo, forever?"

"I wish I knew the answer, Annie . . . sorry. Anna."

She threw herself at him and hugged him. Tight. "You call me that all you want, Daddy. You call me that all you want."

When he left her room, she was studying her *Sound of Music* script and Carole King was softly singing "You Need a Friend." All was right with their father-daughter world again . . . or as right as a world could be without her brother in it.

This was Monday, his first day back at Cal-Neva — he had virtually not set foot out of his house since that staff sergeant arrived with the news — and now Michael sat at his desk staring out the picture window at the green pines and sparkling lake and brilliant blue sky, which hadn't changed at all, despite the Satarianos having their universe upended.

Tomorrow was May first and the casino resort would be open for business, so many of his staff were here, not just maintenance but kitchen and bartending and . . . well, everybody. Word had gotten around about Mike, and one by one they'd stopped to speak respectfully to their boss. Many of them knew Mike, and these comments were particularly appreciated if painful.

One disappointment was the last-minute cancellation of Bobby Darin, who was having health problems, it seemed; but Keely Smith had been available to take the singer's place in the Sinatra Celebrity Showroom, and she had a long history with Cal-Neva.

The beautiful Smith had even dated Sam Giancana, after her divorce from Louis Prima, though she'd never been an item like Phyllis McGuire. This reminder of Giancana was an unsettling one, however: Michael's confrontation with Momo had taken place just minutes before he'd been called home to deal with the crisis of the notification about Mike being M.I.A.

He had not forgotten or ignored the

Giancana situation — he had even taken certain precautions here and at home, including picking up two handguns belonging to his son and daughter, at the gun club shooting range, and bringing the weapons to the house.

Not that he really expected any retaliation from Giancana: Sam was out of power, if possibly contemplating a return to it, and any overt attempt to muscle Michael — who was responsible only to Tony Accardo himself, now that Paul Ricca was gone — could have severe ramifications for the man they called Mooney.

But here, in the context of work, away from the tragedy of recent days, Michael wondered if he'd been negligent about contacting Accardo. He had once worked for the so-called Big Tuna, and although direct meetings between them over the past several decades had been infrequent, Michael felt certain a mutual respect remained.

If Giancana was contemplating the killing of Mad Sam, Accardo should probably be told. But Michael was so far out of the Outfit loop these days, he didn't really know where to turn — all his contacts were with the late Ricca's people. Accardo was mostly living at his ritzy Palm Springs–area estate, these days. . . .

And Michael barely knew the current Chicago boss, Aiuppa. But was there any reason to think Giancana was up to anything more than just trying to silence that crazy fuck DeStefano, before the madman spilled to the feds?

This Michael was pondering when he heard the sound of stone grating on stone.

He glanced to his right, toward the fireplace, and saw the left stony pillar moving — just a little, as if being tested. . . .

Quickly he was out from behind the desk and, moving silently on crepe soles, went to the fireplace and reached up and plucked the Garand rifle from its perch over the mantel, above the citation from General Wainwright.

His back to the stone of the other fireplace pillar, Michael stood poised like a soldier on a patriotic postage stamp. . . .

Then the pillar swung out, the grinding of stone on stone making a soft unearthly scream, and a heavyset gray-haired black-mustached man in a black raincoat sprang out like a guest at a surprise party, and aimed a .22 automatic with a silver cylindrical silencer, at the empty desk.

As his visitor burst in, Michael lunged and, as if wielding a bayonet, thrust the Garand rifle's nose deep into the man's stomach, burying it there.

The would-be assassin, surprised, did manage to swing the .22 toward Michael, who squeezed the trigger on the rifle; loading it had been one of those precautions he had taken after Giancana came calling.

Fabric and fat served as Michael's own home-made silencer as the bullet bore into the belly, and the sound of the shot was no louder than the .22 clunking onto the floor, unfired.

Then Michael swung the rifle stock up and, with a swift short hammering with the butt of the weapon, smashed the man's nose, jamming bone into brain, killing him quickly, so that no cry would emanate from his guest to bring others in from beyond the office — whether Cal-Neva staff, or an accomplice through the secret passage.

Michael grabbed the man by the arm and — before the literal dead weight could fall to the floor and mess up the carpet with blood and shit (the smell told Michael evacuation had occurred) — dragged him into the passageway, and let him lie there, his stomach leeching blood onto cement to pool.

Then Michael returned to his office just long enough to pick the silenced .22 automatic up off the floor, and paused to see if anyone had heard anything and come checking — it was midafternoon and some of the staff was already gone.

Nothing.

He stepped back into the passageway. His guest had moved through darkness, but Michael found the wall switch just beyond the fireplace, turning on the sporadic caged yellow ceiling lights, and pulled the rope handle on the pillar, shutting himself within the hidden corridor with his dead visitor.

Rifle in his left and .22 in his right, Michael made his way through the hidden hallway. At first the walls were pine and the floor cement, as he traveled through the recesses of the Cal-Neva Lodge itself; shortly the route became a kind of tunnel with cement-brick walls, indoor-outdoor carpeting, the yellowish overhead bulbs providing what struck Michael as a coal-mine effect. A fairly steep descent followed the slope of the hill.

Sinatra had put this underground tunnel in connecting the office with Mooney Giancana's favorite cabin (number 50) as well as various other passageways, including one that led from the star dressing room of the Celebrity Showroom to Sinatra's favorite cabin (number 52).

As for Michael's late guest, the Cal-Neva manager had at once recognized the guy as a longtime lieutenant of Mad Sam DeStefano's, Tommy Aiello, who'd had a spot in the Outfit since the '40s, despite being the cousin of an old Capone enemy. The fifty-something hood had probably iced a dozen victims for Mad Sam, sitting in on countless torture sessions under the ice-pick maestro.

Michael knew how these hit teams (whether Outfit or freelance) operated — almost always in twos, the designated hitter and a back-up who also served as driver. He fully expected the second man to be waiting either inside cabin 50 — which was now the resort's on-site beauty shop, no staff present, day before the lodge opened — or parked somewhere nearby.

At the end of the tunnel, the passageway straightened out, walls becoming pine again, and led to a nondescript white door, the kind that waits atop many a front stoop.

Padding up quietly, Michael propped his rifle soundlessly against the wall, and — the silenced .22 automatic in hand — leaned against the door as he carefully, slowly turned the knob, opening it just a crack, the weapon poised to fire.

A competent second man would have been primed for his comrade's return; if something went wrong, anyone or anything might come bursting through that door — so a good man would either be facing the entry, or outside, behind the wheel of his car, motor running.

But the cracked door, through which the nastily pungent chemical beauty shop odors immediately made Michael's nostrils twitch, revealed something else entirely: another member of Mad Sam's crew, Jackie Buccieri, not ready for anything, except maybe a manicure.

Jackie's late brother, Fifi, had been Mad Sam's right-hand man and hitter of choice, so valuable a player that nepotism granted a third-rate goofus like Jackie a slot on the crew, too.

Right now, Jackie — a skinny, pop-eyed, black-haired, mustached forty-some-year-old in a brown leather jacket, Levi's and Italian loafers — was sitting in one of the beauty shop chairs. He was slouched, to avoid the dryer cone, and his grin was as yellow as the passageway as he lip-smackingly took in various scantily dressed fashion models in *Vogue*, thumbing through the magazine, chuckling to himself, as if it were a catalogue from which he could select any item. The twin of the noise-suppressed .22 automatic rested next to him on a small table, amid hair spray canisters, scissors and more magazines.

Michael came through the door quickly, and was on top of Jackie in an instant, sweeping his free arm across the table and knocking the gun and scissors and some of the cans and magazines clatteringly onto the floor.

Jackie's pop eyes popped some more as he tried to stand, only to collide with a clunk up inside the dryer's spaceman-like plastic helmet, which went well with his fallen .22 and its raygun-like metal-tubing silencer.

Grabbing him by the front of the zipped-up leather jacket, Michael jerked Jackie higher, smacking his head hard against the interior of the plastic dome.

The man was barely conscious when he flopped back down into the chair, and his eyes fluttered, then popped again, as the snout of the silenced .22 in Michael's hand jammed itself uncomfortably in Jackie's throat, under an active Adam's apple.

"Who else, Jackie?"

Jackie's voice was high-pitched and whiny. "Just me! And Tommy!"

So many of these Outfit guys were just

overgrown immature kids — Tommy and Jackie, Jesus. What kind of names were those for a guy in his fifties and another in his forties?

"No, Jackie," Michael said through tight teeth, "just you — Tommy's dead."

"Fuck. Ah, fuck. Fuck *me*."

"Yeah. Fuck you. What's this about? Who sent you?"

Jackie swallowed. "Come on, Saint! You know what it's about!"

Michael reached his left hand over and plucked one of the remaining hair spray cans from the tray-like table; he shook the cap off and then — never removing the snout of the silenced gun from the man's neck — sprayed the stuff into Jackie's eyes, like he was trying to kill cockroaches.

"Shit! Fuck! *Hell!* . . . That shit *burns!"*

"What's this about? Who sent you?"

"We sent ourselves! You fuckin' killed Mad Sam!"

That stopped Michael.

Cold.

"I what?" he asked.

"You killed Sam, Saturday! Blew his fuckin' arm off and splattered his ass! You don't think his crew's gonna *do* something about it?"

So — Giancana had arranged to have

Mad Sam killed by someone else, but got even with Michael by laying the hit on his doorstep.

"I didn't kill your boss."

"Fuck you didn't! Fuck you didn't!"

Was there any way to cleanse this? Could he dump Tommy's body, and send Jackie packing with the straight story?

"It's a frame, Jackie. Giancana came to me for the hit, but I turned him down."

"Yeah, right! You was seen! You was fuckin' *seen!*"

Fuck a damn duck — Giancana had made the frame fit tight.

"Did Accardo approve this?"

"Shit yes!"

Not what Michael wanted to hear; not what Michael wanted to hear. . . .

He removed the gun from the man's neck.

"Give me your car keys, Jackie."

Jackie sat up in the chair, brushing himself off though nothing was there, just trying to regain his dignity and his manhood. He had, after all, pissed himself. When he dug the keys from his jeans, though, and dropped them in Michael's open left palm, no moisture made the trip.

"What are you driving, Jackie? Where is it?"

"What do you want with *my* car?"

"What, Jackie? Where, Jackie?"

"It's a dark green Mustang. Around the side of this place." He pointed.

"Thank you, Jackie."

"You can kill me, Satariano," Jackie said, sticking his chin out, eyes popping, "but it won't do you a goddamn bit of good!"

"It might," Michael said, and stuck the snout of the weapon in Jackie's left eye and squeezed the trigger.

The silencer was aided and abetted by the eyeball, and the squish was louder than the report, death so immediate, nothing registered in the right eye as blood and brain and bone splattered the back of the beauty-shop chair, some of it splashing up inside the plastic dome.

Fortunately the chair wasn't fastened to the floor, and Michael shoved it across the tile floor, Jackie riding along limply in it, and pushed it through the door into the passageway. The blood-spattered hair dryer, on its separate stand, he wheeled through there, too. For the time being he left the door open, as he found a small rag with which he rubbed his prints off anywhere, anything, he might have touched.

This was for the sake of the police. Though his prints might be expected to be found all sorts of places at the resort, the beauty shop wasn't one of them.

The notion of using Jackie's car to get rid of both bodies had occurred to him, but he knew such an exercise would be futile. The Cal-Neva was dead to him now; he couldn't even return up through that passageway into his office and leave with his own car. He would be seen, and possibly the place would be under surveillance — Outfit guys or even the FBI.

He retrieved his rifle, shut the tunnel door on the corpse, and went to the phone at the stand by the door where the cash register and appointment book resided. Impossibly beautiful women with impossibly beautiful manes smiled fetchingly at him from framed color photos hanging here and there, but empty chairs with hovering hair dryers stared accusingly.

"Satariano residence," his wife's voice said.

"Pat," he said, gently, "is everything all right?"

"I'm fine. I know you're worried about me, Michael, but —"

"Take the station wagon and meet me at the bank. *Inside* the bank — bring the safe-deposit key."

"I'm not even dressed . . ."

"Get dressed. Don't talk to anyone. Anyone comes to the door before you have a chance to leave, don't open it. Car's in the garage?"

"Yes," she said, alarm in her voice. "What is it, Michael?"

"What we've talked about. What we hoped would never come. Just use the garage door opener and drive straight out."

"Oh my God . . . after all these *years* . . . ?"

"It may blow over. See you soon."

They said 'bye and hung up.

Perhaps he should not have been so frank over the phone. Perhaps the Outfit had the line tapped; but he didn't think so. This was the doing of that evil troll, Giancana, who was operating out of Mexico, for Christ's sake. And Mad Sam was freshly dead, so today's assault was all they'd likely had time to mount, so far.

And it would be assumed he'd be out of shape, so long out of harness, the hit would go down like ducks in a barrel; hell, the backup might feel comfortable enough to just sit in a chair and look at magazine babes in their scanties. . . .

If he'd had more time, perhaps Michael could have savored a certain irony that this shop — where women now tried so hard to achieve beauty — had once played host to Frank Sinatra and Sam Giancana, tossing back cocktails and dallying with women so beautiful trying wasn't necessary. But the former Cal-Neva boss had more important things on his mind.

Rifle in one hand, .22 automatic in the other, looking in every direction including up, Michael Satariano stepped out of number 50 into cold late-morning sunshine.

But it was Michael O'Sullivan, Jr., who got into Jackie's car and took off in a scattering of gravel.

4

Patricia Satariano took her daily dosage as religiously as communion, the little yellow pill her host. Dulled as she was by the Valium, she nonetheless felt the panic boiling in her belly, in response to Michael's phone call.

The odd thing was, the medication did not allow that terror to spill over — she had a strange distance from it, just as (over the past week) she had developed an almost serene acceptance of her son's M.I.A. status.

The calming effect of the drug, and the sure and certain hope (as the Bible said) that Mike would return to them one day soon, had given her a state of mind that seemed to her peaceful (and to others lethargic). Thanks to mother's little helper, she'd heard the alarm bell Michael sounded, but at a safe remove.

Still, enough anxiety made it through to inspire her to guide the Ford Country Squire — canary yellow with woodgrain side panels — in record time to the First

National Bank of Crystal Bay, less than five minutes. An advantage of living in such a small town was the ability to get anywhere fast, particularly in off-season, and she actually beat Michael.

Shortly before noon, Pat Satariano — an apparently calm, remarkably attractive middle-aged blonde in an avocado pants suit and matching clogs — selected a seat in a small waiting area between the loan officers and a circular central teller's area, over which wooden ceiling spokes emanated like sun rays. For a bank, the surroundings were warm — cherrywood paneling, cream-color tile floor, woodpatterned desktops, tweedy-paneled cubicles, and the orange Naugahyde cushions of the waiting area's chrome furniture. At shortly before noon, the lobby not quite crowded, Pat sat — leaning on her darker green handbag — and reflected.

In the station wagon, she had been consumed by making good time and chanting in her mind a mantra whose hysteria was reflected only in the words themselves: *oh-shit-oh-shit-oh-shit-oh-shit. . . .*

When she had married Michael, over thirty years ago, she had known that this day might come — that despite the more or less legitimate line of work her husband had been in, the men he worked for remained criminals. And not just criminals — dangerous men.

Killers.

"We have to be ready," he would say — fairly often, in the early years, perhaps once a year this past decade or so. "If it ever became known that I was born Michael O'Sullivan, life could change for us. Or if I somehow wound up on the wrong side of a power play, we might have to run."

This was as close to a speech as Michael ever made, and the wording varied little over the years. She had long since stopped asking him what exactly they would do — had not in several decades asked him to define how they might "run" — because Michael's answer would be a mere shrug.

She had come to think of this as just some residual paranoia on Michael's part — he had after all lost his parents and his brother Peter to the violence of that world. Americans sought security, and yet no such thing existed: accidents could happen, illnesses might come, jobs could be lost and death waited for everyone. So Pat, long before her medication, had learned to shrug off Michael's concerns much as he had her queries.

Now, however, the answers to those questions would come. In minutes, perhaps moments, she'd know just how their life would change; and learn the reality behind the words "we might have to run."

And for the first time since she had begun taking the little yellow pills, she felt the urge for a smoke. She dug out her pack of Virginia Slims and fired one up. On the table before her, in the bank waiting area, were various magazines, and on top was *Better Homes and Gardens*; also in the array of periodicals were *Ladies' Home Journal* and *Life*.

And it occurred to her, as she drew the smoke into her lungs, that right now she had none of that: no home; no life. No garden, either — just an empty swimming pool.

Michael, in a gray suit and darker gray tie, entered with a large black briefcase in his left hand, his dark raincoat over his right arm; quickly he spotted her, motioned for her to join him.

She stubbed out her cigarette and did.

Within three minutes, they had signed the safe-deposit slip with the required signature (Michael's) and followed the young female clerk into the vault, where the large box was unlocked, using both the clerk's master key and the one Pat had brought from home.

The clerk, a brunette in her twenties with too much green eye shadow and a green-and-yellow floral pop-art-pattern dress, said to them, "You can stay here in the vault, if you're just putting in or taking something out . . ."

"We'd like to use one of the cubicles, please," Michael said.

"Certainly."

"If I recall, one of them has a jack for a phone."

"Actually, two have that capability, yes, sir. Shall I bring you a phone?"

"Please."

Michael had to kneel to get at the unlocked box, which he slid out from its niche, using the raincoat-draped arm to cradle and carry it out of the vault, Pat right behind.

Soon, with the door to the cubicle shut, Michael set the briefcase on the table, then — still cradling the deposit box under his arm — dropped the raincoat on an extra chair, revealing a strange-looking gun in his hand, a skinny automatic with an aluminum tube on the barrel. He placed the gun on top of the raincoat, then rested the metal box on the table, next to the telephone the clerk had set there. He sat on one side and Pat on the other, as if about to partake of a meal.

Pat had never seen the contents of the box. She knew their vital papers were kept in a wall safe at home, and had no idea why Michael had felt the need to maintain a safe-deposit box for all these years. Sometimes she had complained about the annual expense, and Michael had merely said, "Please pay it," and she had.

Now, as Michael lifted the lid, she suddenly understood, drawing in a sharp breath . . .

. . . as she beheld the tightly packed stacks of banded bills — twenties and fifties and hundreds.

On top of the money, like a bizarre garnish on a green salad, rested a .45 automatic, which she recognized as the weapon Michael had brought home from the war.

Her eyes large with the green of the money — and the gun — she noted that the bands on the bills were not new, in fact were browned with age, though the bills themselves had a crisp, unused look. This box seemed to have been filled for some time.

She said, "How muuu . . . ?"

He said, "Much? Half a million and change. Not a fortune, but plenty to start over somewhere. It's cheaper in a lot of countries than here."

"What? Where . . . ?"

"Not sure. Haven't thought that through yet. Mexico. South America. Even Canada's a possibility. That might be easier for Anna."

Her brain struggled to process all of this; the medication was not helping. "*Really* start over. Really *truly* start over . . ."

"Yes."

"Anna. . . ." And then, despite the medication, the words came out in rush: "She's a senior, Michael, she has prom coming up, and graduation. . . . She's Maria in —"

He reached across the table, past the metal box of money, and touched her hand. "I killed two men today, Pat."

". . . what?"

"Two men who were sent to kill me."

Again, she struggled to process the information, shaking her head, slowly. "I don't understand. Why, after all this time . . . ? What have you done to them that . . . ?"

"It's what I *didn't* do."

Briefly, he explained that Sam Giancana had come to him, just over a week ago, demanding that Michael perform an assassination.

"By refusing," he said, "by turning my back on the Outfit, I've put us in this position. Pat, I'm sorry."

She was shaking her head again, but quickly now. "No, no, don't say that. I wouldn't have wanted you to — you're not one of those . . . those *people,* anymore."

"But I have to be, now. I have to protect us."

Her brain whirled; her eyes could focus on nothing, the green forgotten. "How, Michael? How . . . ?"

His hand was still on hers. He squeezed. "We may have lost Mike — but we won't lose Anna."

Her forehead tightened; and she tightened her grip on his. "No, no, we can't lose Anna! We *can't.* . . ."

"We agree. She's the priority."

"Anna. Anna. Yes. Yes."

"Pat, if Mike comes back . . ."

"*When* Mike comes back . . ."

"When Mike comes back, we'll contact him. We'll bring him into our loving arms again, I promise you that. But for now we have to put Mike aside, and concentrate on keeping Anna safe."

She began to nod. "How do we start?"

"You start by transferring that money into my briefcase. I have a phone call to make."

He hauled the briefcase up onto the table, snapped it open — it was empty. She began filling it while her husband plugged the phone into the jack above where the table was flush to the wall, and he made a collect call to a name she didn't recognize.

Someone answered right away.

"Vinnie, it's Michael Satariano. . . . Don't pretend nothing's wrong. . . . Are you on a secure line? . . . You have five minutes to call me back. Here's the number."

After Michael hung up — Pat still stacking the banded stacks of cash into the briefcase — he removed the weapon from the safe-deposit box. He was checking it over, examining the clip of bullets, testing the mechanisms, making sure everything was working properly, she supposed, and then the phone rang, and she jumped a little.

Michael held up a hand to her, in a calming fashion, almost as if in benediction; then he answered the phone.

"Hello, Vinnie. . . . I called you because you, like me, were Paul's man. Are you orphaned, too? . . . Really? Well, good. It's good you're in solid with the new bunch, because you can pass this message along to them. . . . First, I didn't kill Mad Sam. . . . I don't care who says they saw what, think it through: would I do a hit for Mooney

Giancana? . . . You're right, Momo's a crazy prick, keep in mind he's also a lying prick. Much as DeStefano needed killing, much as he deserved to suffer for days and days and then die, I didn't do the honors. . . . I'm glad you believe me. Question is, can you make anybody else believe me? . . . Here's the thing: Sam's boys Tommy and Jackie came around to the Cal-Neva to see me this morning. . . . Right in my god-damned office, is where. . . . Where are they now? In that passage Sinatra built, between the office and Momo's favorite cabin. . . . Going anywhere? Not unless Christ comes, and resurrects their sorry dead asses."

Task almost finished, Pat glanced over at her husband; this was a tone of voice she barely recognized, a kind of talking she knew not at all, coming from Michael. His eyes were tight, the right one as hard and cold and unreadable as the glass one. Only the faintest trace of scar remained from the long-ago war wound, a teardrop of flesh at the outer corner of his left eye — Pat had made him get plastic surgery decades ago.

"Vinnie, I'm giving you boys the opportunity to clean up after yourselves. . . . All right then, it's DeStefano's crew, but shit runs both up- and downhill, in our thing.

I'm a made guy, Vinnie, they didn't do that without approval way up the food chain. . . . I find it hard to believe Joe Batters would sanction that myself, but he must have — do you see Tommy and Jackie doing this under their own steam? . . . Good. Good, you see my point. . . . *Do* about it? Whether I ever go back there or not, the Cal-Neva is not well served by dead *goombahs* cluttering up the joint. What kind of heat do you think is gonna come down, they're found? . . . Probably they were gonna haul my dead ass through the Sinatra tunnel, and stick me in their trunk and dump me, how the fuck should I know. . . . What do I suggest? I suggest you get one of your Sicilian clean-up crews out here, toot sweet, and get Tommy and Jackie checked out of the Cal-Neva. . . . You'll find Jackie's wheels in the parking lot of the Christmas Tree."

That was a well-known local restaurant.

"No, Vinnie, I'll call you."

And he hung up the phone.

He looked at her. "Ready?"

She nodded. All the cash had been transferred.

"My Corvette's back at the Cal-Neva," he told her. "I don't dare retrieve it. Drive to the high school. We need to pick up Anna."

"It's the middle of her school day. . . ."

"When we get there, it's the end of her school day. You up to driving?"

"Yes."

"Good." He stood, and so did she. "Pat, be strong for our girl, okay?"

"Okay, darling."

He smiled a little; he seemed to like hearing her call him that.

"I'm relieved you're not mad at me."

"I love you, Michael."

"I love you, baby. We're gonna be fine . . . but the next days, weeks, even months, may be a rough ride."

He punctuated this news by shoving the .45 automatic into his Sansabelt waistband, where it wouldn't show under the gray suitcoat.

"Could you carry the briefcase, dear?"

She said she could.

He closed the case and pushed it to her, and she took it.

A few minutes later, after the (now empty) safe-deposit box had been locked pointlessly away, Michael — the raincoat again over his arm, hiding his hand holding the automatic with the silver snout — followed Pat to the station wagon. She noticed that he seemed to be looking everywhere, though she doubted anyone else would have picked up on that.

He asked her to take the wheel, which she did, after depositing the briefcase on the seat between them. The sun was shining and the small, pseudo-rustic downtown — surrounded by mountains, under a perfect blue sky with smoke-signal clouds — seemed to her idyllic to the point of irony.

At Incline Village High, Michael slid over and took the wheel as the car waited at the curb, Pat going in to tell them at the office that a family emergency had come up, and she needed to collect Anna.

When Pat walked her daughter down the endless sidewalk to where Michael waited in the BUSES ONLY lane, Anna let go a barrage of questions.

The seventeen-year-old — in her denim pants suit with floral iron-ons and bell-bottoms, lugging her books before her in both hands — didn't mind getting out of school (what teenager would?); but she immediately jumped to a false conclusion.

"It's Mike, right? Is it good news? If it's bad news you can tell me, Mom. . . . Mom? What's going *on?* What is *going* on?"

But Pat could only think to say, "It's all right . . . it's all right. . . . Your father will tell you."

Then Michael was driving them home, and Anna was sitting forward behind them, asking questions that Michael was answering evasively.

"We have no news about Mike," the girl's father said. "But we've had something serious come up, and we'll sit and talk about it at home."

"Did somebody die? Some relative or something? I didn't know anybody was *left!*"

Mama and Papa Satariano had both passed away well over ten years ago (Papa first, Mama two weeks later); and Michael had no brothers or sisters. Well, of course Pat was aware of the one brother, who had died a long, long time ago. . . .

"Daddy, I have a right to know what is going on in this family!"

"Yes, you do," he said.

But that was all he said.

Their daughter was in full pout mode (*"Fine!"*) by the time Michael pulled into the driveway — slowly; he was looking all around again, less subtly now. A few neighboring home-owners were out in their yards, one filling the air with the army-of-bumble-bees buzz of a Lawn Boy.

Down the block a ways, two men in khaki jumpsuits were also doing yardwork

— one trimming bushes, the other seeding. A panel truck, about the same shade of avocado as Pat's pants suit, sat at the curb; bold white letters proclaimed GREEN THUMBER'S LAWN CARE with a cartoon thumb as an apostrophe and a Reno-exchange phone number.

Michael, his eyes on the jumpsuited men, said to Pat, "Aren't Ron and Vicki off somewhere?"

"Yes. Fifteenth anniversary. Hawaii."

"Do they usually have their yardwork done? I thought they did their own."

"No, they get help, this time of year."

"Do you recognize that service?"

"It sounds familiar. From Reno, I think."

"That who Ron and Vicki regularly use?"

"I don't really know."

Michael grunted something noncommittal.

Anna said, "Is this the big news? The Parkers are getting their lawn looked after?"

Michael turned to her. "Do you remember what I talked to you and Mike about?"

Anna's upper lip curled in a kind of contempt reserved only for parents of teenagers, by teenagers. "Sure, Dad — I remember the *time* you talked to Mike and me. . . . Little more help, please?"

Michael's expression had a terrible

blankness. "I went over this subject more than once — I think the last time was right before Mike enlisted. About the kind of people I work for. And the problems that could lead to."

Anna's smart-ass tone vanished. "Oh, Daddy . . . is *that* what this is . . . ? Is something bad . . . about the people you. . . . Daddy, don't scare me."

"Right now," he said, "being scared is not such a bad idea."

And he took the tube-snout silenced automatic out from under the black raincoat — folded between him and Pat in the front seat, on top of the briefcase — knowing Anna, leaning up in the back seat, could see it.

The girl sat back, hard and quick; then she covered her mouth with a pink-nailed hand.

"We'll put the car in the garage," he said.

Pat used the remote opener for him, and the Country Squire slid into place, Michael's eyes everywhere; the door closed behind them. They sat in near darkness for a few moments.

"I'm going to check the house," he said to Pat.

She nodded.

He looked back at his daughter. "Anna, I'm going to leave this with you . . ."

And he handed back the silver-snouted weapon.

But Anna was shaking her head, holding her hands up and shaking them. "No way, Daddy — no way."

He half-crawled over the seat and pressed the gun in her hand and held her eyes with his. "Your mother doesn't know how to use this. You do."

"Daddy . . ."

Somehow Pat's own protestations could not make the trip from her mind to her mouth. *This* was why Michael had insisted his two children become familiar with firearms, despite all her objections. And he'd been right, hadn't he?

Just as now he was right to give the gun not to his wife, but to his seventeen-year-old daughter, who was after all *trained* to use the goddamned things. . . .

"Nothing's going to happen," father was telling daughter. "This is . . . just in case."

Anna swallowed; her dark eyes were huge and unblinking. "I've never shot at anything but a target, Daddy . . . you know that."

With a nod, he said, "If someone tries to harm you or your mother, that's your target. Do you understand?"

She swallowed again, and nodded; the pistol was in her two slim hands, its grip in her right, silver tube cradled in her left.

Michael turned to Pat. "I need you behind the wheel. If something happens in the house, you don't think about it — you just get out of here."

"Michael, I'm waiting for you . . ."

"No. If you hear gunfire, you get out — now. Drive to the end of the block — Country Club Road? You can still see the house from there. Wait three minutes. If anyone comes out of the house but me, go. *Go.*"

Mind whirling, shaking her head, Pat asked, "And what then?"

"Head to Reno."

"Reno!"

"Yes — the church parking lot at St. Theresa's. Wait there for two hours. If I don't show, check into a motel somewhere."

"*Where* somewhere?"

From the back seat, Anna was saying, "Daddy, please, please, you're scaring me . . ."

Michael said, "Good. . . . Pat, any motel anywhere, but drive at least two hundred miles first."

"How will I know . . . ?"

"Watch the papers, TV. If the news about me is . . . bad, then you take this briefcase and . . . remember, Pat, what we talked about, at the bank. Okay? And you two . . . you two'll be fine."

Pat didn't think she could cry, not as long as she was on this medication; but now she began to.

He did not comfort her, exactly — he just put his hand on her shoulder and squeezed. "Time for that later. Right now, be strong. For yourself and for Anna. . . . Anna, you be strong, too, for you and your mother. We may have many moments like this — when I walk into that house, it's probably going to be empty."

Pat got out a Kleenex from her purse and nodded and dried her eyes and her face.

Anna wasn't crying. She'd found resolve somewhere, and just nodded once, curtly.

He smiled at them, one at a time — Pat first. "I love my girls."

"I love you, Michael," Pat said quietly.

"Daddy, I love you."

"See you in a minute."

And Michael, looking every bit the respectable resort manager in his gray suit and tie, got out of the station wagon, moved to the door that connected with the kitchen, and, just like always, stepped inside the Satariano home.

Just like always, except for the .45 automatic in his hand.

5

Afternoon sun slanted through the glass patio doors as Michael paused, having just stepped from the garage into the yellow-and-white modern kitchen. Sun rays, floating with dust motes, were bright enough to make him squint, lending a surrealistic unreality to the mundane surroundings, the world within the Satariano home that seemed as normal as the loaf of Wonder Bread on the counter.

He toed one slip-on shoe off, then the other, and moved on in his socks, the silence broken only by such innocuous household sounds as refrigerator hum, dishwasher rumble and various ticking clocks.

First he checked the pantry and laundry, just off the kitchen at his left — nothing. The adjacent door to the basement stairs made him wonder if he should check down there — semi-finished, the basement consisted of the laundry room (beneath where he stood), a storage room, and a big open space with a Ping-Pong table and a small sitting area on an old carpet with a second

TV and a '60s hi-fi. He decided the cellar could wait for last — unlikely any intruders would be down there, unless they'd ducked out of sight upon hearing the station wagon come into the garage.

So he would have to watch his back.

The kitchen fed both a formal dining room, off to the right, and the rec room, straight ahead. He had good clear views of both, though in either case he had to lean in to get a good look — not that there was any place for anybody to hide in that open dining area, with the Bauhaus chairs and marble-top table and ankle-deep white carpeting that had meant only the rarest meal had ever been taken here.

The rec room — with its comfortable bench-style sofa against the wall (behind which no one could hide) facing the wall of shelving he'd built to house the TV and stereo and all his LPs and Pat's Book of the Month Club selections — was also a mostly open area. The carpet was a shag puce and on one side was a window on the back yard, sending in more mote-floating sun rays, and on the other a wall of the tin Mexican masks Pat had been collecting, strange faces watching him in blank judgment.

With the .45 in front of him, like a flashlight probing darkness, Michael padded through the living room, Pat's current modern approach finally pleasing him — not the yellow and white geometry of it all, but the lack of hiding places this cold European style provided an intruder. The red and green and black and white abstract paintings screamed at him as he passed, as if warning of what might lie beyond. He tiptoed through the foyer into the hallway that split the horizontal house vertically, side by side bedrooms for Anna and Mike, then a bathroom, the master bedroom, another bathroom, and his study.

He began with the bedroom on the far end, Mike's, which after their son left for the army, Pat had said she intended to keep "just as it was." But of course first she had cleaned it, so now it was nothing like when Mike lived in it, when you'd have found a floor scattered with LP covers (Hendrix and Joplin) and books (Heinlein and Asimov) and of course dirty clothes, his bed rarely made; for all his young Republican talk, and despite his skill with weapons, Mike had not been a likely candidate for the military life — the posters of Mr. Spock, cavegirl Raquel Welch and Clint Eastwood from *A Few Dollars More* would not be welcome at a barracks, nor could these quarters have stood up under inspection, before Mike's mother had tidied them up, anyway. . . .

The only place to hide was the closet, but it was empty save for Mike's clothes and the shelf where the kid had stacked the *Playboy*s his parents weren't supposed to know he collected.

Anna's room — which the girl kept tidy without prompting from her mother — was likewise empty of intruders, though the closet provided considerably more clothes for someone to hide behind, and checking without making rustling noises was no small feat.

In the hall again, he listened carefully. No sounds other than the electronic pulse of any modern home; and yet he could swear someone was here. *Was he so out of shape that he was prey to paranoia, now?* Just because he'd maintained his fighting weight, that didn't mean his instincts might not've gone flabby on him. . . .

He continued on, with the bathroom.

Handgun at the ready, he nudged open the glass door on the shower stall — nobody, not even Janet Leigh, jumped out.

Starting to feel foolish, Michael pressed forward, their bedroom next, the master bedroom.

Which had plenty of places to hide —

under the antique four-poster bed, for example; Pat's walk-in closets; behind the black-and-red oriental dressing screen (a rare holdover from an earlier interior decorating scheme); and their large bathroom connecting from the bedroom, with the double shower stall. . . .

No one.

Nothing.

Nobody.

Finally he came to his study, and opened the door quickly, to find a stocky man in a dark business suit sitting at his desk; the man — bald with black-rimmed glasses that magnified dark eyes — smiled pleasantly, as if Michael had finally showed up for his appointment.

And when Michael thrust the .45 forward, a hand came from behind the door and locked onto his wrist, and twisted.

The .45 popped from Michael's hand, clunked onto the carpeted floor (not discharging, thankfully); and Michael spun to meet his attacker, an athletic-looking tanned guy with a somber face cut by Apache cheekbones. Even in the heat of the moment, Michael was taken by the strange calmness of the intruder's sky-blue eyes.

An automatic — nine millimeter? — was

in the intruder's other hand, and he shoved the snout in Michael's belly and shook his head as if advising a naughty child to reconsider that cookie jar.

Because the man did not immediately fire the weapon, Michael knew this was not a hit — not unless someone had decided to take him and torture him and then kill him, always a possibility in the Outfit life — and acting upon this assumption, kneed the son of a bitch in the balls, at the same time gripping the intruder's wrist and shoving the snout of the automatic down, to where it was pointing at the floor.

Apparently the pain was enough — Michael's knee had come up with speed and force — to cause a reflexive loosening of the man's grip on the weapon, and then Michael had the gun in his own hand . . . it *was* a nine mil, a Browning . . . and in one fluid motion retrieved the .45 from the floor, backing up into a corner between his bookshelf walls and pointing the nine mil in his left hand at the bent-over blue-eyed bastard, and the .45 at the bald-headed prick, who was still just sitting there at the desk smiling a smile made wolfish by prominent eyeteeth.

"Stand up," Michael said to the irritatingly pleasant man. "Hands up, too. And get away from my goddamn desk . . . no, other way . . . closer to the wall. That's it."

He waved the nine mil at the other guy, who was bent over, hands on knees, breathing hard; motioned for him to stand nearer to his bald associate.

The blue-eyed guy managed to comply, and even straightened up and put his hands in the air. He was tall, maybe six two, perhaps thirty-five, certainly no older than forty; the other man was pushing fifty, and he still had that disquieting toothy smile going, as if he were the one holding a gun on Michael, the eyes behind the glasses magnified enough to give their bearer a buggy look.

What made this fucker think he *held the cards here?*

Their threads were off-the-rack, but not cheap. The tall younger one had a dark blue suit and blue paisley tie, and the bald guy wore undertaker black, though his tie was a cheerful shades-of-green striped number. They were conspicuously well groomed; professional-looking.

"Daaaaamn," the tall one said, and the reference seemed to be his bruised balls, as he was hunkered over slightly. His expression was that of a man who'd been forced to stare at the sun.

148

"You're not Outfit," Michael said. "What are you? Federal?"

The bald one beamed and nodded, a professor pleased a backward student had provided a correct answer. "Yes, Mr. Satariano."

Michael motioned with the .45. "Put your gun on my desk . . . take it out slowly, and then hold it by the barrel."

Now that goddamned smile turned sheepish. "I'd like to accommodate you, Mr. Satariano — but I don't carry a weapon."

"Hold open your jacket. Let's see the lining — pretend you're Merv Griffin."

In the manner of that obsequious talk-show host, the bald man complied, saying, "We're not breaking and entering. We do have a warrant. May I reach inside this pocket and get it for you?"

"Stop smiling," Michael said, "and you can."

The fed did his best to contain his happiness and carefully reached into his pocket and withdrew several folded sheets of paper.

"Toss it on the desk," Michael said. "What's the charge?"

"No charge — not yet. The document gives us the right to enter your home for a specific purpose. And it's *not* to search the premises."

"I believe that," Michael granted, moving his gaze from man to man — the tall guy seemed to be recovering. "Or else you're the tidiest damn cops I ever ran across."

"We're here to talk to you," the bald fed said. "To you and your family."

"My family?" Michael stepped forward, thrust the gun at the bastard. "What the fuck, my family . . . ?"

The smile returned and he patty-caked the air. "No reason to be concerned; in fact, quite the opposite. My name is Harold Shore — Associate Director of the OCRS. That's the —"

"Organized Crime and Racketeering Section," Michael said, backing up. "Justice Department. Let's see your credentials."

Shore nodded, and again gingerly withdrew something from an inside jacket pocket, a small wallet.

"Step forward," Michael said, still training both guns on the two men, "and hold that up where I can see."

Shore did so.

The credentials were Justice Department, all right; no badge, but a photo I.D. — the son of a bitch was even grinning in the picture!

"You can step back now," Michael said. To the other intruder, he said, "What about you?"

"I'm with him."

"Really? You didn't just bump into him, in my study? Name."

"Don Hughes. Donald."

"Let's confirm that, Donald."

Hughes held up his photo I.D. — and a badge, this time. But the credentials weren't what Michael expected.

"Deputy U.S. Marshal. . . ." Michael frowned, shifting his gaze to Shore. "Not the first team — not FBI?"

Hughes, putting his credentials away, seemed vaguely hurt.

"The marshals work with me," Shore said, "on my unit."

"What unit would that be?"

"Some people call it the Alias Program." That awful smile again, the prominent eye-teeth conspiring with the buggy eyes to create the opposite effect intended. "We call it WITSEC."

Michael, his voice almost a whisper, said, "Witness Protection Program," and lowered the guns. "That's what this is about?"

"Yes, Mr. Satariano. But I wonder if I might call you Michael? And you call me

Harry. All my friends do. Why don't you put your guns away, and invite your family in the house."

Michael ignored that, saying, "Those gardeners down the street? They're yours?"

Shore nodded. "But we wouldn't stop you, if you left. This is not an arrest. We're here to talk, that's all. Give you an option you may not have considered."

What did they know? Were they aware of the two dead Outfit slobs in that passageway at the Cal-Neva? The call he'd made to Chicago could not yet have resulted in the removal of those stiffs. . . .

"That 'option,' as I understand it," Michael said, "would start with immunity for any crime I might have committed prior to this meeting."

"Correct," Shore said. "You can sign those papers today. And we can work out the details later."

"Don't get ahead of yourself, Harry." He turned to the marshal. "Here's your gun, Don. Button it under your coat."

Carefully, Hughes did as he'd been told. But the marshal's eyes met Michael's, acknowledging this as a gesture of trust.

Then Michael said, "You two know where the living room is?"

They nodded.

"Go sit in there and wait for me. I'm going to bring my girls in the house. I don't want either one of you saying a word to them. We're gonna restrict this to guy talk for now, got it?"

Shore gestured with open hands and, of course, smiled. "I would have suggested that very thing."

Hughes said, "We only want the best for you and your family."

Michael laughed. "Yeah, well, that's sweet as fucking hell. I'll wipe my tears and get back to you."

He stuck his father's .45 in his waistband and motioned to them to exit his office, which they did, Michael right behind.

Walking his wife and daughter to the kitchen, Michael suggested that they go ahead and prepare dinner, while he would talk to the two government men in the living room — and he did acknowledge these were federal agents, but that they were not here to make an arrest.

Both Pat and Anna were unnerved, of course, but he had said, "They may be able to help us," and that seemed to calm them both.

In the kitchen, Pat nodded toward the

living room. "Should I make enough for our . . . guests?"

"No. I'm not ready to break bread with them, just yet."

"Well, we could at least offer them coffee."

"No."

Anna was at his side suddenly. "Daddy — are we in danger?"

"With these men in the house? Not at all."

In the living room, Michael took the chair where not long ago had sat the young recruiting officer who'd reported on Mike's M.I.A. status. The two feds were on the couch across from him, Shore sitting forward, fingers intertwined, while Hughes leaned back, arms folded. The bald OCRS director tried so hard to be nice, it came off vaguely sinister; while the marshal was so low-key, you might miss how sharp his spooky blue eyes were, watching you.

"First," Shore said quietly, "I need to bring you up to date on your situation."

"Why don't you do that."

Eyes big behind the glasses, eyeteeth exposed, flecks of spittle on his lips, Shore said, "Considering your caution this evening, I am guessing that you are aware that your Chicago friends . . . perhaps I should say *former* friends . . . are blaming you for the death of Mad Sam DeStefano."

"I am aware of that. But I didn't do it."

Now Shore's eyes tightened and the grin vanished. "We don't believe you did, either . . . but there are certain people in law enforcement who don't agree with us."

Michael crossed his legs, ankle on knee; his hands gripped the arms of the easy chair. "And what people in law enforcement would that be?"

"Police in Chicago who found a weapon discarded a block from the DeStefano home . . . a weapon with your fingerprints on it."

Michael did not bother to hide his surprise. "What the hell . . ." Then he laughed, once. "Ridiculous."

Shore said nothing; both he and Hughes seemed to be studying their host.

He did his best to level with them, within reason: "My son and daughter each have a handgun — they participated in gun club competitions — and those are in my wall safe. And I only own two other guns — one's the .45 you saw earlier. The other is an old war souvenir."

Shore nodded, and then leaned forward, eyebrows hiked above the dark rims of his glasses. "And, by the way, don't think your war record hasn't encouraged your government in giving you this second —"

"Stuff it. *What* weapon has my fingerprints?"

Shore turned toward Hughes, who spoke for the first time since they'd moved to the living room. "A double-barreled shotgun. A Remington."

"I've never owned a weapon like that."

Hughes shrugged. "It was stolen from a pawn shop in Reno — your backyard — about two weeks ago."

Michael grunted. "Somebody went to real trouble, making a fancy frame like this."

The marshal shook his head. "Maybe not fancy enough — our techs tell us the fingerprints were likely planted . . . lifted from a drinking glass, say, and placed on the weapon."

Michael frowned. "That's an opinion, though — not a fact."

Shore nodded. "A prosecutor could look at a jury and say, straight-faced, that your prints were found on the murder gun." He shifted on the couch. "And we understand that you have no alibi — other than your family — for the day of the shooting."

Michael moved his head, to take Shore in better — his mono-vision could be limiting. "Harry, nobody's been around from the Chicago police or anywhere else asking me about that. . . ."

"Some checking was done by phone — Cal-Neva employees confirm you were not at work that day . . . for several days, in fact."

"There's a reason for that."

Shore, who'd mercifully stopped smiling so goddamned much, assumed a somber expression that also tried a little too hard. "We are aware of the sad situation with your son, by the way. He appears to have been a very brave young man. You should be proud."

The marshal, his expression suddenly grave as well, said, "I lost a nephew over there."

"Yeah, thanks, but Mike's listed missing, not killed; so you're saying, if I don't cooperate with you, I might be facing a murder charge in Chicago?"

Shore shrugged. "Good possibility. They have two eyewitnesses placing you at the scene."

Michael already knew this, from talking to Vinnie on the phone; but he said, "Who?"

"Sam's own brother, Mario, and Anthony Spilotro."

Again Michael laughed. "Tony the 'Ant'

157

and Mario? You mean, the same two guys who were gonna have to stand trial with Mad Sam? Who now don't have to worry about what that lunatic might spill?"

Shore nodded. "Our theory is that they were involved themselves."

"You think?" Michael let out a short laugh. "Interesting alibi — do the crime, then say you saw somebody else do it, when you just *happened* to be in the neighborhood."

Hughes said, "They said they saw a Corvette like yours, with a ski-masked guy at the wheel that could've been you, half a block from the house, driving away fast."

Shore said, "They didn't catch the license plate number, though — we figure they're being just vague enough to cover themselves should you come up with a better alibi."

Michael grunted another laugh. "Anybody else around there see this mysterious Corvette?"

"No."

"Imagine that. Did Mario and the Ant find the body?"

"No. The killer shut the garage door after him. Mario and Tony say they went to the front door and knocked, but nobody was home."

Shaking his head in disbelief, Michael

asked, "And those two would make credible witnesses in a murder trial?"

Shore sighed. "Well, it *is* Chicago. . . ."

"Couldn't your tech guy testify that the fingerprints were fake?"

"Only if the prosecutor calls him. Look, the fact that the Chicago P.D. will likely come calling isn't your only concern."

Hughes put in, "Isn't even your *main* concern."

Shore continued: "DeStefano's crew wants blood, and apparently Tony Accardo has sanctioned that action. We understand that Sam Giancana . . . still in Mexico, for the moment, in his mansion down there . . . has designs on making a comeback Chicago-way. He's put half a million of his own money into an open contract for his old friend Mad Sam's killer."

"That would be you," Hughes said, and pointed a finger — Uncle Sam Wants You, Witness-Protection-Program-Style.

"So," Shore said with a weary shrug, "that means you face not just Mad Sam's own people . . . not just contract killers . . . but any asshole with a gun and the guts."

Hughes said, "And who are you to these young punks? They don't know the Congressional Medal of Honor from a Boy Scout merit badge. You're some over-the-hill casino manager. Easy rubout. Like picking money up in the street for 'em."

Michael's question was for Shore. "Your . . . informants. They're reliable?"

That awful grin again. "Mr. Satariano . . . Mike. I'm in the reliable information business. That's what I do. That's *all* I do."

"And they say Accardo himself goes along with this?"

Shore studied Michael, then said, "You were fairly tight with him, I hear. Not as tight as you were with Frank Nitti . . ."

Hughes sat forward. "Frank Nitti?" The marshal had an amazed expression as he asked Michael, "You knew Frank Nitti? From TV?"

Drily Michael said, "Don? Despite Walter Winchell, *The Untouchables* was not a documentary."

Mild embarrassment colored the marshal's angular face.

But Michael noted from this exchange that Hughes was not as familiar with the background here as Shore; that the marshal truly was a flunkie.

Shore was saying, "According to reliable sources, you and Frank Nitti were like father and son. And a similar relationship grew between you and Paul Ricca . . . only Ricca's gone. Your protector is dead.

Which begs the question: are you tight enough with Accardo to risk going to him now, and making your case?"

This thought Michael had been mulling, since driving away from Cal-Neva in the moments following the attempted hit. Hearing it from Shore, however, forced it forward, his other option for help, for sanctuary — if not the feds, Tony Accardo.

Suddenly Michael was eleven years old sitting in a car in front of the Lexington Hotel in Chicago, his father going in to see Frank Nitti, showing good faith by meeting Nitti on the ganglord's own turf. And in less than half an hour his father emerged having shot his way back out, his face spattered with the blood of Outfit goons — because Frank Nitti had turned him away, putting business before loyalty. Then after the Angel of Death and his kid getaway artist had hit all those mob banks, Nitti made a deal. Nitti gave up Connor Looney, the murderer of Mama and Peter, to Michael's father, and promised that the war between the O'Sullivans and the Outfit was over . . .

. . . only then Nitti had sent a contract killer to end the life of the Angel of Death.

"I'm not going to talk to Accardo," Michael said.

"Good." Shore nodded enthusiastically. "Good, good, good — because, Michael, if we can't work things out here, now, then . . . well, I'll have to make a phone call. And the courtesy that's been provided to us, in this matter, by the Chicago Police Department . . . that will, shall we say, expire."

"And they'll come after me," Michael said.

"Yes. And whether they can try you effectively for the murder of Sam DeStefano or not . . . you *will* be back in Chicago, a town where every cheap punk and for that matter expensive hood knows that killing you is worth a small fortune."

Hughes put in, "Even with inflation, half a million dollars can take you places."

Funny.

Michael was just thinking that.

Because there was in fact a third option: running. Disappearing. Changing identities *without* the federal government's help. . . .

"What can you offer me?" Michael asked.

Sitting forward, a little too eager, Shore said, "In broad terms, a fresh start — a new name, a new job, a new house every bit as nice as this one. You are in an unusual position, Michael — most of our witnesses are, shall we say, not the most reliable individuals one might hope to meet."

Half a smile dug a hole in Michael's left cheek. "I thought that was your business . . . reliable witnesses?"

"Reliable *information*. Sometimes the sources are . . . well, we have had some difficulty in WITSEC with the criminal types we of necessity must deal with. Individuals who are used to making big money on the streets, who are unemployable in the straight world. We give fresh starts to some very stale individuals, Michael — most of them wind up working as grocery clerks or security guards."

"Thieves hired as guards. Cute."

"But you, Michael — you're smart, you're honest, you have a remarkable background in business. You're not some dese-dem-and-doser with a broken nose and cauliflower ears."

"I do clean up nice."

Shore's grin grew to grotesque proportions. "You will clean up *very* nicely. Usually we work for months to find anything remotely acceptable to our . . . clients. In your case, we have a situation that's perfect for you, *and* us — a restaurant that needs a manager, an establishment that the government wound up owning, thanks to an IRS matter. We also have a lovely home, almost as lovely as this, waiting for you in the same area."

Michael narrowed his eyes. "You'd provide these lodgings?"

With an expansive shrug, Shore said, "We would arrange for your home, *this* home, to be sold. Until that time, you'd live in the house we provided, rent free. Then we'd ask that you use the proceeds from the sale of this place to purchase that one."

"You can't just hand me a house, huh?"

Shore shook his head, his expression regretful. "No. We can't pay for testimony. But we have . . . leeway in seeing to it that you're able to trade this life for a comparable one."

"And all I have to do is testify."

Shore was beaming again. "You see, Michael? You are not like the people we normally deal with. You didn't say 'rat out,' or 'squeal.' You said 'testify.' You, like us, have no love for these people. You just happened to go down a road that put such people in your life . . . specifically, in the role of your employers."

Michael held out open hands. "I don't have much to give you, Harry. I've worked on the legit end."

The buggy eyes flared. "For over thirty years, in the employ of the Outfit — confidant of Nitti, Ricca, Giancana, and Accardo? . . . I think you'll make a most . . . reliable . . . witness."

Michael said nothing.

"I know you'll want to talk to your family," Shore said. He looked toward the kitchen, from which the fragrance of spaghetti sauce was wafting, Papa Satariano's recipe. "Or would you like us to . . . ?"

"No. I'll handle it." Michael sat forward, elbows on the arm rests, fingertips touching prayerfully. "Do you have the papers with you? That I can sign today? Tonight?"

That caught Shore off balance; he exchanged looks with Hughes, then said, "Well . . . yes. But I thought you . . . well, yes, I can provide those papers. Certainly I can provide those papers."

If those two killings today, self-defense or not, came to light in the next few hours, the immunity offer might be withdrawn. . . .

Michael stood. "You get those papers ready. I need to talk to my family."

Shore stood, and then so did Hughes.

"Would two hours do it?" Shore asked.

"Yes."

"I'll be back with the papers."

Michael pointed to the picture window,

where the curtains were drawn. "In the meantime, will you leave your gardeners out there, in that panel truck, and keep an eye on this place?"

"Certainly."

Michael turned to Hughes. "How did you boys come in?"

The marshal, gesturing, said, "Through the back door off the garage. We'll use that again."

"Good." He turned to Shore. "And, Harry — one other thing . . ."

"Yes?"

"When does this go down? When do we leave?"

"Oh." The question seemed to surprise Shore. "Haven't I made that clear? Right now."

"Tonight?"

Shore put a fatherly hand on Michael's shoulder. "This life is over. You're starting a new one. And the longer you give those little ladies to think about this . . . the worse off you, and they, will be."

Michael shook his head. Blew air out.

"Well," he said, "I'll be damned."

"Perhaps not," Shore said, his smile a restrained one, for him, anyway. "You'll be on the side of the angels now — see you in two hours. Pack your toothbrush."

BOOK TWO

PARADISE OF DEVILS

Two Months Later

6

The Michael Smith family of Tucson, Arizona, lived in a development known as Paradise Estates four miles southwest of the city. Theirs was one of fifty homes, red-tile-roof pueblo ranch-styles from a short list of cookie-cutter designs, each with a swimming pool and a generous lawn of Bermuda grass that required a lot of watering.

In fact, the first thing Anna had said, when they'd emerged from their new family vehicle (a wine-color Lincoln Continental), was: "Paradise Estates, huh? Paradise with crab grass."

They had come from Tucson International Airport with only the bags they'd packed that first sudden night in Crystal Bay, having lived out of them for two weeks in various motels and one hotel, all deemed "safe" by WITSEC.

And what a surprise it was to walk into their new home and find their old furniture waiting.

Among the missing were any personal items — identification, snapshot albums, letters, bills, and no clothing other than what had been frantically packed. The furniture was arranged in essentially the same manner as in their Lake Tahoe place, including a spare bedroom that had already been set up as Michael's study, complete with books on the shelves (missing any that had been inscribed to him as gifts). Even his precious 16mm film collection had made the transition (though framed signed photos to him from Sinatra, Darin, Dean Martin, Shirley MacLaine and Keely Smith had not).

Later Michael asked Harold Shore about the surprise party their old furniture and household goods had thrown for them.

"Well," Shore said genially as they sat in the living room area of a hotel suite in Phoenix (where Michael had flown for a Sunday meeting with his federal friends), "our movers went in the morning after we took you out. They crated everything up and lugged it over to a storage facility in Reno, which we watched until we were certain no one else was. . . . And then another set of movers hauled everything to a military base — you don't need to know where — until finally the crates were delivered and unloaded to your new home at Paradise Estates. We even sent along a female agent to lend a woman's touch."

"Slick," Michael said. "*If* you weren't followed."

"Oh, we take great care," the fleshy fed said, those eyes buggy behind the goggle-like black-rimmed glasses, flecks of spittle on his terrible smile. "You're very valuable to us, Michael. We have big plans for you."

"So does the Outfit," Michael reminded him.

Initially the three family members had been taken to a motel near San Francisco and kept under discreet but heavy guard by that blue-eyed Apache called Hughes. Then the Satarianos — not yet Smith — were flown to Washington, D.C., where the family was put up in a nice hotel, again protected by Hughes and other marshals.

Hughes made an interesting point, early on, to Michael: "Tell your family to be careful around my guys. We're on strictly a need-to-know basis. Keep that name 'Satariano' to yourselves. I'm the only one privy to who you really are."

"Thanks for the tip, Don. Don't you trust your own people?"

"It's not that, Michael." The voice coming out of that sharp-cheekboned face seemed genuinely concerned for the little family. "Director Shore will tell you the same — even in the OCRS, only a handful are in the know. We're up against dangerous people. But I guess I don't have to tell *you* that."

"No. But I don't mind hearing that you feel that way, too."

At first, Pat and Anna just ate room service and watched television (*Days of Our Lives* and *Match Game* among the favorites) while Michael answered question after question in Room 2730 at the Justice Department. A few days in, however, mother and daughter began working with a female agent, who briefed them about their new identities.

Standard operating procedure was that family members would retain their real first names, with a new last one providing the familiar initial. This helped prevent slip-ups, giving the re-christened Satarianos a chance to catch themselves if they started saying or writing their old names.

Or, as Anna said, "Saves on monograms."

When Michael returned to the hotel room each evening, he, too, would study the fake backgrounds provided them. Fabrication was kept simple, just the basics, should new friends or employers or teachers or whoever ask the usual innocent questions.

The Smiths needed to know where they were from (St. Paul, Minnesota — a city none of them had ever even visited) including street address and description of home and neighborhood; also some key names (of nonexistent grandparents and real schools, including colleges for Pat and Michael).

And "Michael Smith" had to be familiar with various things about the assorted businesses he'd worked for, over the years; and be aware of his undistinguished military service — he'd been stateside during WW II, a company clerk (oddly, the same fake post their son Mike had fooled his mother with, when he'd really been in combat).

A blond, bland, friendly OCRS agent named Michael Reddy counseled the family, individually and as a group, on various difficult aspects of the WITSEC program.

"You can't maintain contact with any relatives or friends," Agent Reddy said. "You'd put them — and yourself — in danger."

"But what about when our son comes back from Vietnam?" Pat asked.

"We'll bring you together, of course. He'll be over twenty-one, so joining you in your new identity would have to be his own choice."

"I understand," Pat said, apparently mollified.

Privately, however, Reddy admitted to Michael that the U.S. Army did not hold out much hope for Lieutenant Satariano's return — apparently, WITSEC had checked the missing soldier's status, as a matter of course.

"How frank you want to be with your wife," the agent said, "I'll leave up to you. . . . You might not want to put her under any more pressure right now than necessary."

Reddy also told Michael, privately, that exceptions were often made to the "no contact" policy where parents and grand-parents were concerned. Letters could be forwarded on, sans return address, and even phone calls arranged through a Justice Department switchboard; but since both Michael and Pat had lost their parents, this service would only be made available, discreetly, to Pat . . . should she want to maintain contact with her sister, Betty.

Pat and Betty were not close — the once wild Betty was now a Republican, and married to a born-again pastor — but "Mrs. Smith" did arrange for one call to be made, just to keep Betty from being concerned.

The biggest problem, of course, was

Anna, who was going steady with a boy named Gary Grace.

"You'll have to watch her like a hawk," Reddy said. "She *is* a teenager."

"No kidding," Michael said. "Can't she even write the kid a goodbye letter?"

"We advise not. Make it a clean break. Right now."

"Do you have any kids, Agent Reddy?"

"Why, yes."

"How old?"

"Grade school — third and sixth."

"Why am I not surprised?"

"Until she's twenty-one you can control her, of course, and . . ."

"You *really* don't have teenage kids, Agent Reddy."

". . . and if you want to allow her to write the boy, her letters will have to be read by both you and your wife, and by WITSEC personnel. There can be no hints of where your daughter has moved."

"I understand. Let's not even give her that option."

"That's a good call, Mr. Smith. A very good call."

Another trauma dropped at their feet was the need to make a legal name change: they wouldn't just be pretending to be the Smiths, they would legally *be* the Smiths

. . . Satariano no more.

Shore himself explained this to Michael: "We can't have you lying when you fill out legal documents, real estate documents, for instance, or loan papers. The Justice Department can't be party to fraud. You will have to use your real name . . . which is now Michael Smith."

Court records would be sealed, protecting the old and new identities alike. Pat and Anna hated this whole legal-name-change thing, though Michael didn't really care. He'd been through it before.

The intensive combination briefing and debriefing lasted almost two weeks. Toward the end a stream of new official papers flowed: birth certificates, Social Security cards, driver's licenses, even school and college transcripts. The Smiths had history.

They had documents.

They were real.

Pat and Anna were in a better mood working at memorizing their new backgrounds than they'd been watching TV, a hotel-room existence which had in particular begun to bore Anna, whose every other sentence was a report of what would be going on back home ("Prom committee is meeting now — *right now!*"). That, and

"I can't *believe* that *The Waltons* is the best thing on!"

Michael was not told who he'd first be testifying against, and in what trial, just that it would be at least six months before he had to take the stand, though thereafter he'd likely be involved in at least one trial a year for the foreseeable future. Just having a foreseeable future seemed a good start to Michael.

He would testify as neither Michael Satariano nor Michael Smith, rather as "Mr. X."

Suddenly I'm starring in a Saturday afternoon serial, he thought.

That the government had been able to make Michael the manager of a restaurant that Uncle Sam owned (due to an IRS takeover) made it particularly easy for their witness to miss work. He had no monthly stipend from WITSEC because the restaurant salary ($40,000 a year) outstripped it.

The meetings with Shore in Phoenix would be occasional, perhaps once a month, never longer than a single afternoon. Shore had to fly in from D.C. for these, and Michael was only one of dozens, perhaps hundreds, in WITSEC the Associate Director was dealing with.

"We're going to let you hang on to that

.45 auto of yours," Shore advised Michael, on the first of these Phoenix confabs.

"It's a sort of a family heirloom," Michael said, unaware they knew he'd kept it. Did they know about the half-million, too?

"I can understand you wanting some protection at hand," Shore was saying, "but no other guns, Mike. Don't make your new home a fortress or an arsenal. If you have a problem, if you have any suspicion that you've been made, let us handle it."

"Harry, all due respect — you don't even have an office in Tucson."

"No, but I can send a marshal, straightaway. One thing they have plenty of in Arizona, Mike, is marshals. You'll have a 'panic number' to call."

"Let's say I call it. What happens then?"

Shore shrugged. "Marshals will swoop down, and you and your family will be whisked away to safety again."

"What . . . to start over? New names and . . . ?"

Shore's nod was somber. "Yes, Michael. You may have to relocate several times. We hope that won't be the case, and we haven't broached the subject with your family . . . but it may happen."

"Christ."

"But know this: we've never lost a witness or a family member in WITSEC. Never." The awful smile formed. "We wouldn't be in business long if we did."

Michael was shaking his head, a sick feeling in his belly. "I'd feel better if you were using FBI, not these damn marshals."

Marshal Don Hughes was not in the room with them; he was in the bedroom next door, but did not sit in on the conversations between Shore and Michael.

The WITSEC director's face dropped in disappointment; he almost looked wounded. "Michael, they're good people!"

"Harry — you and I both know that these marshals are the bottom of the Justice Department barrel. Just because you're sending us to Arizona, don't go thinking this is my first time at the rodeo."

"Our marshals have —"

"No standards for employment — they're former city cops or sheriff department deputies with enough political clout to land themselves a federal plum. . . . Am I lying, Harry? Or exaggerating?"

Shore's normal shit-eating grin was nowhere to be seen. "No. No, Michael, you're not. But I handpick these men, from what's available."

"From what's available."

"I go over their records, thoroughly. We have the best of —"

"A bad crop? Harry, just know this: if you can't protect my family, I will."

Shore leaned forward. "I *can* protect them, Michael. I can protect *you* and *them*."

"Okay, then." He smiled just a little and locked eyes with the fed. "I'll do my end of the deal. You better do yours."

Breathing deep, Shore reared back. "You know, Michael . . . with all we're doing for you? I don't think threats are called for."

"With all I'm doing for you, Harry? I do."

So only a little over two weeks after their midnight exodus from Crystal Bay, the Michael Smith family walked into a living room set up remarkably like their previous one had been. Even the layout of the house was similar, right down to a patio off the kitchen with a pool.

Anna had taken time out between bitch sessions to take her father by the arm and, in a little-girl voice, say, "Daddy, it's weird — it's so weird. I feel like a ghost, haunting my own house."

He slipped his arm around her shoulders. "Annie, it is odd — no getting around that. But maybe it'll help us, you know . . . get back in the swing."

She said nothing, but hugged him and went off to her room — one of the few moments with Anna in this house that he would treasure.

Michael knew how hard it was for her — missing the last two months of her senior year; taken away from her friends, her boyfriend, no *Sound of Music*, no prom that she would have been queen of. For a girl her age, could anything be worse?

She wouldn't even be valedictorian of her class. The transcripts from St. Paul that would eventually go to the University of Arizona would have a 3.7, so Anna would have a strong academic record without attracting the attention such an honor would bring. Strangest of all, she wouldn't really finish high school — it was too late in the year to transfer to anywhere in Tucson, so WITSEC would cook up a diploma for the girl from Minnesota, saying she'd graduated early in anticipation of the Arizona move.

All of this served to put Anna in limbo, not to mention a deep, sulky funk.

In addition to homesickness for her boyfriend and the life she'd had to run out on, Anna was annoyed that she was a "prisoner in her own home."

She had made this clear to Michael when he took her for an afternoon drive in the Lincoln around the university campus, an oasis of learning in a residential section between Speedway and East Sixth. Wearing a yellow tube top and cut-off jeans, her long dark hair in a braided pony-tail, Anna would fit in fine with the kids on this endless acreage — she already had a dark Indian tan, and they'd only been here a week.

As father and daughter wound through immaculately landscaped drives, rambling red-brick buildings nestling among sun-shine-dappled trees and shrubs, he ex-tolled the virtues of the school, with its great programs in the arts; she'd have every opportunity here to pursue her music and acting. . . .

"I feel like goddamn Gilligan," Anna said suddenly, slumped against the rider's side window.

"Who?"

"Gilligan! Stranded on his island with the Skipper and a bunch of other idiots? . . . Daddy, here I am eighteen, and you're driving me around like I'm a little kid."

"Honey, you know I intend to buy you your own car, in the fall, when you start college. . . ."

The dark eyes flared. "If I *behave* myself, you mean!"

"I didn't make any conditions. . . . That's the auditorium over there — largest in the Southwest. You'll be on that stage, before you know it."

"I'd rather be on the first stage *out* of this hick town."

"Annie . . ."

She cast an outrageously arch expression his way. "And why, pray tell, will I *need* a car?"

"Well, Annie . . . because Tucson sprawls all over the place. You'll have to be able to get around."

"If I was living in one of the dorms, I could get by without a car. But you don't *want* me living in a dorm, do you, Daddy? Like any other *real* college student! You want me at home . . . under your thumb."

He pulled over in front of a three-story red-brick building, the library, leaving the car and its air-conditioning going. He looked at her hard and yet lovingly, though her gaze flicked from him to this and to that, her half-smirk digging a dimple in one pretty cheek.

"I'm not trying to smother you, sweetheart. You know this is no game — we're in danger, all of us. I have to make sure we're safe."

"Will we *ever* be safe?"

Not really, he thought, but he said, "I think so. But let's just . . . settle in, okay? And make a new life for ourselves?"

She grunted something that wasn't exactly a laugh. "What, I'm supposed to make a new life for myself in my *bedroom?* You make me leave everything behind but you won't let me *replace* it with anything!"

"It's early, Annie. . . . Day at a time, okay?"

"Easy for you — you've got a job, a *really* real new life! I'm just at home with Mom, who these days has about as much interest in life as one of these cactuses or cacti or whatever the fuck!"

He sighed. "Your mother will adjust."

"You really think so? She's just this, this zombie Donna Reed, any more."

"She'll adjust. And so will you. You're already making friends, right?"

"Yes, and if it wasn't for Cindy living across the street, I'd be insane by now!"

"And I haven't stopped you from going out with Cindy and her friends, right?"

She swallowed and granted him a look that acknowledged him as a human being. "No. I appreciate that. I do. And it's fun out here, sort of."

"You liked the horseback riding, right?

You said that riding trail was really beautiful . . ."

"It was okay. It was fine."

"And you and Cindy and those kids went off together, and I didn't have any trouble with that, I wasn't a jerk about it or anything, right?"

"Right."

"It's beautiful out here. You know it is. We can make a new start here, all of us."

"I know."

"We can go out for golf. You wanna go golfing with your old man?"

"Sure, Dad." She seemed worn down by the conversation. "Let's keep looking. At the campus."

"Sure, sweetheart."

But Anna was right about her mother, this Michael knew.

Pat was going through the motions, not much else. Her grooming remained typically immaculate, even if she did look like she'd aged ten years in the last few months. Her uniform had become pale pastel pants suits, the colorful, western-style clothing of Tucson not to her tastes; she looked as pale as her clothes, sitting by the pool sometimes, but in the shade, avoiding the sun.

She did the cooking and the shopping

and even the cleaning, saying she'd prefer not to have any housekeeping help. All of the housewifely stuff she took in stride, and seemed to get lost in.

When she wasn't keeping house, she sat and drank orange juice (she promised him it was *just* orange juice, since alcohol with her medication was not a good idea) and read paperbacks she'd picked up at the supermarket or watched television. She had gotten hooked on several soaps, particularly *General Hospital*, during the Washington, D.C., hotel stay; and she liked some game shows, the ones with celebrities like *Hollywood Squares* and *The $25,000 Pyramid*.

"Did you ever meet Peter Lawford, dear?" she asked him once. "He was on the *Pyramid* today."

"Yeah, a couple of times."

"He's an idiot, isn't he?"

"Pretty much."

This was what her life had become — TV, housework, cooking, the occasional inane comment. She had made no move to get involved in anything political or with a church. Her political impulse seemed limited to saying, "Fucking Nixon," whenever the president came on the TV screen; and they had not yet found a church, which was a major shift for the

Satariano . . . the Smith . . . family.

"Wouldn't you like to join somewhere?" he'd asked her one evening, at the supper table, after Anna had gone off to her room to listen to Deep Purple (the rock group, not the song).

"I don't think so," his wife said, drinking her coffee, not looking at him, or anything, really.

"Several nice possibilities on this side of Tucson. We could even go to one of these funky old mission churches."

"No." She made a slow-motion shrug. "We're supposed to keep a low profile, right?"

And that was all she'd say on the subject.

He hoped Pat would indeed adjust. And he would do his best to help her. He knew she was lying about the orange juice, because the vodka bottle in the cupboard wasn't draining itself; and he doubted Anna was snitching it. Right now, so early in this new life, he didn't have the heart, the will, to confront his wife about it.

But he would. He would. Gently. One of these days. Nights.

He felt almost guilty about how well he was adjusting himself. He had made harder adjustments before — when he and his father left their house in the middle of the night, several lifetimes ago, they'd had more than just a threat of violence hovering, they'd left behind the corpses of Mama and brother Peter. Going to a great town like Tucson in a beautiful state like Arizona was hardly as hard as living out of a Ford and sleeping in Bonnie-and-Clyde motels and robbing banks, on the road to Perdition.

He'd been Michael O'Sullivan, Jr., a kid in Rock Island, Illinois. He'd been the Angel of Death's getaway driver, written up in newspapers all over. He'd been Michael Satariano, a teenager in DeKalb. He'd been Michael Satariano the war hero. He'd been Michael Satariano the mob enforcer. And he'd been Michael Satariano the casino boss.

Being Michael Smith, the restaurant manager, was no strain.

And Tucson — its nine square miles stretched over the broad desert valley of five mountain ranges — *was* a great city, the best place he and his family had ever found to live; the girls would surely come to love it as he already did. He found the stark, arid city strangely soothing, and relished the dry heat, the wide-open sky, the horizon jagged with mountains of ever-shifting shades of red and deep blue.

The Tahoe area had wrapped itself in a pretend frontier feeling; but at heart it was a great big tourist trap. Tucson, on the other hand — with its wide, paved streets, dotted with pepper and orange trees, feather-leafed tamarisk and even Italian cypress — had a genuine easygoing vibe, informal, unhurried, blue jeans and short skirts year around. In his suits and ties, Michael was a regular dude in this culture, with its Spanish, Mexican and American Indian roots; cowboy hats and sombreros were common in Old Pueblo, as the long-time residents called the town.

Other old-timers had another name for Tucson: "Paradise of Devils." This dated back to outlaw days, when the horse thieves, gunslingers, gamblers and other "varmints" called Tucson home; the Clanton gang, Wyatt Earp and Doc Holliday had walked these streets when dusty hard dirt had been underfoot — that is, when they weren't over in nearby Tombstone (Earp had been a marshal, too).

Michael related to this, on a deep, secret level — hadn't he and his father been among the last of the great outlaws? He remembered when an old-timer at Tahoe had told him that Baby Face Nelson and

John Dillinger had used the Cal-Neva as a hideout in their heyday; and he'd thought, *You mean . . . in* my *heyday. . . .*

The Cal-Neva, of course, was history — as ancient as Baby Face and Dillinger. If Michael no longer had the responsibility of a casino resort and all its wide-ranging problems — and its considerably bigger paycheck — he was nonetheless content with his new command, a restaurant on trendsetting North Campbell Avenue.

Vincent's — whose namesake had been an embezzler and tax dodger, hence the current owner being Uncle Sam — was, as the boys back in Chicago would say, a class joint. Floor-to-ceiling windows provided a view of the city lights in a hacienda-style facility, though the cuisine was not Tucson-style Mexican, rather Continental specialties like lamb Wellington and veal Sonoita. The chef — a Russian Jew who called himself Andre — was four-star, and made a salary equal to Michael's . . . and worth every penny.

Michael, like most men of his experience, had expected to walk in and immediately begin making notes about sweeping changes. Instead, he'd found nothing not to like, and his gaze took in only perfection: fine china with pale pink linens, fresh flowers, classical music. Everywhere he looked he saw elegance — from the beamed, vaulted ceiling with its glittering chandeliers to the stone floor, from the framed western landscapes to a massive fireplace, which saw action only in winter.

He was a general stepping in to take over an army from a retiring general of great skill. Vincent may have been a crook — with a gambling habit — but he had certainly also been a fine restaurateur. Michael could not have hoped for a better situation. The job took time and expertise, but for all of that was not stressful.

The staff had been so well trained by the former owner that the place — overseen by the assistant manager for six months — was running quite well on fumes. The only person having difficulty was that overworked assistant, who was glad to be relieved of some of her duties, anyway.

The assistant, Julie Wisdom — a lovely divorcée in her early forties — was aptly named but for a troubling tendency to flatter and flirt with her new boss. He found himself attracted to this intelligent brunette, and fought stirrings that weren't helped by Pat's somnolent behavior at home.

Michael had always been a faithful

husband, but with the world at work so much more pleasant and fulfilling than the one at home, he was tempted. Already he was falling into justifications and rationalizations . . . *with what I've been through, with the stress I've been under, who could blame me?*

But he had not yet acted on these impulses. Perhaps he was still "Saint" Satariano, at heart; or maybe he just still loved his wife, the woman who had taken this dangerous road with him even though he had warned her of his deal with the Chicago devil, the woman who had given birth to Mike and Anna, the pretty prom queen from DeKalb he had fallen in love with so many years ago. . . .

On a Thursday evening, two months into their new life, Michael took Pat to Vincent's for a romantic dinner. In part, this was to send a signal to his flirtatious assistant manager; but he also wanted to encourage Pat to rejoin the world. His world. Their world.

While not Pat's first visit to Vincent's, this was the first time their daughter hadn't been along. Tonight Anna was staying with the neighbor girl, Cindy — desert-trail riding followed by a slumber party. And Michael and Pat were anxious for Anna to expand her circle of friends.

They shared Chateaubriand and an especially expensive bottle of French wine from Vincent's cellar of over one thousand. In the candlelight, against a window of sparkling city lights, Pat looked lovely and even happy. They mostly talked about Anna, since Pat didn't have anything else going in her life right now, except television and the household.

"This is going to be a hard weekend for our little girl," Pat said.

"Really? Why?"

"Saturday night — back home? Prom."

". . . Oh."

Pat sipped her wine. Then she shrugged with her eyebrows and said, "She still carries the torch for that Gary."

"Well, he's a handsome kid, nice enough. Star quarterback, president of the class. . . . Hasn't been any contact, has there?"

This time Pat shrugged her shoulders, which were bare; she wore a chic white dress, lace over a satin shell. "If so, she's hiding the letters well. I've been through her things a thousand times."

"Terrible." He shook his head.

"What choice do I have?"

"Oh, I'm not being critical. It's just . . .

what this . . . situation reduces us to."

She sipped her wine.

He nodded toward the city-scape in the window beside them and said, "Pat, if you gave this town half a chance, you'd really love it."

"I don't have any problem with this town."

"Honey, you've barely seen it."

"I'm just keeping a low profile, that's all. Aren't we supposed —"

"Actually, we're supposed to *live* our lives." He reached across the linen-covered table and took her hand. "And, darling, you need to start living yours. *We* need to start living ours."

She smiled just a little. Her eyes flicked toward the assistant manager, who wore a white shirt with tux tie and black trousers, mannish attire that made her no less a strikingly attractive woman. "Has she moved in on you yet?"

". . . what?"

"Your little minx assistant. Has she made her move yet? She's had her eye on you from the beginning."

He waved that off. "Don't be silly. I'm not interested in anybody but you."

Her mouth twitched a bitter knowing smile. "I wasn't talking about you, Michael. I was talking about that little preda-tory bitch."

He sighed, gave her half a grin. "Let's just say I haven't *let* her make a move."

"Don't." Now she reached her hand across and squeezed his. "I know I . . . haven't been very romantic lately. . . ."

They'd made love perhaps half a dozen times since moving in at Paradise Estates, strictly perfunctory.

"No problem," he said.

She shook her head. "No. No, I'll make it up to you. Michael, I will make it up to you. . . ."

Several hours later, she did.

Like all the Paradise Estates backyards, theirs was fenced off. Just a little drunk, they swam nude in their pool under a swatch of blue velvet flung across the sky, scattered with jewels, held together by a big polished pearl button. He dogpaddled after her and chased her and cornered her and kissed her, sometimes on the mouth. They crawled out, and without drying off lay on a big beach towel on the Bermuda grass and necked and petted like teenagers.

He sat on the edge of the towel, heel of his hand wedged against the cloth and ground beneath, and he gazed down at his still-lovely wife, with her slender fine body pearled with water, the breasts full firm handfuls, the legs sleek and long and soon to be wrapped around him.

"I love you, Patsy Ann O'Hara," he said.

As she lay on her back, her blonde hair splayed against the towel, her pale flesh washed ivory in the moonlight, she held her arms open, her legs, too, and her eyes were wide, her lips parted, in an expression perched at the brink of smiling, or perhaps crying.

"I love you too, Michael Satariano," she said.

He lowered himself into her embrace and indeed those legs locked around him as he entered her, and he kissed her mouth and her neck and her breasts, and she laughed and sobbed and held on to him so tight, it was as if she were trying to meld herself with him, disappear into him.

He came harder than he had in many months, perhaps years, and her cries of pleasure may well have alarmed the neighbors. They lay together, laughing quietly, stroking each other's faces, and kissed a while.

"Everything but the fireworks," he said.

"Huh?"

He played with a lock of blonde hair. "In the moonlight, you remind me of that first night, after I got back from service? . . . We were in your father's Buick, backseat, parked by that cornfield . . ."

"Fourth of July!"

"Yes, and we could see the fireworks."

"Oh, Michael . . ." She smiled at him and her look was so loving, she broke his heart even while warming it. ". . . *I* saw the fireworks. Didn't you?"

The coolness of the night got to them after a while — Arizona could get damn cold after dark — and they padded into the kitchen. She got robes for both of them — after all, Anna was just across the street at Cindy's — and they sat and had decaf.

He was trying to find the words for something when she said, "What, Michael? What is it?"

"Would you . . . please think about starting to go to mass again? And getting involved with a church?"

Her face fell. "Oh, Michael."

He leaned forward, patted her hand. "Honey, it would be so good for you."

She smirked. "You mean, keep me busy?"

"Is that bad? It's not busy work, it's . . . meaningful."

She studied him; she was almost staring. "Don't tell me. . . . Oh, Michael, don't tell me you still *believe*."

"What do you mean?"

Her eyes were huge. "You believe in *God?* After all this, you really still believe in *God,* and the fucking Catholic Church, and all that pomp and circumstance?"

He shrugged; oddly, he felt embarrassed. "Tradition isn't a bad thing. It gives things an order. Puts a framework on."

She laughed humorlessly. "Then you *don't* believe. It's just . . . social. Like a country club without the golf. A nice thing for a family to do. A way to expose your kids to a moral outlook on life, and give them some . . . some structure."

He was shaking his head. "You're wrong, darling. I *do* believe there's something out there, something bigger than us, a father who loves us and understands us. And forgives us."

She arched an eyebrow. "If so, He hasn't exactly been breaking His hump doing anything for either the Satarianos *or* the Smiths."

"Pat. . . ."

She sighed, then leaned forward, and her smile was not unkind. "Michael, if it makes you feel better to believe this ridiculous superstitious nonsense, go right ahead. Just don't ask me to go along with you."

"Then you *have* lost your faith?"

She reared back. "Are you for real? Whatever 'faith' I had died when we got that telegram about Mike! Jesus, Michael — look at our life! Look at *your* life! Your mother and brother, shot down like animals. Your father dead on a kitchen floor. These gangsters you've worked for, for so many goddamn years, they're ankle deep in blood . . . *knee* deep!"

He cradled his coffee cup in both hands; couldn't look at her. "None of it's God's fault."

"Whose fault *is* it, then? *Ours?*"

"Yes."

"Oh, because we're born sinners? Give me a break. . . ."

"My father chose his path. I chose mine."

She grunted. "Revenge?"

"Yes."

"Would you do it any differently?"

"What?"

She shrugged. "You wanted to kill the men who killed your father. Just like your father wanted to kill the men who killed your mother and Peter. Would you do it any differently today than thirty years ago?"

". . . I don't know."

She sipped her decaf, thought for a moment, then said, "You told me once that you thought it was sad that your father felt he could commit murder, then walk into a confessional, fess up, get forgiven and walk back out and commit murder again."

"I remember."

"Is that how *you* see it?"

"I . . . I don't know how I see it. I . . . I haven't had to see it, look at it, for a long, long time. We've had a good life, Patsy Ann, for a lot of years now. We had two great kids."

"Have two great kids."

"*Have* two great kids. All I've been doing over the years is trying to keep my head down and provide for us. And all I've been doing these past couple months is trying to keep my feet under me."

"Me, too. Me, too."

"But I don't think I could do that, if I didn't think that . . . that there was something out there, bigger than this, better than us. A heavenly father. Forgiveness."

She shook her head, smiled distantly, but her eyes were locked on to him. "You really do still believe."

"I guess so." His eyebrows went up. "But I never thought you'd think less of me for it."

Her expression dissolved into concern, and she reached both hands out and took one of his. "Oh, I *don't,* darling. Really I don't. I think it's . . . sweet. Naive. Kind of cute."

"Cute?"

She shrugged. "Or maybe I envy you. Because if I believed what you believe, I could handle the days better. And the nights." She sipped the decaf again. "Maybe even . . . face the thought that I may never seen Mike again."

"It's not a crutch, Pat. It's —"

Shaking her head firmly, the blonde locks bouncing, she said, "No, Mike, it's a crutch. It is a crutch. And God knows I could use a crutch. Because, Mike — most of the time? I feel like I'm falling down."

"I'm here to catch you, baby."

"I know. And I do love you. You're not gonna let that little bitch at the restaurant come between us are you?"

"No. Hell no."

She smiled; there was love in it. "Good. Take me to bed, why don't you? Let's fall asleep together in our four-poster bed like the old married people we are. And we won't talk religion anymore. Or bitches."

"I can dig it," he said.

"Ha! Aren't you the hep cat?"

She was laughing as they walked arm in arm to the bedroom. Pat hadn't laughed like that for a long time, and Michael found the sound pleasing, and chose not to recognize the desperation in it.

7

In the shimmering distance, a dazzling white edifice seemed to hover over the beige expanse of desert to meet a violet ragged ribbon of mountains and rise into cloudless blue.

The castle-like Mission of San Xavier del Bac was no mirage, rather a Moorish monument whose stately dome and proud parapets contrasted sharply with an otherwise stark Arizona vista. In the midst of the hell of an American Sahara, the church promised paradise, burning bright and white, stucco covering adobe bricks to conspire with the intense desert sunlight to create that ghost-like glimmer.

Michael had driven out Mission Road, onto the Tohono O'odham Indian Reservation, through a severe landscape of tiny houses and tilled fields that made Paradise Estates seem a world away, not just a few miles. The White Dove of the Desert, as the mission was called, was a tourist attraction, but it was also a working church, holding mass daily, four times on Sunday.

This was Friday, the morning after Michael and Pat had discussed religion, among other things, and he'd asked her to come along and she, in her robe at the kitchen table with coffee and a cigarette, had declined.

"But by all means, darling," she said, "you go."

And she'd waved a hand in a regal fashion reserved for monarchs, popes and wives.

Things had gone so well the night before that he knew getting back into the touchy subject of church attendance — much less the existence of God — was no way to start their day. But he had gone to mass regularly for as long as he could remember; even on the road with his father, all those years ago, they'd stopped at churches, if not for mass for confession and to light candles for those Michael's father had dispatched to final judgment.

Almost two months of no mass had put Michael into a kind of spiritual withdrawal. He needed a God fix.

The mission sat on a slight elevation — to call it a hill would be an exaggeration — which had encouraged that optical illusion of hovering that Michael had, from a distance, noted. The parking lot was about half full, separating the mission buildings from a plaza of craft shops and stalls selling American Indian snacks, the fragrant food aroma and displays of pottery, jewelry and baskets emphasizing the tourist aspect of San Xavier.

But the churchgoers making the pilgrimage to the mission for mass were a mix of sightseers and locals, the latter comprised of Indians and Mexicans.

Many of these wore suits and ties, however humble, while the tourists wore sportshirts and slacks and sundresses, including western-style apparel picked up on their Tucson trip, right down to cowboy hats and brand-new boots. Michael — the only Anglo in a suit and tie — could not avoid feeling he was, with these other whites, invading the land of the natives once again.

On the other hand, the collection-plate contributions would stay here, in this parish, just like the money made across the way, selling fried bread and friendship bowls.

At the edge of the parking lot, Michael paused to take in the magnificent wedding cake of a structure, which was a series of arches and domes, every surface elaborately decorated. The only use of wood he could see was in the window frames and doors; otherwise, all appeared to be burned adobe brick or lime plaster.

Twin towers — one lacking a crowning dome, as if to say God's work is never finished — bookended the finely carved Spanish baroque stone entry, which was a weathered red in contrast to all the surrounding white, embellished by gifted if naive native artisans with arabesques, shells and swirling scrolls.

Past the weathered mesquite doors, Michael felt a welcoming warmth that was in part his relief to again be inside a church but also this particular church, with its ornate carvings, painted statues and faded frescoes. Even if the colors had dimmed over time, indications of a vivid interior remained, as on the corner supports of the dome before the sanctuary, where large wooden angels perched, bearing bright banners.

He slipped into a well-worn wooden pew at the rear, on the aisle, next to a Papago family, the father with his straw hat in the lap of his threadbare brown suit, the mother in a dark blue dress touched gently with lace at collar and cuffs, and two boys, perhaps nine and eleven in black confirmation suits that hadn't had a chance to get worn out yet. They were obviously comfortable here, in this warm and lived-in sanctuary, suffering the presence of tourists with quiet dignity.

The church interior was more elaborate than your typical Spanish mission church. Colorfully painted religious statues filled niches, and on the ceiling and walls were panels detailing Christ's life and death and resurrection. The somewhat crude execution indicated these were likely the work of primitive painters, but though the faces held little expression, Michael found the depictions deeply moving.

When he took communion, Michael got a closer look at the altar, which — beneath the wide sanctuary arch — was vividly painted, polychrome with gilt touches, and arrayed with images of the patron Saint Xavier and of the Virgin, as well as scrolls and cherubs. The altar itself was backed by an intricately carved brick and stucco retable.

The service lasted forty minutes, but Michael lingered afterward, sitting alone in the sanctuary but for an occasional tourist, who climbed to the choir loft for a better look and to flash photos.

He prayed for his family. He prayed for forgiveness for himself and his father. He prayed for a miracle for his boy, Mike. But mostly he prayed for guidance and strength. When he settled back in the pew, he felt a presence beside him — it was Father Francisco, a Mexican American in his late forties with a dark brown face, creped by sun and responsibility; his eyes were large and dark and kind.

The father sat beside Michael in the pew and said, "You don't look like our typical tourist."

"I'm not a tourist, Father." He introduced himself, shaking hands with the priest, then said, "I'm local. My family and I just moved here."

"And you're looking for a church?"

"We are. But I've missed mass for a few weeks, and I'd heard about your lovely church . . . it really is quite beautiful . . . and, well —"

A wonderful smile broke through the leathery face. "You needn't apologize for stopping by to see us, Mr. Smith. And you and your family would be welcome here."

"My wife has lost her faith."

It just came out.

The kind dark eyes did not tense. Gently, the priest said only, "Why?"

"Lot of reasons. Starting with our son is M.I.A. in Vietnam. And . . . we got rather violently uprooted from our old life, and dropped down here in Arizona, kind . . . kind of like Dorothy in Oz."

The priest nodded. "A move takes adjustment. And the loss of a son is an adjustment we never really make. It's the kind of wound that doesn't heal. But if your wife could find her way back to the loving embrace of our Lord, that would be a start."

"I know. I know."

"If you'd like to take confession —"

"No! Uh, no. Thank you, Father. You really do have a beautiful church here at San Xavier. Pleasure meeting you."

The priest took his cue and rose and allowed Michael out of the pew. "As I said — you and your family are always welcome here. We do have several Anglo families who are members."

"Thank you, Father."

Outside, Michael moved quickly to his Lincoln in the parking lot. Across the way, tourists were buying trinkets and finger food — somehow it cheapened the experience. No way would he give confession, though he had two more killings on his conscience, Tommy and Jackie, those DeStefano crew would-be hitters he'd taken out at Cal-Neva.

But that had been self-defense, or at least in defense of his family (admittedly he'd pretty much just whacked Jackie), and he felt he could sort that out with God personally. He would make do without an intermediary in a collar. Besides, even after all these years, he had vivid memories of the pale faces of the priests who emerged from their side of the confessional after his father, the legendary Angel of Death, had dropped by to cash in his latest sins for forgiveness.

Still, Michael felt refreshed somehow, as he drove back to Paradise Estates. Relieved that he and the Man Upstairs were on speaking terms again. He found the pageantry and the Latin liturgy and the Host on the tongue all reassuring; he was taken back to his childhood, before his mother and brother were gone, when the world was big and unknowable but his life had been small and secure.

A stray thought popped into his mind: after Connor Looney killed Mama and Peter, his father had gone to the Looney mansion, to beard the lion in his den; but, before leaving the boy to sit in the car in the dark, Papa had given him a gun and said, "If I'm not back in an hour, go to Reverend Dodd at First Methodist for sanctuary."

Papa did not want Michael going to Father Cailoway at St. Pete's, because mob money had built that church.

"No sanctuary there," he'd said.

And one other thing Papa had made very clear: Heaven was the next life; this life was Hell, and just navigating through its flames was enough to keep a man busy.

When Michael pulled the Lincoln in the drive, Pat came flying out the front door, a whirlwind in a yellow pants suit. For a split second he thought she was glad to see him, and wanted to rush into his arms as a result of last night's rekindling.

And she *was* glad to see him, but not because their love had been renewed or that she'd reconsidered about joining a church. . . .

Her eyes were wide and hysterical, and her voice quavered with terror: "Oh, Mike — Anna's *gone! She's gone!*"

She gripped his arms with steel fingers.

His hands found her shoulders. "Easy, baby, easy. Go slow."

The words were a rush: "I called across the street, at the Parham's . . . to see if Anna wanted to have lunch with us."

"Right. She and Cindy and some girl-friends were having a slumber party . . ."

"But they *weren't!*" Her eyes and

nostrils flared, and words streamed: "Molly Parham said she thought Cindy was staying with *us* last night — Molly's fit to be tied, too, but *she* isn't part of the Witness Goddamn Fucking *Protection* Program, with gangsters wanting to kill her and her whole fucking family!"

He took her into his arms and patted her gently, saying into her ear, "Settle down, honey, settle down — it's nothing. Just a couple of high school girls putting one over on their parents. Just a bunch of kids trying to . . ." He remembered Anna's words. ". . . get out from under their parents' thumbs for one night."

Pat pulled away to look at him, her dark blue eyes showing red-tinged white all around. "No, no it's *worse* than that. She's gone, Michael. She's run off!"

"What makes you think that? Did she leave a note?"

Pat shook her head, her blonde locks flouncing, as if the hair itself were as hysterical as its owner. "No . . . but come inside, Mike. Come inside."

His wife dragged him by the hand through the living room and down the hallway to the bedrooms, and into Anna's. She yanked the closet open, dramatically, and then opened several doors, and showed him.

"Most of her clothes are gone," Pat said, working to control herself now. Making her case. "Not everything — she left enough for me to maybe not notice, right away. And her little powder-blue suitcase, *that's* gone, too."

Michael drew in a breath, let it out as he took in the room. "How did she sneak the stuff out of the house?"

"I don't know! She says we patrol her like Nazis, but it's not really true. I've left her here alone lots of times, when I've gone to the store or whatever."

He moved closer to Pat. "Do we think that girl across the street helped? Cindy?"

She shrugged helplessly, saying, "Maybe. Cindy told her parents the same lie Anna told us."

"What about Cindy? Is *she* gone?"

Eyes flared again. "Well, she's not *home!*"

"No, honey, I mean — has Cindy run off, too?"

Pat threw up her hands. "I don't know . . . I don't know. I only know the Parhams are pretty upset."

"Let's go talk to them."

They did.

Sid Parham was in life insurance and his wife was a substitute grade school teacher;

they were solid citizens, and wonderful, generous parents, whose daughter hated them.

But Cindy's clothes were all present and accounted for, as well as her suitcase. The Parham girl did not seem to have taken off with Anna, though probably had aided and abetted the getaway.

The two sets of parents sat in the Parham kitchen, which was much like the Smith's, looking out on a familiar fenced-in backyard with pool.

"They took off together yesterday afternoon," said Mrs. Parham, a slender not particularly attractive strawberry blonde in a blue-and-white floral-print-shorts outfit, "in Cindy's new little red Mustang."

"We bought Cindy a Mustang," Sid Parham said pointlessly, a bald heavyset Uncle Fester–ish fellow, dressed for yardwork. "For graduation."

"She hasn't graduated yet," Michael pointed out.

"Well, there are a lot of things going on this time of year," Parham said defensively. Suddenly Cindy having a car seemed to be the problem. "Her having it early made sense. Senior parties and prom and —"

"Prom," Pat said.

Michael looked at her and their eyes

locked. He said, "Tomorrow night's the prom, back at —"

But he stopped. He'd come very close to saying Crystal Bay.

"Back where you used to live?" Sid said, finishing Michael's statement with a question. "St. Paul, isn't it?"

"Yeah," Michael said. "St. Paul. . . . If you hear from Cindy, let us know right away. Right away!"

"You'll be the first," Sid said.

"Don't be worried," Mrs. Parham said. "Cindy does this kind of thing all the time."

Back in their own kitchen, Michael and Pat sat and held hands, tightly.

"You think she's gone back home for prom?" Pat asked, shaking and on the verge of tears. Hope and despair fought for control of her voice as she said: "She's gone back for prom, hasn't she?"

"It's a possibility."

"Where *else* could she have gone?"

"It is a real possibility." He sighed and shrugged. "But it's a long damn drive . . . twelve, thirteen hours."

Shaking her head, Pat said absurdly, "She doesn't have that kind of *driving* experience!"

"Easy, Pat — remember, she doesn't

have a car. If Cindy didn't drive her, she'd have to take a bus or plane. A girl her age can't rent a vehicle . . . unless she has fake I.D., which I suppose —"

Pat squeezed his hand so hard it hurt. "What are we going to *do?* Oh my God, Michael — what in hell can we *do?*"

"I'm not sure."

"That panic button!" Her eyebrows climbed her forehead. "We'll call the federal panic button, and they'll go get her!"

"We could do that. Are you prepared to move again?"

Pat, half out of the chair, froze. "What?"

"If I call our friend Assistant Director Shore, he'll help us out — send marshals to Lake Tahoe to grab her up . . . *if* our assumption is right . . . but in any case, they will consider our cover blown."

Still frozen, she asked, "So what?"

"So . . . it means another name change. Another move. Another city. Another new life — for all of us."

She sat heavily down. Her eyes stared at nothing. "Oh, Christ . . . but what *else* can we do?"

"If we're right about where Anna's gone, we retrieve her. I'll drive or fly back home, and get her. The prom isn't till tomorrow night."

Pat was looking at him now, guardedly hopeful. "We'll go together?"

"No. I think . . . I think the first thing we do is call some people back home."

Nodding decisively, Pat said, "I can do that."

"No." He held out a cautionary palm. "I don't want those calls on our long-distance charges. Hell, for all I know, the feds have our phone tapped."

Indignation tweaked her expression. "I thought we were the *good* guys!"

"No — we're not the good guys, and we're not the bad guys. We're the poor bastards getting squeezed between. . . . I'll go to a phone booth, and call every neighbor back there I can think of, to see if anyone's seen Anna."

Nodding again, frantically, she said, "Start with the Grace house! She's gone back to be with that Gary, I just know she has!"

He nodded, too, but slowly, reassuringly. "That's where I'll start. Can you think of anyone who lives next door to the Graces? Or even in their neighborhood?"

Her eyes tightened. "No . . . No, his family lives in Incline Village. That Pineview development, but I don't know anybody there. Damn!"

He held his palm up again. "Pat, it'll be all right. Do we have a picture of Anna since we moved here?"

Turning her head toward the hallway, she said, "There are some snapshots on her mirror, from when she and her wonderful-great-good-friend-that-little-bitch-of-a-brat Cindy went horseback riding."

"Get me one, will you?"

"All right." She stood, then hovered. ". . . What are you going to *do* with it?"

"I'm going to hit the bus stations, train depots and the airport."

"You make it sound like . . . like she's a runaway."

"She is, sort of. But just for the weekend, I think. This is just about prom."

Again her eyes tightened, in confusion this time. "But didn't Cindy drive her . . . ?"

"We don't know that. And that's a long way to drive, whether Cindy's along or not. The picture?"

"All right."

Rising, he said, "I'll be in my study."

She eyed him with mild suspicion. "Doing what?"

"Getting something."

"Getting what, Michael?"

"Pat — just fetch the picture, okay? And stay calm. Stay steady."

She went off to Anna's room, and he slipped into his study and from a locked desk drawer got the .45 automatic — the gun his father had taken on the road, the gun he had taken to Bataan, the gun he'd used as an Outfit enforcer — and slipped it in his waistband, in the small of his back, covering it. He wasn't sure he would need it; he wasn't even really sure why instinct said to take it with him.

But that's what instinct said.

And he listened.

He'd just finished snugging the gun away when he heard Pat in the hall. Then she was standing framed in the doorway, holding up the snapshot.

"Everything else we have of Anna," she said glumly, "didn't make the trip from Crystal Bay."

She stepped into the study and he took the snapshot, dropped it into his suitcoat pocket, then wrapped her up in his arms and looked earnestly at her.

"Darling," he said softly, "it's going to be fine — she's just a teenager who didn't want to miss her senior prom. Can you blame her?"

Frustration and something like anger colored her face. "Doesn't she know what she's done? How she's put us all at risk?"

"No. Like I said, she's a teenager. . . . And even when we get her back home, safe and sound, we may have to seriously consider telling Shore all about this."

Alarm again widened the dark blue eyes. "You said bringing WITSEC in was *dangerous* . . ."

"It may be more dangerous *not* moving on to another identity. I'm going to want to talk to Anna and her boyfriend about just how much contact they've maintained, and how they did it. And then, remember . . . we have another option."

Confusion tensed her forehead. "Which is what?"

"We still have our half-mil nest egg. We can start over like we were planning to, before WITSEC stepped in — a new life in Mexico or Brazil or some damn place. Without the federal safety net, but also without the federal hassle."

Her eyes were so tight with thought, they were almost closed. "What will Anna think about *that?*"

He smirked. "What does she think now?"

She fell into his arms and held on to him tight and shivered. "I want to go with you."

"Back to Tahoe?"

"Everywhere — to the airport and —"

He held her away, just a little, and locked her eyes with his. "No, honey. You need to stay here. By the phone."

She thought about that, then said, "You're right."

"Anna may call, or the Parhams may hear from Cindy, or Cindy may show up and —"

"You're right. Go." She managed a crinkly smile, somehow. "Get out of here and find our little girl . . . ya big lug."

"I love it when you call me that."

"Find our daughter." The smile from a moment ago was ancient history. "I couldn't take . . . *find* her."

He nodded, and then he kissed her lightly.

She clutched his face in one hand, roughly, in an almost accusatory fashion; and then kissed him — hard.

"I love you, Michael. You'll come through for us. You always come through."

"I love you, Patsy Ann," he said, and kissed her.

And went off to find their daughter.

8

Michael started with the Greyhound Terminal on South Church, talking to every clerk and vendor and even a guy with a broom. The snapshot of Anna was fairly close up and she was an attractive girl whose heart-shaped face, big dark eyes and endless brown mane made her distinctive enough to be remembered. But no one did.

American Trailways on East Tenth drew the same disappointing results, though Michael did catch one slight break. The same clerks were working today, at both terminals, as had been on duty yesterday afternoon. Which was exactly when his daughter would have come around to buy a bus ticket (based on when Cindy's parents saw the girls drive off in that red Mustang).

Otherwise, Michael would have had to spend much of the day tracking down off-duty bus-station tellers, all over Tucson.

The identical combination of good and bad luck awaited him at the Southern Pacific railroad station on East Toole: same clerks on duty as yesterday, none of whom recognized Anna's picture. This was repeated at Tucson International, six miles from the city, out US 89, though it took a while — he had to query busy clerks at American Airlines, TWA and half a dozen other lines major and minor.

From a pay phone at the airport, already pushing four p.m., he called the Parhams to see if they'd heard anything from their daughter Cindy. They had not.

So he called home.

Pat answered the phone with a painfully eager, "Yes?"

"Just me, sweetheart." From the sound of her voice, he knew the answer to his next question, but he asked, anyway: "Hear from Anna?"

"No. Any luck with the snapshot?"

"Afraid not." He quickly filled her in about the air, bus and train terminals. "I think we can be reasonably sure she didn't travel that way. I just called the Parhams and they haven't heard from Cindy, either."

"You think Cindy drove Anna to Tahoe?"

"Well, it's just the idiotic kind of road trip a couple of teenagers might take. And with that many hours facing them, two drivers, trading off behind the wheel, would suit the plan."

"Michael, we don't know for *sure* she went home. . . ."

"No we don't. She and Cindy could be hanging out with some of their friends at some mountain cabin, taking their rebellion out with beer or pot or something."

"That doesn't sound like Anna."

"Not to me, either, but a kid frustrated about her life . . . on the weekend of the prom she can't attend . . . could behave seriously out of character."

"Oh, Michael . . . what now?"

The frustration and desperation in his wife's voice broke Michael's heart, but he kept his own tone positive.

"Do me a favor, sweetheart. Call across the street and get that Parham woman to phone the parents of every friend of their daughter's she can think of. If Anna's still in Tucson, we need to find out. . . ."

He left unstated: . . . *before I go running around the Tahoe area, breaking our cover, looking for her.* Just in case the feds *were* tapping the Smith line. . . .

"Yes," Pat was saying, "yes, that makes sense. I'll get her to do that right away. . . . What about those calls we talked about?"

Pat, too, was being cautious about what she said on the phone. She was referring to the long-distance calls to friends in Tahoe that Michael had said he'd make. *Good girl,* he thought.

"I'm doing that next. . . . Listen, I know it's no picnic for you, staying home by the phone. But it's important."

"I know it is. And I love you, Michael, for . . . for springing into action like this."

"Listen, she's fine. You just hang in there, baby. I love you, too."

They said goodbye and hung up.

Before he left Tucson International, Michael bought a ticket on the red-eye to Reno — the flight, on American, would leave at one a.m.; in Reno he would rent a car and spend Saturday in Crystal Bay and Incline Village, tracking down their wayward daughter; and would *she* be thrilled with her father, when he pulled the prom rug out from under her. . . .

On Congress he found a drive-in bank that stayed open till five, and just made it in time to trade paper money for rolls of nickels, dimes and quarters.

His next stop was the library on South Sixth. In the massive two-winged red-brick building, he found a wall of shelves with out-of-town phone books — including one labeled LAKE TAHOE AREA. He hauled the relatively slender directory out onto a stone table in the library patio and sat in the sunshine for twenty minutes copying numbers onto a piece of scratch paper.

At a pancake house on Stone, he pulled in to the parking lot and soon was making phone calls in a nearby booth.

He'd already prepared a speech for these friends and acquaintances who'd been abandoned when WITSEC whisked the Satarianos into the Smiths's new life.

"Yeah, well, I got this job opportunity on the East Coast and I had to jump at it. Didn't mean to leave you folks in the lurch."

That was all he intended to share, other than, "Look, I promise I'll call again under better circumstances, but Pat and me, we're crazy with worry, trying to find Anna. We think she got homesick and ran back there to go to the Senior Prom. Have you seen her?"

This, with minor variations, was how he steamrolled over any questions, and elicited support, since most of those he called were also parents. Then when whoever-he'd-called said he or she hadn't seen Anna, Michael would say, "Thanks, anyway, sorry, gotta keep looking, 'bye," and hang up.

This approach was successful in all ways except the key one . . .

. . . no one had seen Anna.

Worst of all: no answer when he dialed the number of boyfriend Gary Grace's parents. And he tried them in between every other call, getting nothing but an endless ring and then the coins rattling back down.

The need to keep the calls brief prevented gathering any other information, such as whether the Graces were out of town. But some information Michael already had: for example, he knew that little groups of the kids always went out to dinner before the prom, nothing organized by the schools, just cliques, socializing; and that after prom, parties (mostly at the homes of various kids) would go on till dawn.

Sometimes the prom itself was held in the Incline Village High School's gymnasium, but all the crepe-paper streamers in the world couldn't turn that echoey, sweat-sock-smelling cavern into the kind of romantic wonderland the students had in mind. So most years, the Prom Committee found some other, more appropriate venue in the area; and of course Tahoe offered many nice possibilities.

Several months (that seemed like years) ago, Michael had taken the booking himself, helping out his daughter, who after all had been on the committee: the 1973 Incline Village Senior Prom would be held in the celebrated Indian Lounge of the Cal-Neva Lodge.

This fact may have eluded Pat; in any case, Michael had no intention of reminding her. . . .

When he emerged, unsuccessful, from the phone booth, night had settled over Tucson, and the neon SAMBO'S sign had replaced the sun. Still in the suitcoat, he raised the lapels against a cool evening that threatened to turn cold.

He pulled into the driveway just after seven.

Pat met him at the door, a beautiful woman who looked terrible, her make-up long since cried off, her eyes webbed with red, her usually carefully coiffed 'do a tangle of greasy blonde worms and snakes; only the yellow pants suit looked crisp, polyester holding up under any tragedy.

He had never seen her look worse, nor loved her more.

"Nothing from the calls," he said.

"Not a word from Anna," she said, voice cracking.

He looped an arm around her and walked her into the house, nudging the door shut. Her head leaned on his shoulder.

They settled onto the Chesterfield couch in the front room, their target-like abstract paintings seeming particularly ugly to him at the moment.

"Have you heard from the Parhams lately?" he asked.

She swallowed and nodded. "Yes, Molly claims she called everybody she could think of, going back to friends Cindy had in junior high. All the parents were supportive, of course, but nobody knew anything."

"No big party last night?"

"No. And no other lies about a slumber party at somebody *else's* house. This looks like strictly a scheme of Anna's and Cindy's."

"Really looking that way."

Pat craned her head. "Do you think Anna went somewhere else?"

"Other than Tahoe, you mean?"

"Yes. I mean, if she's really fed up with us, maybe she went out to California or something. Lot of kids live on the street out there — Haight-Ashbury or something?"

He shook his head. "Our girl's no hippie. She likes her creature comforts. Really, we're probably over-reacting."

She reared back. "How can you say that?"

"I mean . . . because of our specific . . . situation, we're reacting in a way that . . . makes sense." He shrugged. "But if you take WITSEC out of the equation, Anna's just a teenager whose parents moved and made her miss prom."

"You mean . . . she hasn't run away for good, just to go back to prom?"

"Right. If we didn't do a thing, she'd probably come strolling in that front door tomorrow night or Sunday, and face the music."

Pat's eyes narrowed. "You could be right. I think . . . I think you *are* right. She's just run away for the weekend. But with our . . . like you said, 'situation' . . . it's so very awfully, terribly dangerous."

"Yeah."

He held Pat and she cried into his chest.

For a long time he squeezed her, patted her, then he said, "Should we eat something? I haven't eaten all day."

"*Could* you eat? I don't think I could eat *any*-thing."

"We probably should."

He was thinking of keeping her busy; but he was also thinking about keeping himself sharp and straight — he'd be flying via that red-eye tonight, after all. With a big day tomorrow. . . .

Fifteen minutes later they were eating ham and Swiss-cheese sandwiches at the kitchen table. Pat was drinking a glass of milk, Michael a Coke.

"Funny," he said.

She smirked humorlessly, half-eaten sandwich in hand. "I can't imagine what's 'funny.'"

"Took me back a second. When we were kids in DeKalb . . . teenagers like Anna . . . this is what we'd drink. Woolworth's soda-fountain counter. Glass of milk for you, Coke for me."

Her smile was bittersweet. "We've been together a long time, Michael."

"I know. And I wouldn't trade it for anything."

She reached across and squeezed his hand. "What now? I'll go crazy, waiting."

He told her about the ticket on the red-eye.

"You have to stay here," he said.

She arched an eyebrow. "Hold down the fort?"

"Home fires burning," he said, nodding. "I'll keep you posted, every step of the way."

"I know you will. But I . . . I . . ."

She put her sandwich down and began to cry again. He got up and went around to her, knelt by her, slipped an arm around her shoulder and said, "I know it's hard to be strong. And there's not much you can do, now. You really should get some sleep."

"Sleep? I don't think that's possible."

"You didn't think you could eat, either, and what happened to half of that sandwich?"

She laughed a little. "I still have those pills, from when . . . when we heard about Mike."

She meant the sedatives.

"Can you take those, along with the, uh, other?"

"Valium, Michael. It's not a bad word. Yes. The same doctor prescribed both, nothing to worry about."

"Okay. Well, I'll feel better on that plane, not thinking you're tossing and turning and, uh, just . . ."

"A mess?" She sighed, managed a small smile. Then she yawned. "My God, I am tired, at that. . . ."

She took the pills at the kitchen counter, and he walked her into the bedroom. She got undressed and into her preferred night wear, baggy black silk men's pajamas. Either the time they'd spent talking and eating, or the medication, had relaxed her.

He took her in his arms. "You look beautiful."

"Oh, yeah, right."

"But you do." He kissed her on the mouth, tenderly. "Get some rest. And *I'll* hold down the fort. . . ."

"Love you," she said, and got under the covers of the four-poster. She switched off the nightstand lamp, and he slipped out of the dark bedroom into the hall, closing the door, tight.

He went back and finished his sandwich. Considering what she'd been through, Pat was doing all right; he was glad she'd had the presence of mind to get some sleep, even if a somewhat medicated one. He cleared the kitchen table, put the dishes in the sink and ran water over them. He got out of the suit he'd been wearing all day and into a black Banlon shirt, some gray Sansabelt slacks and crepe-sole loafers. Then he took some time getting an overnight bag together, including a change of clothes, some toiletries and a box of .45 ammunition.

Though exhaustion was nipping at his heels, he didn't allow himself to fall asleep; he sat in his recliner in the rec room, sipping another Coke (the caffeine was just the ticket) and watched television, volume low so as not to bother Pat. *The Rockford Files* he enjoyed — Jim Garner was just doing *Maverick* again, but that was okay with Michael — but half-way through *Police Woman*, he was thinking that Angie Dickinson's good looks weren't enough to justify this nonsense when, on the end table beside him, the phone rang.

He looked toward the hall, and the bedroom, wondering if it would wake her, expecting Pat to come rushing out.

"Smith residence."

"Say," an amiably gruff male voice said without preamble, "it's Sid Parham. Listen, Cindy's come home."

He sat up. "What does she say about Anna?"

"Why don't you come over and talk to her yourself. She says Anna's fine, but . . ." Embarrassment colored the perhaps too-friendly voice. ". . . you come talk to her yourself."

He went in to tell Pat, but she was sound asleep.

Deciding not to disturb her, he shut her back in, and soon stepped out into another chill, clear night, though the streetlamp on this block was out and the full moon was on its own. Almost running, he crossed the street to the Parhams; on the front stoop, he glanced at his watch, thinking about the red-eye flight: quarter till eleven.

Stocky bald Sid Parham, in a two-tone burnt-orange leisure suit (was he going skydiving?) met Michael at the door and led him, once again, to the kitchen. Molly was wearing an identical leisure suit. *And parents these days wondered why kids rebelled. . . .*

All four chairs were taken at the square glass kitchen table, mother and father framing the daughter, with Michael across from the girl, a small, petite blonde who had drawn the best features from both her parents, and still wasn't pretty.

But maybe that wasn't fair — the girl looked tired, and sat slumped with more than just sullenness. Her light blue eyes were hooded, emphasizing her robin's-egg eye shadow, their industrial-strength mascara matched by dark circles that could pass for Halloween make-up.

She didn't look at him, at first. He'd seen this teenager with his daughter numerous times, and she'd always been well groomed, for the type; but tonight her hair — blonde with dark roots, straight to her shoulders — looked unwashed and bedraggled. She wore a green tank top, which flattened the perk out of her small breasts, and cut-off denim short-shorts and sandals.

She was playing with her car keys.

Had he been her father, Michael would

have already taken those away from her.

But he kept his voice friendly. "Cindy, what's the story? Where is Anna?"

"How should I know?" Cindy asked.

Her father said to her, "You told me she's all right."

"Well, she is."

Michael said, "When did you see her last?"

"Yesterday."

"Where is she?"

Half a smirk dimpled a cheek. "When was *I* put in charge of her?"

"You weren't. Where is she, Cindy?"

A weight of the world sigh came up from her toes; my gaaaawd, adults were stupid! "Look, I dropped her off at a Denny's on Speedway yesterday evening."

"Why?"

"She met up with some friends in the parking lot. They were going to a party."

"What friends? What party?"

"I don't know — I didn't go to it. And they were *her* friends, not mine. I had this other party to go to."

Michael shook his head; but he kept all anger and irritation out of his voice. "Cindy, you're Anna's only friend, her only contact in this town. We've only been here six weeks."

"What's the problem?" She looked up in mock innocence and batted her eyelashes at Michael, which might have worked if he were eighteen and her baby blues hadn't been so bleary. "Didn't she come home or something?"

"You know she didn't."

Her father said, "Cindy! You told us Anna was *fine!*"

She gave him a dirty look and went back to playing with her keys.

Michael said, "You do know where she is."

The girl said nothing.

"Where is she, Cindy?"

"I told you I don't know."

"Would you rather talk to the police?"

She looked up sharply. "What did *I* do?"

Michael shrugged. "My daughter's been gone long enough for me to file a missing-persons report. You're the last known party to've seen Anna. So you're the first they'll be talking to."

". . . What if I *do* know where she is?"

"Then you should tell me."

She shook her head. "I'm not going to tell you."

"Why not?"

"Because I promised her. You guys are terrible to her."

"Then I'll tell *you*. She's in Lake Tahoe."

Cindy said nothing, but her eyelids flickered.

Sid Parham said, "Where have you been since yesterday, Cindy?"

"Driving."

Molly Parham said, "Driving where? You're going to get in trouble, young lady!"

Michael closed his eyes.

Then he opened them and said, "Cindy, I know Anna went back to Crystal Bay so she could attend prom."

Sid Parham said to Michael, "You're from St. Paul."

Michael said, "Sid, I know I'm a guest in your home. But you need to let me handle this."

"Well . . . sure . . . but. . . ."

Michael rose, gave Parham a nod to come talk to him, out of the girl's earshot. Near where the kitchen fed the living room, Michael said softly, "I have a big favor to ask, Sid — and I'm asking as one father to another. May I please talk to your daughter alone?"

"Oh, now, I don't —"

"I'm not going to browbeat her, and I certainly won't touch her. But I think having you and your wife there makes it harder for me to get through to Cindy."

"Why would that be?"

"Kids this age take an attitude with their parents around. I've talked to Cindy half a dozen times, and she's never been like this with me before. I think I can get her to relate to me . . . one-on-one, if you'll give me the chance."

Parham drew in a deep breath, looking more than ever like Uncle Fester; when the man finally spoke, Michael half expected it to be in a high-pitched whiny voice.

But the voice was Sid's usual baritone, and so gentle as to be almost sweet. "Listen, Michael — I know you love your little girl. Like we love ours. And I know all about how difficult it can be. . . . So you go ahead."

"Thank you, Sid."

"Understand, if it gets loud, I'm coming in!"

"I understand."

Parham nodded. "I'll talk to Molly. . . . Give me a minute."

The man of the house went over, whispered in his better half's ear; she frowned, started to say something, but he whispered again. And finally, reluctantly, she nodded.

Sid, walking his wife away from the kitchen table, a gentle guiding hand on her elbow, said, "We'll be in the front room, if you need us."

"Thank you," Michael said.

As they left — looking like janitors in an art museum in those leisure suits — Cindy frowned. She seemed confused and perhaps a little worried.

Michael said to her, "How much did Anna tell you?"

Cindy looked past him and shrugged.

"Did she tell you that she was putting herself in danger?"

Cindy looked at her keys; fiddled with them.

He plucked the keys from her fingertips and set them down, with a small clunk, out of her immediate reach.

"Did she tell you that she was putting her mother and me in danger?"

Cindy folded her arms over her small flattened breasts. "She wanted to go to her prom. What's so *dangerous* about that?"

Relieved to finally have confirmation of his theory, he asked, "How did she get there?"

The girl shrugged. Her emotions seemed on the verge of breaking through the sulk; the tiredness helped — it took energy to maintain a good pout, even for a kid.

"Did she tell you everything?"

". . . Maybe."

"Did she tell you the kind of people this involves?"

The girl looked away.

Were her eyes damp?

"You didn't drive her there. If you had, you'd still be in Tahoe, staying till after prom, to make the round trip."

She smirked, but the curled lips quivered. Somehow the blue eye shadow and mascara only made her look younger.

"What did you do, Cindy?" he asked, casual. "Meet the boyfriend half-way?"

The girl's forehead tensed a little.

Thinking out loud, Michael said, "You drove half-way, and met Gary at a rest stop or gas station . . . ? And he drove her the rest of the way, right?"

"Why ask if you know?"

"Not a rest stop. I'm going to say . . . Las Vegas. That's about half-way, and that sounds like fun. But all that desert driving, it's no picnic, is it?"

Tiny chin jutted. "What if I *did* drive her? I'm eighteen."

"Without stopping it'd be maybe six, seven hours to Vegas. With pee breaks, and grabbing quick bites at diners, maybe eating in the car. You must have air-conditioning in that little Mustang your folks got you. . . ."

"So what if I do?"

He sat forward. He kept his voice even, flat, only vaguely threatening. "Why are you back so late? Why didn't you stay in Vegas longer?"

"You're so smart. You tell me."

". . . Well, it sounded like more fun than it was. You're right, you are eighteen, and you have to be twenty-one to get into the casinos. And those security boys can spot fake I.D. at a hundred yards."

Her eyes tensed; she was staring down through the glass table.

"So you drove up and down the Strip, taking in all those bright lights, and you had some food, drive-in maybe, and maybe shopped a little. Couple nice new malls, there. Did Anna and Gary spend the night in Vegas?"

She said nothing; but she swallowed.

"And then you kids fooled around Sin City this morning, nice breakfast, maybe a little shopping — there's a record shop Anna likes there, with lots of British releases . . ."

Her eyes flashed a little. He was obviously dead-on. Seemed to frighten her that he had Anna pegged like that.

"I'm not psychic, Cindy. Our family's spent a lot of time in Vegas, over the years, is all — I've even worked there. So the two of them headed out for Tahoe today, about mid-afternoon maybe? Three or four? Some more nasty desert driving ahead for 'em. But they ought to be there, by now. Like you're here."

She leaned an elbow on the glass table, rested her head against a hand.

"Where are they staying, Cindy?"

"I don't know."

"Cindy, how much did she tell you?"

"What do you mean? About what?"

"You know what I mean. And about what."

She swallowed again; she was trembling. "Everything, I guess. That, that you . . . you ran casinos and stuff. And you're testifying against these Corleone-type guys, so you're, like . . . hiding here? In Tucson?"

"Right. And now Anna's actions . . . and your actions . . . have put her and Gary, and me and Anna's mother and even you and your parents, at terrible risk."

"What? That's crazy."

"It is crazy. These people are ruthless. They take a human life like you might swat a mosquito. Means nothing to them."

She covered her face with a hand whose hot-pink nails were chipped a little. "I . . . I really don't know where they're staying. . . . I just know they . . . they're in

Tahoe. I just know . . . just know Anna wanted to go to her prom." She looked up with eyes soaked with tears, the mascara streaming in dark ribbons. "Why is that so wrong? Who's gonna care about that, but her stupid parents? . . . S-sorry."

"Anna told you not to tell anybody about us — about my being a witness, didn't she?"

"Y-yes."

"Well, that includes your parents, Cindy. Do you understand? That includes your parents."

The girl nodded a bunch of times, then rose to get some Kleenex from a dispenser on the kitchen counter. He rose and went to her, put a hand on her shoulder.

"I'm not mad at you."

She was still crying, but not hard.

"I know you were just trying to be Anna's friend."

"I . . . I am Anna's friend."

"And that's why you'll keep everything we talked about between us — just you and me, Cindy." He took her face in a hand, gently. "Just you and me? Friends?"

She swallowed and nodded. "Friends."

He was going off to join her parents when her voice called out, "Mr. Smith! . . . I'm sorry. Didn't you ever do anything stupid, when you were a kid?"

"No," he said, and smiled at her.

She laughed a little, choked on snot, blew her nose, and was crying at the glass table again as he stepped into the living room.

Molly, reading *House Beautiful* magazine, was seated on a squat low-backed red-and-black sofa that was like a massive unhealed wound against the pale pink walls. A squat ugly cactus decorated an end table, and a pop art print of a crying comic-book woman was framed on one wall next to shelves of stereo gear and LPs, opposite another wall of silvered panels reflecting the room back at itself, distortedly.

Sid was at the front picture window, the dark-pink drapes drawn, peeking around an edge. "Goddamned hippies," he was saying.

Michael stood beside him. "Cindy gave me the information I needed. She was very helpful. . . . What's wrong, Sid?"

He nodded toward the street. "I noticed this pothead scum earlier today, driving around the neighborhood."

Leaning in next to his neighbor, Michael looked out and saw a van parked just down the block, almost directly under the burned-out streetlamp, straddling where the Smith property ended and their next-door neighbor's began . . . an old faded red panel truck with flowers and peace symbols and the KEEP ON TRUCKIN' guy painted on it, badly.

Sid's upper teeth were showing and he wasn't smiling. "What are they doing, coming around a respectable neighborhood like this for, anyway? Making their goddamn drug deals. . . ."

The back of Michael's neck was tingling, but he said, "Don't worry about it," and patted Parham on the shoulder. "I'll check it out."

"Would you, pal? You, uh . . . want me to go with you?"

Michael smiled and shook his head. "No. I'll just run over and tell 'em to go peddle their papers someplace else."

"Rolling papers, you mean!"

He managed a polite laugh, and said, "Why don't you two check on your daughter? She's a little upset."

Parham nodded, and he and Molly went off in their unisex uniforms, toward the kitchen.

Michael turned off the front stoop light before slipping out of the house.

That van had not been here when he'd crossed the street half an hour or so before.

Head lowered, he walked down the sidewalk on the Parham's side of the block, away from his house. When he came up from behind, along the driver's side of the battered van, he stayed down, hoping not to be picked up noticeably in the side mirror.

Like a carhop with a gun, Michael thrust the .45 through the window into the chest of the driver and without even getting a good look at the hippie behind the wheel, harshly whispered, "What the hell is this about?"

But the hippie behind the wheel was not a hippie.

He was a hood in his forties from Chicago in a bad Beatle wig and an old paisley shirt and tie-dye jeans and a fur vest Sonny Bono might have considered cool in 1966.

Jimmy Nappi was Giancana's man, a driver on scores mostly, with tiny eyes, a long nose, a wide mouth and plenty of pockmarks. He was not known as a tough guy, not somebody generally enlisted for killings, though he was a made man, so had killed at least once.

But if *Nappi* was here — parked just down the street from the "Smith" house, with his hands on the wheel of a van that tried much too hard to look like it belonged to hippies — it could only be for one reason.

No time for discussion; no reason to give Nappi a chance to go for the .38 on the rider's seat beside him.

Michael buried the snout of the .45 in the hair vest and fired and all that Sonny Bono fur served well as an impromptu silencer.

Heading around back of the house, Michael again stayed low, .45 in hand. With the Lincoln in the driveway, they would have figured he'd be home. He prayed he was not too late. He climbed over the fence and lowered himself to the cement patio by the pool. The sliding glass doors on to the kitchen were locked, he knew, but another conventional door was down off the laundry room, and he used his key on it as silently as possible, easing the door open, making only the slightest creak.

Laundry room was empty.

Kitchen, too — just as he'd left it, right down to the dishes in the sink.

Padding through on his crepe soles, he could faintly hear Ed McMahon saying *"Heeeeere's Johnny,"* the audience responding with the usual applause; he'd left the TV on in the rec room, when he left. That might actually help — it would cover him. . . .

In the trashed living room, standing next to the slashed, stuffing-spilling Chesterfield sofa, using a can of red spray paint on the wall, was another Giancana hood playing hippie (in a wig and jeans and Hendrix T-shirt) — Guido Caruso, a big fat-faced fuck who took pleasure in beating on deadbeat welshers, when they were smaller than him, anyway.

Sprayed across one of the abstract green-and-black-and-red-and-white geometric paintings, Guido had written: OFF THE PIGS! On the wall over the couch, he had already written HELTAR [*sic*] and had just gotten to SKEL when Michael blew the top of his head off and made another abstract painting on the wall, albeit lacking a frame and heavy on the red.

Michael barreled into the hallway and almost ran into the third "hippie," this one with a fake beard to go with his Beatle wig, and faded striped red-and-blue jeans and an American flag T-shirt — Frankie Inoglia, a sadistic enforcer in the Mad Sam mode. As skinny and wild-eyed as Manson himself, Inoglia had just exited the bedroom where Michael had left Pat not long ago.

Inoglia had a blood-dripping butcher knife in his Playtex-gloved fist, and when he saw Michael coming, raised the blade high, a pearl of blood flicking off the poised-to-stab point onto Michael's cheek like a single tear as he shot the intruder in the right kneecap, and — as Inoglia was going down — shot him in the left kneecap, too, then kicked the knife out of the fallen, screaming man's hand as he passed, heading into the bedroom.

Michael would re-live this waking nightmare many times, but it would never be as vivid as in this moment.

The nightstand lamp was switched on, its shade spattered and streaked with red. KILL THE PIGS was fingertip-scrawled in blood on the wall just over the headboard of their four-poster, and Pat, on her back, was slashed to ribbons on the bed itself, the sheets soaked, her black silk pajamas shimmering with the life that had been spilled. He stood beside her and looked down and saw that her throat had been cut, slashed ear to ear. The other wounds — save one, over her heart — were not so deep. They were window dressing, part of the hippie masquerade. The chest stab had killed her, and — judging by the placid expression on her lovely, untouched face, eyes closed — in her sleep.

This small saving grace would be for

Michael the only thing, in days ahead, that would stave off madness.

He kissed her forehead.

"Goodbye, baby," he said.

In the hallway, he knelt beside Inoglia, who was still screaming in pain, the faux hippie an overgrown fetus now, grabbing first one ruined kneecap, then another, a process he kept repeating, mixing his own blood with what had already been on the dishwashing gloves he wore.

"She was asleep when you killed her?"

"Fuck you, rat! Fuck you!"

Johnny Carson was getting big laughs in the rec room.

"She was asleep?"

"Yes! Yes! Yes!"

"That's why I'm doing you this favor," he said, and shot his wife's assassin through the left temple, the bullet smacking into the wall on the other side, its kiss puckering the plaster.

The shots and the screams — on the heels of Sid Parham's paranoia about hippies in the neighborhood — would have the police here soon.

Never looking at his dead wife, he returned to the bloody bedroom and transferred the contents of the overnight bag into a larger suitcase, threw in more clothes and made room for the briefcase with half a million dollars in it, which he retrieved from under the floor boards in the closet of his study.

From the same hiding place he took his Garand rifle — a souvenir the feds didn't know he'd hung on to — which was field-stripped into barrel, buttstock and trigger group; also tucked away were four boxes of .30 ammunition, twenty cartridges each. The parts of the rifle and the small white ammo boxes he wrapped up in various articles of clothing within the suitcase.

In the kitchen he grabbed the rest of his wife's pill bottle, figuring the sedatives would come in handy. In the bathroom he peed, then checked to see if he had any blood on himself or his clothes, and didn't. Finally he took a .38 long-barreled Smith & Wesson revolver off the corpse of Inoglia, and left this house, and the woman he had loved for over thirty years, behind.

A white-faced Parham was in the window across the way when Michael pulled out in the Lincoln, suitcase in the backseat, and four cop cars siren-screamed past him on US 89 on his way to the airport.

He had a red-eye to catch.

9

Under vaguely yellow lighting, Michael —
in the black Banlon sportshirt and gray
slacks with a dark-blue windbreaker —
parked the Lincoln Continental in the
Tucson International lot, and got his suitcase out of the trunk.

Six weeks ago, the '72 Mark IV had been
deeded over to "Michael Smith" by
WITSEC Associate Director Shore — a
confiscated, luxury, low-mileage number
poised to go on a federal auction block,
where it would likely now end up again.

Just in case anyone was watching, Michael
made a show of locking the automobile,
although he would be walking away from
what had once been a nine-thousand-
dollar ride.

Michael did not relish entering the airport, and taking his red-eye flight, unarmed; but with the rash of skyjackings the
last couple years, airport security had been
beefed up. With these new metal detectors,
and search of carry-on bags, he dared not
tote his .45. The gun was in his Samsonite

suitcase, along with his field-stripped Garand rifle, various boxes of ammunition and a briefcase filled with half a million in cash.

This was a bag he hoped the airline could manage not to lose.

Michael checked it with an attractive blonde in stewardess mufti at the American Airlines counter in the outer terminal, who set it down with another half-dozen bags. Then he headed for the nearby bank of telephone booths — he had a long-distance call to make.

This time not even a dime was required, much less an elaborate handful of change; he closed himself in, sat and dialed O, asked for the charges to be reversed . . .

. . . and gave the operator the "panic button" number.

"Yes?" a male voice answered.

"A Mr. Michael Smith calling," the operator said, "station to station — will you accept the charges?"

"Yes."

Michael said, "I need to talk to Associate Director Shore immediately."

"Where can you be reached?"

Michael read the number off the phone.

"He'll be with you in five minutes."

"Make it sooner."

It was — about three.

"What's wrong, Michael?"

Anxiety undercut the pleasant, business-like surface of the WITSEC director's tone.

"You haven't had any reports?"

"No. What's *wrong,* man?"

Michael gave Shore a brief dispassionate description of what had gone down at the Smith residence.

"Oh my God," Shore said, sounding not just shaken but genuinely saddened, over Pat's murder.

After completing the story — the only details he skipped were such private matters as packing guns, money and sedatives — Michael said, "Don't ask me where I am. You probably already know."

"I don't, but of course it would be easy enough to find out. Let's agree to work together in this dark hour. You stay put, and —"

"No. I don't like your level of protection."

"Michael . . . I can understand that. . . . Jesus Christ, I can understand that, but *nothing* like this has ever happened before in the program! I *swear* to you!"

"Imagine how comforting that is to hear."

"I . . . I can't imagine what you're going through. How's . . . how's your daughter taking it?"

Unless Shore's acting rivaled George C. Scott's, the fed was honestly unaware of the girl's disappearance, a state Michael was not about to spoil by sharing information.

"Her name is Anna, Harry, and how do you think she's doing? Her mother was butchered."

"Michael . . . I guarantee your safety. Yours and Anna's."

"I thought you already had."

The words came in a fevered rush: "I don't know what you have in mind, but you can't make it alone out there. You need us. You . . . need . . . *us*."

"No. You need me, maybe. This is just a courtesy call, so you can clean up out at Paradise Estates, if you want. And to, you know, say so long and fuck you."

A sigh breathed through the receiver, then: "Michael, you have to come in from the cold, you just *have* to . . ."

"I like the cold. Getting colder."

Shore tried another tack. "You said these were Giancana's men? Not DeStefano crew, like before?"

"All Giancana insiders. Hard asses. Formerly."

Shore's words continued to leap desperately out of the receiver: "Michael, since last week, Giancana is back in the United

States — our intelligence indicates he's trying to position himself for a return to power. *That's* why he's done this — he thinks you're a threat to him."

"He's right."

"I meant in court."

"Don't worry, Harry — he'll be judged."

"Michael, no. What happened at your home was self-defense. Anything you initiate now —"

"Do we know how Accardo feels about this? Would he have sanctioned this hit?"

". . . Not likely. Accardo rules from the sidelines, through weaker men he can control. He's probably telling his people that Giancana's time is over, but —"

"But what he's thinking is, Mooney's too strong."

"That, and the Big Tuna probably doesn't like having somebody as high-profile as Mooney Giancana back in the press."

"Since when is Giancana making headlines?"

A brief pause in the fed's fast flow of words indicated, perhaps, that Shore had to consider whether or not to share what he said next: "Mooney'll be a media darling again, within days — he's set to testify at a committee meeting in Washington next week."

"*What* committee meeting?"

"Senate Select Committee on Intelligence. It's that old rumor about the CIA working with the mob to assassinate Castro."

"Not to mention Jack Kennedy," Michael said.

Shore ignored that, and blurted, "We have a golden opportunity here, Michael! Giancana is no Mad Sam DeStefano — he'll be testifying under oath, selling out the CIA, but revealing nothing at all about the Outfit. *Omertà* runs deep in an old made guy like Giancana."

"So, Harry, you see my wife's murder as a golden opportunity?"

"No, no, no. . . . It's just, Giancana is full of himself, thinks he's smart and clever; but he *will* perjure himself in the process . . . and with you on our side, Michael, with your knowledge, your testimony, we'll take him down."

"On perjury."

"That will just be a *start!*"

"I'm looking for the finish, Harry," Michael said, and hung up.

The metal detector was a tunnel four or five feet long, and he had to walk a ramp up inside, and back down. On a trip to Hawaii six months ago, before everything went wrong, he and Pat had talked about how airline travel just wasn't fun or special anymore; once-upon-a-time, two or three years back, passengers wore suits and dresses, and the food was decent, and the stewardesses were friendly, and anyone with the price of a ticket was a kind of jet setter. Now you had to submit yourself and anything you carried onto the plane to a frisk.

"Like a common criminal!" Pat had said. "All the romance is going out of it."

His wife and her voice in his mind, Michael walked casually toward his gate and didn't spot Marshal Don Hughes until nearly too late.

The lanky, Apache-cheeked Hughes, his back to Michael, was at the check-in counter talking to a stewardess, showing her something — a picture of Michael probably. Two other guys in off-the-rack suits and snapbrim hats — *who the fuck wore hats, anymore, but feds!* — were bookending Hughes, and fortunately both men also had their backs partly to Michael.

One marshal began to swing around, probably on the lookout for Michael, who lowered his head and fell in with a few other passengers, and moved on past the gate.

The airport was fairly dead this time of night and it wasn't as if a crowd was available to get lost in. But finally he found another small group to walk with and headed back. He watched in the reflection of a closed newsstand's window to see if Hughes and/or his Joe Fridays were on to him.

Apparently they weren't, because soon Michael had made it back out into the terminal lobby, his mind clicking through a thousand things, including wondering if Shore had been keeping him on the phone so Marshal Hughes could arrive and nab him.

Then he stopped in his tracks. *Oh shit,* he thought, sick with visions of his money and his guns catching the plane without him, going to Phoenix to make the connecting flight on their way to Reno. . . .

He went directly to the American Airlines counter, where he sucked in a relieved breath as he saw his Samsonite still waiting amid half a dozen others to be passed through for loading.

"I've got a sick kid at home," he told the woman at the counter. "I have to scrap this flight. Can I get my bag back?"

He waved his boarding pass.

"No problem, sir," she said, with a

friendly apple-cheeked smile. The blue-eyed blonde looked just a little like Pat — or was he reading in? "I remember you — you seemed distracted. I hope your, uh . . . little boy?"

"Little girl."

"Hope she gets better. You can use your ticket at a later date, no problem."

Within two minutes he was again in the yellow-lit parking lot, unlocking the driver's side of a wine-color Lincoln that he had never expected to see again. He unlocked and opened the back door, and threw the Samsonite in on the seat. He clicked the suitcase open, got the .45 out, stuck it in his waistband, closed the case and soon was driving out of Tucson International Airport.

The terrible reality was he had only one option: driving to Lake Tahoe. The trip would take at least a dozen hours, possibly more, and he'd already had a long, traumatic day. His soldier's detachment had saved him so far, but fatigue could eat away at that, and emotions could get out of their cage. . . .

Right now, as he headed north, he tried to decide whether Anna was in any immediate danger.

She was not Giancana's target. But if the

261

"Smith family" cover had been blown due to Anna keeping in touch with Gary Grace, the girl's current whereabouts would be known to the Outfit. The nastiest scenario he could come up with was Giancana goons snatching her and using her to get at Michael. If they already knew where she was, such a kidnapping had probably already taken place.

Bad as that was, she stayed alive.

Associate Director Shore seemed unaware of Anna's status, although admittedly that could have been a scam. If WITSEC did know about the girl running away, and where she'd gone, Michael could do nothing about it. And the feds were no threat to her, really.

Perhaps he should call that panic number again, and send Shore after Anna, to protect her in case Giancana sent his forces after her . . .

. . . but what if it hadn't been Anna's indiscretion with Gary that had blown the Smiths' cover?

What if WITSEC had sprung a leak?

Pushing the panic button in that case meant handing Anna over to their betrayer.

No.

His only option was to go after his daughter himself; and she wasn't going anywhere, not until after prom, which was Saturday night at eight p.m.

At Cal-Neva Lodge.

One-eleven a.m., still near the airport, he pulled into a Standard station and told the gawky high-school-age attendant, "Fill 'er up."

The Lincoln's gas tank was what, twenty-one gallons? But he was getting around ten miles to the gallon. So he bought a cannister of gasoline and two quarts of oil, as well as several big jugs of water, and put them in the trunk.

The coveralled kid, in the process of cleaning the windshield, grinned as he chewed his gum and said, "Must be gettin' ready to do some desert driving."

"Yeah."

"Well, you're smart to do it at night."

"Not sure smart is the word. You got any coolers? Something on the small side?"

"Sure."

"Throw some ice in one, and toss half a dozen cans of Coke in there, too. And a couple Snicker bars."

"Sure thing!"

He gave the kid a twenty-keep-the-change, and then bore north on 89, going straight up through Tucson, barely no-ticing the slumbering city. He started with the windows rolled up and the air conditioner on low — cool enough outside without it, but he didn't relish the rush of wind. Wasn't like he was setting out in a buckboard into the wilderness — the Lincoln had comfy bucket seats, a Cartier clock and plenty of headroom, not to mention horsepower.

Washed ivory in moonlight, the open plains of the desert, bordered by blue-tinged mountains, had a soothing, other-worldly beauty. Few other cars were on the road, and he had the two-lane stripe of concrete mostly to himself, often driving straight down the middle. He and Pat had taken this route to Vegas now and then, because they liked to spend the quiet time together, listening to music, enjoying the strangely peaceful landscape and the feeling that they were the only two people in the entire world.

He thought about her, various little incidents over the years, jumping from high school to just last year, from their early days in Chicago to Crystal Bay — nothing major, just tiny anecdotes that his mind kept playing for him, one memory triggering another and another.

An odd detached calmness settled over him as he drove and drove and drove.

Whenever he came to a gas station, he would stop and fill up, since one never knew in the desert; many of these stations were twenty-four-hour, but the desert didn't listen to reason, so better to keep the tank as full as possible.

Some stations had diners still open, but he didn't eat, other than a Snickers bar about two hours in; and he drank Cokes, their caffeine helping out, and would stop and pee alongside the road, feeling weirdly serene as he sent a yellow arc into the ivory landscape under a vast sky of stars.

The third roadside pee break, he had his first bad moment. He looked up at the sky and said, "She was right, wasn't she? Either you're not fucking up there at all. . . . Or worse, you *are* up there and we're just some goddamn ant farm you lost interest in! *Fuck* you!"

He yelled all of this, and it sounded hollow in the night, not echoing exactly, more floating.

Despite the caffeine, he was getting tired, and about four hours in, the monotony stopped helping and started hurting. Suddenly he was weaving and ran off on the soft shoulder and woke himself up. He reached into the cooler on the otherwise empty rider's bucket seat, and got

265

another can of Coke going. He turned the air conditioner up until the car's interior was damn near freezing. Then he stuffed a random four-track into the tape player and Johnny Mathis came on.

"Chances are," Mathis sang, and he remembered how much Pat liked the song — wasn't her favorite or anything, just a song that when it came on, she'd always say, "That's so pretty," and he began to cry.

Losing control of himself and the vehicle, he had to pull alongside the road and get out and he knelt on the sandy desert floor in the big empty cathedral of the night, cacti here and there like prickly votive candles. He wasn't praying. He was weeping.

Ten minutes later he got shakily to his feet, pouting like a kid who suffered an unfair parental spanking, flashed the sky a middle finger, and again got behind the wheel.

The idea had been to tough out the whole twelve or thirteen hours, but by just after dawn, when the Lincoln rolled through suburban Henderson into Vegas, Michael had decided he needed a new plan.

His route didn't take him to his one-time home-away-from-home, the Strip, where the Vegas of the Sands and Stardust and Sahara were in the process of displacement by the overblown themed likes of Circus Circus, Caesar's Palace and the MGM Grand. Howard Hughes had talked of Vegas becoming a "family" town (not meaning "family" in the Syndicate sense, either), a concept that longtime casino manager Michael knew had great potential.

In some respects the Cal-Neva had anticipated that, with its genuine resort-in-the-mountains attributes, boating, hiking, horseback riding; yet a certain nostalgic fondness for the Rat Pack glory days lingered in Michael even now, perhaps because on his periodic Vegas stints, he and Pat had shared laughter and love in this neon paradise, hobnobbing with celebrities, enjoying fine food and the lush life.

Near downtown, practically in the shadow of that leering electric cowboy Vegas Vic, he pulled into the Lucky Seven Motel, one of those space-age two-story courtyard affairs with glass flecks in the cement serving as glitz.

The young man at the desk was skinny with bored brown eyes and an untrimmed mustache and shaggy dark hair, and seemed less than thrilled with the short-sleeve white shirt and snap-on blue-and-red striped necktie he was required to wear. "Stairway to Heaven" was playing a little too loud on a cheap radio behind him.

Michael spoke up, requesting a room on the first level as far away from the street as possible, and the clerk complied, possibly because that was the easiest thing to do. After signing in as John Jones, the former Michael Smith paid the twenty-five dollars in advance, and said to the clerk, "I need a nine a.m. wake-up call."

The clerk frowned in thought, which was an obvious inconvenience. "Tonight you mean?"

"No — *a*.m."

"Oh, you mean tomorrow morning?"

"*This* morning."

The frown deepened. "Three hours from now?"

"Right. Will you still be on duty?"

"Yeah, just came on. So what?"

Michael summoned a smile for the sullen young man. "Because if I get that wake-up call, nice and prompt? I'll be another twenty-five bucks grateful."

The clerk brightened. "No problem, Mr. Jones!"

Locked inside the room, curtains drawn tight, air conditioner up, Michael placed the .45 on his nightstand, stripped to his underwear, slipped between cool sheets and was asleep in seconds.

He dreamed he was driving.

Dreamed he was back on the endless highway through the desert, following the ribbon of concrete under a beautiful starflung sky and a moon-bleached landscape. Pat was next to him, smiling over at him, wearing that lacy white dress from their evening at Vincent's.

As dreams went, it wasn't a bad one, other than his mind providing him with more of the same experience that had sent him into this motel room; a kind of delirium accompanied it, giving him an awareness of being in a dream but no power over that dream. Still, having Pat beside him, not talking, just smiling over at him, occasionally touching his shoulder or leg or hand, Johnny Mathis singing a non-existent love song on the four-track, was comforting.

Then he glanced over at her and she was someone else, another woman he'd loved once, a long time ago. *They had killed Estelle in a terrible way, tortured her and burned her to death and he had found her body, when he was just a kid in his early twenties who had admittedly seen horrible things in war but nothing to compare to a beautiful woman tortured and burned,* only in the dream Estelle was pristine in her loveliness, blonde and green-eyed with a '40s hairstyle and make-up and a blue gown with sequins on the bosom; and then she was Pat in the '40s hairstyle and make-up and blue gown, and his eyes returned to the highway, and then to her, only Pat was smiling like a skull now, her hair a frightwig with clumps yanked out and her face battered and bruised, nose bloody-broken, mouth punched to a pulp, one eye slashed, ice-pick punctures on her cheeks, throat cut ear to ear, bare arms a welter of welts and gashes and contusions until finally the lower half of her was a charred mass dissolving to cinders, and he drove off the highway and the phone rang shrilly and he sat up in bed, sweating in the air-conditioned room.

But he'd had his rest, and the long-haired clerk (sullen no more) got his twenty-five, "Stairway to Heaven" playing again (or still?), and Michael set out — on Highway 95 now — for Reno.

The Pineview development in Incline Village ran to rustic lodge–like dwellings built against a rising wall of pines, a stylistic world apart from the rambling ranch-styles of the Country Club subdivision with its golf course view where the Satarianos had lived.

Typical of these, the Grace home had a driveway that swung around to a side double-garage in the basement, sloping landscaping designed to give the first floor a nice elevated rear look at the green scenery. This enabled Michael to pull in and park his car on a downward slant of cement, the Lincoln out of sight of anyone passing by.

The desolate drive from Vegas to Reno had taken over seven hours; with full-bore June heat beating down, he'd been careful not to overwork the air conditioner — Highway 95 skirted the edge of Death Valley — and again kept his gas tank topped off and his eye on the radiator. He even had a meal around two, a diner that would serve you breakfast any time of day, which was what he craved.

He'd listened to music, tapes mostly, Sammy Davis, Ella, Bobby D., Joanie Sommers — he'd pitched his Sinatras in Walker Lake, during a fit of anti-Outfit pique — and he'd again fallen into a groove of monotony that worked for him, the traffic scant all the way to Sparks. Long though the drive and the day had been, he came sharply awake when he hit Reno, "biggest little city in the world," and his familiar home area. This sensation only increased on the half-hour drive to the Tahoe's North Shore.

Now he was peering into the Graces' garage — no cars. He cautiously walked around the rough-wood-sided house — he'd slung a dark gray sportjacket over the black Banlon to hide the .45 in the waistband of the slacks — and checked windows. Within five minutes he was convinced the house was empty.

Steps up to an elaborate wooden deck took him to glassed-in sliding doors onto the kitchen that, for all the rustic trappings of the mini-lodge, were the same as in the last two homes Michael had lived in. He forced the door open, without having to break the glass.

The interior of the home was phony farmhouse, starting with a mostly pine kitchen interrupted by calico wallpaper, avocado appliances, shelves of flea-market crocks, and a window of various wooden spoons hanging vertically and horizontally.

A sink filled with dirty dishes announced the aftermath of meals prepared for two. A wastebasket brimmed with empty cans of

Tab, his daughter's drink of choice. A big calendar with a picture of a covered New England bridge had bold notations, including a line drawn through five days including today and tomorrow — "Bob and Janet/Caribbean!"

So Bob and Janet Grace had gone on a cruise and left high school senior Gary — the only one of the three Grace children still at home — to fend for himself for a few days. And Gary had done so by driving to Vegas to bring his girlfriend back here to shack up and go to prom . . .

. . . a theory the girlfriend's father confirmed when he got to Gary's room and found a double bed that had been slept in on both sides. In this all-pine room, with exposed beams, the walls wore posters of the Beatles walking across Abbey Road, the Dallas Cowboys cheerleaders, O.J. Simpson in his uniform grinning as he cradled his helmet under an arm, and Muhammad Ali in boxing trunks and I-Am-the-Greatest grimace, raising a padded-gloved fist.

He felt parental rage rising as he noted the open box of Trojan rubbers on the nightstand, as casual as a pack of open cigarettes; four ripped-open individual packets were tossed there, too, like chewing gun wrappers. But a luxury like fatherly disapproval wasn't available to Michael right now.

He found her powder-blue overnight bag, with various articles of clothing in it, all clean — she'd done her own laundry, apparently, even if she hadn't done the dishes — but one item was conspicuous by its absence: no nice dress for the prom, much less a formal.

Which meant that though it was now only a quarter to six, she had already dressed for the prom; she'd already left here — for the Cal-Neva? Then he remembered: the Incline High kids usually went out for a nice dinner before prom. So Anna and Gary were probably dining somewhere in North Tahoe.

He returned to that nightstand, where earlier his eyes had only been able to focus on those condoms; now he noted the football-shaped phone and a small message pad.

On the pad it said: RENO SAT *RESERVATION* — 5 PM!!!

Which meant Anna and her rubber-sporting beau were at a restaurant in Reno, or on their way back, or possibly even were already at the Cal-Neva. . . .

But Gary's otherwise specific note (the handwriting was not Anna's) did not indicate *what* restaurant. . . .

He sat on the edge of the bed, but for just a moment, standing up as if the sheets had been hot; he looked back at the rumpled bedding and shuddered. As he left the boy's bedroom, he knew that any hope of heading them off here, at the Grace home, before the prom, was as empty as those Trojan wrappers.

The house he'd already prowled before checking the bedroom — making sure he was truly alone — and had seen enough slate floors, knotty pine, rush-matting and cane-seating to last a lifetime. But back in the kitchen a pile of unopened mail on the counter tweaked his interest; among various bills, he found one from the phone company.

Within seconds he was staring at the Grace's monthly Ma Bell damage — which included ten long-distance calls to the number of the Smith family in Tucson, all in the last two weeks, juxtaposed beside dollar-and-cents figures sure to dismay the Graces when they got home . . . unless four-hundred-buck-plus phone bills were the norm around here.

He helped himself to some sandwich meat in the Amana fridge and settled for a can of Tab to wash it down. Then he gathered his daughter's overnight bag — carrying it in his left hand to leave his right free for the .45 if need be — and returned to the Lincoln in the driveway. He stowed her bag in back with his Samsonite, which he opened, withdrawing a white shirt and a dark blue tie, putting them and his gray sportjacket on; he stuck the dirty clothes in the suitcase and snapped it closed.

Poised to get in on the driver's side, he looked at the sky. Dusk had given over to night, and the same clear starry tapestry with full moon that accompanied him across the desert was waiting for him at Tahoe.

He said silently to the sky, *This isn't a prayer. But if Pat was wrong, and you are out there, not dead like some people say . . . I could use any help you want to give me, getting Anna out of here to safety.*

Dispensing with the "amen," but this time not giving God the finger at least, he left the Grace home and Pineview development and headed for Crystal Bay. Driving up the pine-framed "strip" of Lake Tahoe, the familiar glowing garish neons — CRYSTAL BAY CLUB, NEVADA LODGE, BAL TABARIN, CAL-NEVA — welcomed him home; but they seemed unreal — was he asleep behind the wheel of the Lincoln, out in the desert, dreaming and about to run off the road . . . ?

The Cal-Neva lot was brimming with luxury cars; but here and there a Chevy II or Plymouth Fury or GTO nestled between vinyl-topped Eldorados and Rivieras — one indication of the prom going on in the Indian Lounge tonight. Another was the steady stream of sideburned guys in tuxes (red or white or light blue, never black) with ruffled shirts and bow ties the size of small aircraft, arm-in-arm with shellac-haired gals in frilly pastel Guinevere gowns heading into the A-frame lodge under a banner shouting: WELCOME CLASS OF '73!

Near the front a Mercedes pulled out and glided off, and Michael slipped the Lincoln into the spot, gaining a perfect clear path to the front entry; then he sat in the dark watching teenage couples go in, and considered his options.

If Anna and Gary weren't back from Reno yet, he could simply wait for them, and grab the girl on the Cal-Neva doorstep. But that Reno reservation was for five, and the two kids could have eaten and made it back to the Cal-Neva by as early as six-thirty or seven.

And it was almost eight o'clock now. . . .

Michael exited the Lincoln, his manner seemingly casual, but keeping his right hand ready for the .45 in his waistband. He strolled around the side of the building where fir trees and darkness conspired with a recession in the building, between added-on sections of the lodge, to allow him to climb a drain pipe to the slanting roof, walking Groucho-style up to where it flattened out.

Sinatra's most grandiose excess awaited Michael — a rooftop heliport atop the Celebrity Showroom that had not been used since the days (and nights) when the Chairman of the Board had flown Jack and/or Bobby Kennedy in from Sacramento, or Dino or Marilyn or the McGuire Sisters from Hollywood. As the moon lengthened Michael's shadow across the rooftop, he ran on those quiet crepe soles to the dormer housing a doorway to a stairwell.

Padlocked on the other side, the door had panels so weathered and thin that Michael tapped one with an elbow and it splintered.

The unlighted stairs were not difficult to navigate; they led to a landing with off-shoot stairs down to performer dressing rooms as well as a side door to the Sinatra Celebrity Showroom. The main stairs, however, took Michael below to the cement-block-walled tunnel with its indoor-outdoor carpeting and nest of overhead pipes. From this juncture the tunnel snaked under the kitchen, casino and Circle Bar, coming back up to provide a pathway to what had been Michael's office.

As far as Michael knew, the last time the secret stone-pillar fireplace "door" had been used, an assassin had come into the office and got immediately shot and killed for the trouble. He hoped the new Cal-Neva manager, whoever that might be, wasn't as quick on the trigger; at least he knew the Garand rifle wasn't over the mantel anymore — it was in the suitcase in his car, in pieces.

The scraping of stone on stone was unavoidable, so Michael shoved it the hell open, and burst in the office, fanning the .45 around what appeared to be an empty room, illuminated only by the picture window filtering in moonbeams and their reflection off the lake.

The new manager wasn't here, at least not in his office. Nothing much seemed to have changed, but for a wall arrayed with celebrity and politician photos; they were hanging crooked, which was nothing new for the politicos, anyway.

He cracked the door and looked out into a dark hallway of offices; busy casino noise, and the laughter of those high school kids, echoed down from the lodge — the Indian Lounge was nearby.

He recalled what Anna had said about their home in Paradise Estates — that she felt like a ghost haunting her own house. Michael had that same bizarre sensation setting foot in the Indian Lounge again — his ten years at the Cal-Neva had been his single longest stint at any one facility, and no job had pleased him more, no work-place could have been a better fit.

Now the most familiar face at Cal-Neva over the last decade relegated himself to the shadows of the lounge, which was suitably darkened for the occasion. That was why he'd put on the shirt and tie with sportjacket, to better fit in with the parent chaperones who would be staying on the sidelines, not bugging the kids.

The lounge had the usual streamers and crepe-paper balls in green and gold, the school colors, and another banner over the stage — where a cover band in pirate shirts and bell-bottoms bellowed, *"Free ride, take it easy!"* — said, PROM '73 — HIGH-LAND FLING! (the school teams were the Highlanders).

But the open-beamed lounge's natural decor would have overwhelmed the most ambitious decorating committee, with its black California/Nevada state line painted on the floor through the massive, sixty-foot granite-boulder fireplace, and natural wood walls arrayed with deer, elk and bear trophies and Indian art and blankets.

At least fifty couples were out on the dance floor and at the round tables with gold or green cloths, and the sea of red, white and light-blue tuxes and froufrou pastel gowns made the kids fairly interchangeable in the dim green light. The cover band was doing a badly out-of-tune "Bridge Over Troubled Waters" now, but the couples clutching each other out there didn't seem to mind. He moved along the periphery, trying to get a better vantage point, hoping to spot Anna and Gary. . . .

"Mike!"

He turned and saw the father of one of Anna's friends from chorus — Dan Miller, an insurance agent from Incline Village, grinning and shoving a hand at him like a spear.

"Dan," he said with a smile, shaking the moist hand, "nice to see you."

"So you decided to let Anna come back for the prom!"

"Yes — yes."

"White of ya! Couldn't just pull her out of school a few months 'fore the end of her senior year, and expect her to forget her whole damn life! You're a good parent, Mike. Good parent."

"Thanks." Maybe the punch was spiked. "Have you seen Anna?"

"I think they're up near the stage, her and Gary. Great to see you! Where are you folks again, these days?"

"Great to see you, too," Michael said, working his voice up, as if having trouble hearing over the band.

And he edged down the wall, getting nearer the front.

There she was.

His beautiful daughter, looking so much like her mother, her head nestled against the chest of blond athletic Gary, one of the few boys here with shorter hair. They stayed in one spot, moving in a barely perceptible circle, both with eyes dreamily closed, lost in a loving embrace.

Anna wore a white dress with none of the silly frills of these other girls, adorned only by a sheer shawl and the orchid corsage at her wrist, her long brown hair braided and ribboned here and there. Gary's tux was white with slashes of black lapel.

Michael lurched reflexively toward them, then stopped himself. An empty table — its rightful claimants probably out on the dance floor — presented a chair for him to flop into, which he did. Suddenly he felt tired. Old. His eyes filled with tears and he swallowed hard. Beautiful. How beautiful, how sweet she looked. Sweet and alive. . . .

Even the thought of those Trojans on the nightstand only made him smile. Hadn't he and Patsy Ann screwed like rabbits in the backseat of her daddy's Buick on prom night? What had been so awful about that? He had loved Patsy Ann, and she loved him.

He would let them finish their dance.

". . . bridge over troubled waters . . ."

At least the guy was back on tune for the finish. Applause rewarded the band, and most of the kids stayed out there for "Right Place, Wrong Time," a growly fast number. A few other couples threaded back toward their seats, Anna and Gary among them.

The table where Michael sat remained otherwise empty, and while it didn't belong to Anna and Gary, the couple's own seats were nearby apparently, because she spotted her father on the way over.

Freezing.

Emotions, in a rapid wave, traveled her features: anger, worry, terror, indignation, frustration, sadness, even regret.

Gary — petrified beside her, holding her hand — only gazed at Michael blankly. The father knew the look — this boy loved this girl, and he would be a man about any decisions he'd made, regarding her; would not be afraid to stand up to Daddy.

Anna started to pull away, but Gary shook his head and walked her over to his girlfriend's father, who remained seated.

The couple just stood there looking at him, Gary pretending to be calm, Anna with chin defiantly up.

Gary said, "We couldn't let you keep us apart. We . . . I . . . really meant no disrespect, sir. But —"

"Please sit down," Michael said, his voice calm.

Anna and Gary locked eyes.

"Kids — please. Sit. I'm not angry. Really. Just relieved."

"I'm sorry if you were worried," she said, her words cold, her chin crinkly, "but my life isn't about you and Mom, any more, Daddy. My life is about me, and Gary."

"Honey — sit. Gary? Help me out here?"

Gary nodded and guided the girl into the chair beside her father. Still, she sat as far away from him as she could manage.

"Please listen to me, both of you," he said, firmly but with no anger, nothing judgmental. "I understand what tonight is about — I was . . ."

"You were a *kid* yourself once," she said snippily.

Gary said, "Anna, please. . . . Give him a chance."

"Thanks, son. Annie, back home, our —"

"*This* is home."

He sat forward, "Sweetheart, our new identities have been exposed."

She frowned. "I don't understand."

"Our cover's been blown, back in Arizona. Very bad people know the Smiths are really the Satarianos. You're in danger. Right now. Right here."

Her eyes flew wide. "My God. . . . Is Mom okay?"

He said, "Baby, we need to leave. Cal-Neva's just about the worst place on the face of the earth for us, right now. Gary, you should probably stay."

"I'm going with you," he said.

"Gary, that's not —"

"*Daddy!*"

Her hand was clutching his arm. Tight. Her eyes were big and wet. Her lips were trembling.

"Daddy. . . . Is Mom . . . is she . . . ?"

"We lost her, baby," he said gently, and he began to cry. He covered his face with a hand. "I'm sorry . . . I'm sorry . . . I have to be strong for you. . . ."

And his daughter was in his arms, holding him tight, and she was crying, too. "Oh, I'm sorry, Daddy, I'm sorry, I'm so sorry. . . ."

He held her away from him. Shrugged off the emotion. Cold again, he said, "Listen to me — this was *not* your fault. You didn't do this to us, to your mom. If anyone did, it was me."

"Daddy, Daddy. . . ."

"Listen!" And he shook her, just a little. A few eyes were on them now, so he kept his expression neutral and his voice soft. "We don't have time for recriminations. We don't have time to take any blame. A very long time ago, I sat where you're sitting — I thought I'd caused *my* mother's death."

"Gran'ma . . . Satariano?"

"No — my real mother." He turned to Gary, who looked like he'd been pole-axed. "Son, I told Anna and Mike that I was adopted, but I lied to them about something. I didn't tell them that I knew my real parents, that I grew up with my real parents."

Anna was shaking her head, tears streaming, ruining her make-up. "I can't . . . I can't . . . I can't. . . ."

"Baby," he told her, "my father told me, 'It's not your fault — it's the business I'm in.' He told me I wasn't responsible for my mother's death, and that neither was he."

But I am responsible for their retribution, the Angel of Death had said, so long ago. . . .

This memory Michael did not share with his daughter.

"Right now," he said, "we have to survive. We have to leave this place, and we have to go somewhere else, somewhere safe."

"*Where* is safe, Daddy?"

"Anywhere. Anywhere is safer than here. . . . Gary, you shouldn't come with us. We'll contact you. You have to trust me, son, you have to believe me."

The boy was shaking his head. "I love Anna, sir. I can help you. Let me help you."

"Gary, please."

"No. I'm coming with you."

No use arguing with him here. Michael would get Anna out of here, and deal with the Gary problem later.

"I'm sorry to spoil your prom," Michael said, "but we have to leave this very moment. . . . You two go on out. I'll meet you in the front lobby."

Gary nodded and, then, so did Anna.

The hundred or so kids in tuxes and formals were dancing slow again, to "The Morning After," which sounded even worse when a male sang it.

Michael hugged the wall, kept his head down, hoping no other chaperone would recognize him, among these numerous familiar faces — other parents, and some teachers, too.

In the front lobby, he joined the boy and girl. Behind the check-in desk, an assistant manager of his, a pretty young woman named Brandi, squinted at him; he shook his head at her, and somehow she got the signal. She said nothing, God bless her.

"The car's close, right out front," he said to the young couple, standing between them, a hand on each one's shoulder. "I'm going out first. If there's no problem, I'll pull right up to the door. . . . Gary, open the front for Anna, Anna you get in, and Gary climb in back, it'll be unlocked."

Gary nodded. "And we'll book it out of here."

"We will indeed," Michael said, and squeezed the hand on the boy's tux shoulder. "Just look after my little girl."

Their eyes met.

Gary understood: *if Michael didn't make it, Anna would be his responsibility.*

"Be careful, Daddy," Anna said.

He kissed her on the forehead and went out.

Trotting to the parked Lincoln, he swiftly scanned the lot for anything suspicious. A few casino goers, couples, were heading for their own cars. Some kids from the prom were out front catching a smoke in the cool crisp pleasant breeze.

Behind the wheel of the parked Lincoln, he made sure the seat was clear in back for Gary, moving the suitcases over; he unlocked the doors on their side, and powered down the window on his own side, and Anna's.

Then he started the car, backed out, and swung around, pulling right in front. Gary came out first, Anna right behind him, and the boy opened the door for her, she climbed in, and Gary's head came apart as the gunshot, probably a .45 or maybe .357, caught him in the forehead. His eyes didn't have time to register shock.

Anna screamed, and Gary fell away, a mist of red taking his place, as Michael hit the gas, steering with one hand, yelling, "Close that door, baby!" which somehow, through her screaming, she managed to do, and two little men with big revolvers, Giancana guys who Michael recognized, a stocky kid named Vin and a skinnier one named Lou, came up out from among the parked cars, and were aiming the weapons at the Lincoln when Michael shot Vin and Lou with the .45, bang bang, turning their heads into mush and mist, much as they had Gary's.

Anna kept screaming and the Lincoln was screaming, too, careening out of the parking lot and then flying down the curving mountain highway, leaving behind the dead boy and pair of Outfit corpses and Cal-Neva and neon signs until only the pines and the night and the twisty road and the sobbing girl were his companions.

"Oh, Daddy, Daddy," she said finally, horror and hysteria turning the lovely face grotesque, "we just left him there, we just left him there!"

When he could risk it, he pulled over and took her into his arms and sobs shook her as he said, "We had to leave him, he was gone, baby, he was gone."

"Oh but you don't understand . . . you don't understand. . . ."

"I swear I do, sugar. I swear."

"But you don't." She drew away from him a little, and her eyes and face were drenched with tragedy, her voice a tiny trembling terrible thing, so much older than it had ever been and yet much, much too young.

"That was my husband we left back there, Daddy," the girl in the white prom dress said, gasping, gulping. "Last night in Vegas . . . Gary and . . . we . . . we . . . we . . . got . . . *married* . . ."

BOOK THREE

SAINTS' REST

10

Tony Accardo did not fool around.

Not in any sense of the phrase — as a businessman he was no-nonsense and fair, avoiding violence when possible but (if need be) sanctioning the worst, lesson-setting brutality. As a father he was aces — generous and loving, while not an easy mark; he'd made it clear to his two boys and two girls that his way was nothing they wanted to pursue, that the best that could be said for their papa's profession was it had paved the road to a better life for the kids of a six-grade drop-out son of an immigrant shoemaker.

And as a husband with never-ending opportunities, Tony had never once — not in almost forty years of marriage — cheated on his wife. When he married Clarice in 1934, she had been the best-looking blondie on the chorus line; and when he looked at her now, he looked past the extra pounds (who was he to talk?) and saw his same slender sweetheart.

Just because she'd been a show-biz

honey didn't mean Clarice had ever been a bimbo. She had a sharp mind and took college classes, educating herself, traveling the world to increase her knowledge, sometimes dragging Tony along. Her handling of the children was caring but disciplined, minus any favoritism; and when the Accardos hosted a party — Tony loved such gatherings — she was the most gracious hostess in Chicago.

Clarice was back home in Chicago, that is River Forest, in their ranch house on Ashland, the smaller (sixteen-room) digs he built when his Tudor mansion on Franklin caught too much media heat — God he missed his "Palace," with the basement bowling alley and all that room for his antiques, and its vast back yard where he could throw wingdings like his annual Fourth of July bash.

But guys he trusted, including Murray Humphries, Paul Ricca, and his attorney Sidney Horshak (smartest man in the world) had preached to him of going more low-key — and Tony listened; like Frank Nitti, he knew that attracting attention was a bad thing. So — when federal heat and publicity made it necessary to send Giancana packing to Mexico, and Tony came off the bench to take the top chair again — King Accardo, back in the lime-light, bit the bullet and sold his Palace.

Clarice didn't mind; she loved the new house as much as the mansion — "It's homey, Tony, it's cozy, and we're getting older" — and she adored the California digs, too, a low-slung, stone-and-wood-and-glass modern ranch number looking over a fairway of Indian Wells Country Club, twenty miles outside of Palm Springs. This second home was nicely se-cluded, no neighbors half a mile in any di-rection, except for the country club. His wife spent lots of time out here with him, but this was a business trip.

So the quartet of cuties scurrying around his swimming pool on this sultry Sunday night in June — two blondes, a brunette and a redhead in bikinis that combined wouldn't make up a single re-spectable swimsuit — were nothing more than eye candy to Tony, and perks for the boys.

Phil and Vic and Jimmy T and Rocco, in swimsuits and open Hawaiian shirts to show off curly hair and gold necklaces, were playing poker at a dollar-bill-littered table, the shoulder-holstered tools of their trade slung over the arms of their beach chairs; though the sun had long since set, floodlights kept the pool and surrounding patio bright as noon.

This was two-thirds of his security force; two other men — UZIs on shoulder straps — were beyond the seven-foot tan-brick wall, taking turns, one staying at the front gate, the other walking the outer perimeter. They wore white sportshirts and khaki shorts, which amused Accardo; he'd said to one of them, Dave, "Kinda takes the edge off the UZI, don't it, looking like a tennis pro?"

"Ah, Mr. Accardo, you're a riot," Dave had said, and snorted a laugh, and waved it off.

Dave was a Chicago boy like all Tony's bodyguards, and your average eggplant was smarter. That was the trouble with security staff: you couldn't waste your best people in a job like that; but, shit, man, you were putting your goddamn life in their hands!

Not that Tony was worried. In all his years in the Outfit, from bootlegger to bodyguard, from capo to top dog, he'd never had anybody hit him at home. Oh, there was that burglar crew who invaded the River Forest place, when he and Clarice were out here having their house-warming party; but that had been strictly money, and anyway all those guys were dead now, castrated, throats slit, all seven of them.

The girls were giggly and cute — starlets Sidney, with his endless Hollywood connections, had rounded up — and seemed to like each other more than the boys they were here to entertain. Tony didn't mind watching their boobies bounce — the redhead was something, a regular Jane Russell — and he liked the way their firm curvy butts didn't quite fit inside the bikini bottoms.

No law against looking.

Tony himself was in a knee-length terrycloth robe — once the sun went down, it got cool, not that these kids noticed — and leaning back in a lounge-style deck chair, watching through big heavy-framed bifocals the size of goddamn safety glasses (Clarice picked them out — said they were "in style"). He was as dark as these sun-crazy starlets, but it came natural, and daytime he usually sat under an umbrella, avoiding the rays. Mostly he sat out here in the evening. Like tonight.

A broad-shouldered five ten, two hundred pounds, Anthony Accardo — "retired" boss of the Chicago Outfit — still had at sixty-eight the physical bearing of a street thug; his hairline had receded some, the hair mostly white now, the oval face grooved with years of responsibility, the nose a bulbous lump, with small dark eyes that had seen too much.

Smoking a sizable Cuban cigar, sipping a Scotch rocks, Tony was talking with Sidney about the Giancana problem.

Sidney sat in a beach chair, angled to make eye contact with his client. The slender, well-tanned, gray-haired attorney wore a yellow short-sleeve golfing shirt, dark green slacks and moccasins with yellow socks, and looked younger than his sixty-one years. His features were unremarkable, small eyes crowding a long nose and a slash of mouth; nothing about him was distinctive except his intelligence and bearing.

Between them was a small round glass-topped table for their ashtrays and drinks; Horshak had a martini but he'd hardly touched it.

"This terrible thing at the Cal-Neva," Horshak was saying, in between drags on a filter-king cigarette, "it's an embarrassment, a public-relations disaster. We have Walter Cronkite talking about us, Tony — it needs to stop."

"I don't know much more than you do, Sid," Tony admitted with a shrug. "Two of Mooney's crew get made dead in the Cal parking lot, and take some poor kid with 'em who didn't have shit to do with anything."

A small smile twitched the lipless line of the lawyer's mouth. "That last, Tony, is not precisely true. Do you know who that kid is? Or rather, was?"

"No. Just some local twerp, not tied to us at —"

"This is *Cal-Neva*, Tony — everything is tied to us." Horshak sat forward. "My people did some discreet checking — the young man was dating a young *lady* . . . by the name of Anna Satariano."

"Satar . . ." Tony sat up, swung around and sat on the edge of the lounge chair to better face the attorney. "Michael Satariano's daughter?"

"That's right, Tony." Horshak blew smoke out his nostrils like a suntanned dragon. "And judging by descriptions of the shooter in the Lincoln? The individual the Giancana assassins were apparently trying to take down could well be Satariano. In fact, I'd say it *must* have been Satariano."

Tony was shaking his head, dumbfounded. "The girl at the scene . . . who climbed in the car and got away with the shooter. . . . *That* was the Satariano girl? But the Satarianos, they fuckin' moved!"

301

"That's one way to put it," Horshak said drily.

"What would they be doin' back in Tahoe, for Christ's sake? They're in WITSEC someplace-the-fuck!"

The attorney offered a tiny eyebrow shrug. "Apparently the girl came back home . . . for prom."

"Shit." Tony let out a huge sigh; he sucked on the cigar, blew smoke, shook his head. "What the hell is that crazy Giancana *up* to?"

"Trying to hit Michael Satariano, obviously — Michael Satariano, who came out of federal protection to go after his daughter. And as I say, I think we can reasonably extrapolate that the child ran off from the new life enforced upon her by WITSEC, to come home for prom."

Tony frowned. "What're you sayin', Sid? That Mooney had people sittin' in Tahoe all these months, watchin', in case Satariano got homesick and turned the hell back up? That's crazy! What the fuck is going on here?"

The attorney drew thoughtfully on the cigarette, then said, "I would say Giancana is trying to protect himself. Michael Satariano witnessed many things over the years."

"Michael knows plenty about me, too," Tony said gruffly. "He was my guy for a couple years, during and just after the war. Top notch, too."

Horshak agreed, nodding. "And with his war hero status, he's been very useful to us over the years."

"Fuckin' A."

"And how do you think his celebrity stands to impact our interests in the public eye *now,* Tony?"

Tony thought about that, clearly an avenue his mind had not previously gone down. Finally he said, "Not in a good way?"

"Not in a good way, no." The attorney gestured with two open hands. "But Mooney Giancana rarely considers such subtleties — he's the original loose cannon. All Giancana knows is he would like to have Satariano removed from the equation — which is understandable. After all, we know Giancana is positioning himself to take over again — with Ricca dead, and you retired, Mooney's a charismatic figure who —"

"Charisma my ass!" Tony chewed on the cigar as he spoke. "He's a demented prick with delusions of grandeur and a talent for getting his ugly mug in the media. We shipped his ass to Mexico because of the attention he was attracting, and now he's back, what, a month? And we got Senate hearings and fuckin' shoot-outs!"

"Actually, Tony, Mexico is the key to this . . ."

Accardo and Paul Ricca had sent Mooney away, out of the spotlight in '66, and allowed him to develop his own interests, internationally — chiefly, cruise ships and casinos. A modest 20 percent tax came back to the Outfit.

". . . a happy arrangement, Mexico — Mooney's out of your hair, and generating income. What could be better? But good things do not last forever."

Both men knew that Giancana's ties to the corrupt Mexican government had made all of this possible, until last month when a new regime came in and decided to seize all of that money and deport Giancana into the arms of the FBI. No outstanding arrests warrants were waiting, but an avalanche of subpoenas were.

"So now Mooney's back," Tony said, "but he's broke, and his mind's on that Senate hearing. Hell, first thing he did was get gallbladder surgery. He's an old man! Washed up."

"Ah," Horshak said, lighting up a new cigarette, "but remember, Tony — a deposed king always has designs on his 'rightful' throne. What other option does Mooney have, but to stage the comeback he was already thirsting for?"

Tony shook his head, hard. "Can't allow that. Can't allow that. Maybe he'd like to retire someplace."

Another twitch of a smile turned that slit in Horshak's face into a mouth. "You tell me — is Sam Giancana the shuffleboard type? Does he walk away from those millions in Mexico, and settle for a pension? This is a man who has enjoyed power . . . and I do mean *enjoyed* . . . for decades."

Tony's eyes narrowed. "They say he looked like a little old man in baggy pants and beard when he turned up at the airport."

"He was yanked out of his bed in the middle of the night and kidnapped by Mexican immigration officials. How would any of us look? Besides, Mooney always was a ham."

Tony's brow beetled in thought. "That was an act . . . what? For the feds who met him at the gate?"

Horshak waved that away with a hand holding the cigarette, making smoke trails. "I just offer it as a possibility. And meaning no offense, my friend, isn't this 'old man' two years younger than yourself?"

"I'm not officially running things. Aiuppa is."

" 'Officially' being the operative term. . . . But even if all we were facing here is Sam Giancana preparing to testify in front of a Senate committee exploring, among other things, the assassination of Jack Kennedy . . . well, Tony? Do I really have to go on?"

Tony said nothing; he just sat puffing his cigar, his eyes on the girls frolicking in the pool, though he didn't really see them.

"Not good," Tony muttered. "Not good."

Horshak drew smoke in, let smoke out. Then he smiled like a patient priest and asked, "How much security do you have here, Tony?"

Tony, still idly watching the pretty girls swim and splash at each other, said, "What you see is what you get. Half a dozen guys. Why?"

The attorney nodded, thought, said softly, "You must have personally approved the hit on Michael Satariano. The *other* hit at Cal-Neva, remember? The one Satariano deflected?"

His eyes flashed at Horshak. "I sanctioned that because Michael whacked DeStefano! What else *could* we do — tell

Mad Sam's crew easy-the-fuck-come, easy-the-fuck-go?"

"I would have advised against it — Satariano was a loyal man, and his Medal of Honor celebrity could have . . . well, that's beside the point, isn't it? You didn't seek my counsel."

"That's right, Sid. When I want your advice, I ask for it."

"Which you are now, right?"

Tony swallowed. "Right."

The attorney sat back; he gestured with a gentle open hand. "For the sake of argument — what if Satariano *didn't* 'whack' Mad Sam DeStefano? What if Giancana framed him for it?"

"Why in hell?"

Horshak shrugged. "Perhaps to get the heat off the real assassins, and put them — and Mad Sam's crew — securely in his debt. And if you're Sam Giancana planning a comeback, wouldn't that make perfect sense? Remove an obstacle — Satariano — and build allies with Mad Sam's fatherless camp? But, then, you're much closer to this kind of thing than I am, Tony. What do *you* hear?"

Tony shifted on the edge of the lounge chair; the girls giggled and splashed. "Well. . . . Gotta admit that some are sayin' Satariano didn't do DeStefano. Some opinion says it was Spilotro and Mad Sam's brother — the Ant and Mario."

The attorney nodded sagely. "The very two stalwarts who fingered Satariano."

"Yeah. Them stalwarts. They neither one wanted to see that crazy sadistic icepick-happy lunatic take the witness stand."

"And speaking of crazy lunatics taking the witness stand," Horshak said, with as wide a smile as the cut of a mouth was capable, "how do we feel about Mooney testifying before that Senate committee?"

Tony grunted. " 'We' don't like it."

"You don't anticipate Mooney pulling a Valachi, do you?"

"No! But he *will* go after those CIA cocksuckers — Mooney's made it known that those spy pricks have been lettin' him twist in the wind. Says those feds shoulda found *some* way to keep him from bein' deported, or at least get his millions back for him from them Mexicans. And as feds themselves, they oughta be able to prevent him havin' to testify to a buncha senators."

A slow nod. "And how do we feel about having this CIA dirty linen exposed to public view?"

Tony threw up his hands. "It's what those bastards deserve, but I don't see how

Mooney figures he can give the spies up without giving *us* up, too! We're too, what's the word? Interwove with those cocksuckers."

"Strange bedfellows indeed."

"Yeah, but who's fuckin' who? We thought they could help us get Cuba back, and how the hell has *that* been workin' out?"

Both men were well aware that for almost ten years, Giancana — using his Mexico City mansion as home base — had traveled all around Europe, Latin America and the Middle East. This put Mooney in a perfect position to facilitate a major cocaine and heroin smuggling ring . . .

. . . but not for Chicago.

Tony Accardo was a legendary holdout in the drug business; he had never allowed the Outfit to get involved with junk — providing working stiffs with recreation like whores and gambling was one thing, peddling soul-robbing addiction a whole other.

But in Mexico, out from under Accardo's watchful eye, Giancana could make side deals with anybody he pleased. Most likely in those Mexico City years, Mooney got in tight with not only the CIA but other syndicate guys, like Trafficante in New Orleans and Gambino in New York, who did not share the Accardo disdain for drugs.

"I respect and admire the stand you've taken on narcotics over the years," Horshak said. "But the press isn't going to make any such distinctions, nor is the general public . . . that Great Unwashed who elect our leaders. To John Q. American, the 'mob' and the CIA will just be bad guys together, and all sorts of structures could come apart . . . meaning lots of things, and people, could fall down."

A sharp crack provided an exclamation point to the lawyer's statement.

Narrow-eyed Accardo sat forward, wide-eyed Horshak reared back. The bodyguards dropped their playing cards and rose, turning toward the noise.

Another crack followed, one second after the first, and Accardo — already on his feet, a revolver from the pocket of his terrycloth robe now in his right fist — said, "Vic, Rocco, that's the gate — check it out. Vic boy, go left; Rocco go around right."

The two bodyguards had already snatched their guns from the shoulder holsters dangling off the beach chairs. Now the hoods in swimming trunks and Aloha shirts ran in opposite directions, out of the floodlights and into relative darkness — a few security spots kept the entire grounds illuminated within reason — and around the side of the house, toward the gate.

The girls were all in the pool, terrified and treading water; eyes and mouths wide open, they were reacting to Tony's words, not the cracks, which they'd heard but did not recognize as gunfire.

Taking a step toward the pool, Tony waved his revolver and said, "Out of the pool, girls."

As they scrambled out, slipping on the watery edges, Tony said, "Go to a bedroom and get on the floor — stay low. . . . Phil, escort them, then watch the front."

Phil, a stocky, curly-headed kid, nodded and — gun in hand — herded the girls inside through the glass patio doors, saying, "Ladies, ladies, don't trip over yourselves, gonna be fine. . . ."

Another gunshot rang in the night, and another.

Then a terrible silence.

Four of his men dead, Tony figured — the single shots followed by no victory cry from either of his boys, well, that told the tale. Whoever-this-was was inside the gate, now. . . .

Nothing left but Phil indoors, and Jimmy

T out here with them.

"Goddamnit, Tony!" Horshak said, waving his hands like a minstrel singer. "We have to *do* something!"

Tony whirled and thumped the lawyer's yellow sportshirt with a thick finger, right on the little alligator. "You just stay close, Sid. Got it?"

Skinny Jimmy T was hopping around like a demented jack rabbit, revolver in hand, looking behind him and to every side, throwing long shadows on the floodlit patio.

"Jimmy," Tony called softly, "trouble will either come around the house, left or right; or through it, out these patio doors — or if it's more than one guy, both; maybe all three. So get yourself some cover, watch the kitchen, and I got the rest."

Jimmy T nodded, and upended a glass table and used it for cover; *yeah,* Tony thought, *real brains these kids — hide behind glass.*

A wooden picnic table near his barbecue pit, close to the wall, Tony turned over, then yanked the attorney back behind it, giving himself a view of the house where the intruder or intruders could come around either side. He also had a decent angle on the patio doors; the pool was off to the left, shimmering with reflected light, and to the right Jimmy crouched like a praying mantis behind his glass-and-steel table. Patio doors off the kitchen were between those two points.

"We need to get in the house," the lawyer advised hurriedly. "We should call the cops, or —"

"Shut up, Sid."

"This isn't my thing, Tony! It's not my thing!"

Tony slapped the lawyer. "Shut the fuck up."

The floodlights went out; darkness descended like sudden night.

As his eyes adjusted, Tony thanked God for having the good sense to invent moonlight; then his nostrils twitched at a familiar odor — cowering beside him behind the overturned picnic table, the lawyer had pissed himself.

A sliding patio door opened quickly, and someone came lurching out.

Jimmy T fired once, twice, three times, and pudgy, curly-haired Phil — shot to shit — stumbled sideways and fell into the pool making a modest splash; Phil floated face down, blood trails streaming on the water's moonlight-glimmering surface.

"Fuck!" Jimmy T said, all knees and

elbows hunkering behind the glass table again, not seeing a crouching figure — which Tony could barely make out — deeper inside the kitchen, aiming a rifle.

Tony called out, "Jim —"

But it was too little, too late.

Three sharp cracks, close enough to the pool to cause some pinging echoes, shattered the glass table, and Jimmy T fell back, table glass shards raining on him, with a shot in the forehead and two chest wounds, any one of which could have killed him.

From the kitchen came a voice, *"We need to talk, Mr. Accardo!"*

Tony, hunkered down behind the picnic table with the wild-eyed attorney, frowned in thought. ". . . Michael?"

"Yes, it's Michael Satariano, Mr. Accardo. I don't have an appointment. Can you work me in?"

The lawyer whispered, "Is he crazy?"

"Unfortunately," Tony said, "no. . . . That rifle can shoot right through this table, Sid. Fucker can kill us any time he likes."

Satariano called out: *"You have your attorney with you, Mr. Accardo. That's good. I'd like Mr. Horshak to sit in on our meeting."*

Tony began to rise, and the lawyer clutched the gangster's terrycloth sleeve and sputtered, "Are *you* crazy? You want him to shoot *you,* too?"

"I told you, Sid," Tony said, jerking his sleeve from Horshak's grasp, "we're dead any time he chooses."

Satariano called out again: *"Come out from behind the table, set it upright, and we'll sit! And talk!"*

Tony yelled, "You want me to throw my gun out, Michael?"

"I don't really care, Mr. Accardo. Fuck with me and you're as dead as your men."

"As a show of good faith, I'm gonna toss it out! Mr. Horshak isn't armed, but we'll both stand with our hands up — agreeable, Mike?"

"Cool with me."

The attorney was crying. "I'm not, I'm not, I'm not . . ."

"Get your shit together, you gutless prick," Tony snarled. "Stand up and stick your hands in the air, like a fuckin' stagecoach robbery, or I'll shoot you myself."

Horshak swallowed. Nodded. Stood, with hands high.

Tony rose — his knees hurt him a little, he was in decent shape, but no spring chicken after all — and tossed the .38 onto the grass (it did not discharge) and raised his hands.

Michael Satariano stood, his silhouette in the kitchen clearly visible. Then he moved through the open doorway onto the patio — he wore black trousers, a black long-sleeve T-shirt and a rifle slung on a strap over his shoulder, a .45 in his hand, trained on them.

Satariano walked over to Jimmy T's skeletal corpse behind and partially under the shot-up glass table, glanced at the body and its redundant death wounds, and didn't bother to stop. His long shadow in the moonlight reached the gangster and lawyer well before he did.

"Gentlemen," Satariano said, "put that table on its feet, and let's have a talk."

The two men did their guest's bidding.

Satariano sat, putting the brick wall behind him, Tony — seated directly across from the intruder — and the attorney both with their backs to the house. The moonlight left Satariano mostly in shadow and washed Tony and Horshak in pale white. Of course, Horshak had already turned pale white. . . .

"Obviously," Satariano said, putting his hand with the .45 in it casually on the picnic-table top, "I'm not going to bother those girls."

"They may call the police," Tony said helpfully. "There's a phone in there."

"No, I cut the phone lines before I dropped by."

Staying out of the conversation, the lawyer just sat with his hands folded prayerfully and trembled no worse than if a fit were coming on.

Tony asked, "You . . . you used that old rifle on Dave and Lou?"

"If that's their names," Satariano said with a nod. "I was in a tamarisk tree on the golf course 'cross the way. I was a sniper during the war, or didn't you know that, Mr. Accardo?"

Tony's eyes tightened. "And you killed all of my men. Six men — just so we could have a meeting?"

"So we could have it on my terms, yes."

Satariano, though a man in his early fifties, had a bland babyish face that Tony found unsettling.

The intruder was saying, "I don't relish killing, Mr. Accardo, but those men were soldiers. I killed fifty enemy soldiers one afternoon, in the Philippines. I'm prepared to do what I have to do tonight, or any night."

"But you're not here to kill me."

A cold tiny smile formed in Satariano's

otherwise blank face. "That's right. I just needed to make a point."

"A point. Six men dead."

Satariano shrugged. "It's something I learned from my father."

Tony barked a laugh. "Your father! Your old man tossed pizza pie in DeKalb, Illinois."

"No," Satariano said matter-of-factly. "That's where you're wrong, Mr. Accardo. I was adopted. My real father was named Michael O'Sullivan."

Tony's eyes tightened. "What was that?"

"My real name, Mr. Accardo, is Michael O'Sullivan, Jr."

". . . *Angel-of-Death* Michael O'Sullivan?"

"Was my father, yes."

Tony Accardo had not truly been scared in many years; hardly ever in his life, in fact — he was a man of strength who usually held the upper hand. *But he remembered a day in 1931 at the Lexington Hotel when he had been a young punk bodyguard and one of a handful of Capone soldiers to survive an assault by the Angel of Death — something like twenty-five men had died, scattered on several floors, in elevators, on stairways, in the lobby.*

"And all these years," Tony said, "nobody knew . . . ?"

"Paul Ricca did," Satariano said.

"Paul was my best friend. He would've told me."

Satariano shook his head. "I don't think so. He and I were close — closer frankly than you and I ever got. Mr. Ricca used me to remove Frank Nitti."

Finally the lawyer spoke. "Frank Nitti committed suicide!"

Turning to Horshak, Satariano flashed a smile as awful as it was brief. "That's the story, isn't it?" Then he returned his gaze to Tony. "But Frank Nitti also betrayed my father. The O'Sullivans have a sort of family trait, you see — *we settle scores.*"

All of it rushed through Accardo's brain: *the loyal Looney family enforcer whose wife and youngest son were viciously murdered by Connor Looney, and when Old Man John Looney stood by his son, the Outfit had backed them up — putting business ahead of loyalty. And the Angel of Death and his son, who'd been all of eleven or twelve, traveled the countryside, robbing banks of mob deposits and leaving a trail of dead Outfit guys behind them like bloody breadcrumbs.*

That was who was sitting across from him: the killer's kid who had grown up into some kind of psycho Audie Murphy war hero. For decades Michael Satariano had been a front man, a non-violent liaison with the straight world, because of his Medal of Honor celebrity; but Mooney Fucking Giancana had to go and wake up the Michael O'Sullivan, Jr., slumbering inside that soft-spoken casino manager. . . .

Great. Fucking great.

"Why tell me this?" Tony asked. "I can better understand you just shooting me — I don't deny letting Giancana sic Mad Sam's crew on you."

Satariano's shrug was barely perceptible. "Giancana lied to you. You thought I'd taken Mad Sam out."

"But you didn't."

"No. Listen, I swam in these waters for a lotta years of my own free will; I understand the kind of barracudas I'm liable to run into. Something bad happens to me, such is the life I chose. However . . . if somebody touches a hair on my daughter Anna's head, I'll stuff the guy's cock and balls in his mouth and *then* kill him."

"Fair enough," Tony said with a knowing nod. Then he turned to the lawyer, who seemed about to throw up and said, "Don't. You smell rank enough already, Sid."

"And let me explain something else," Satariano said. "Something . . . related."

"Please," Tony said.

"Mr. Accardo, no matter what happens — even if you personally sanction the killing of my entire family, including Anna, who is all I have left in this life — I still would not harm your family. Do you understand what I'm saying?"

Tony said, "I think I do."

"You and me, Mr. Accardo, we're bad men. We're killers. But we are not monsters." Satariano shook his head, his mouth twitching in something that was not exactly a smile. "Do you even *know?*"

"Know what, Michael?"

"Know that Giancana sent three men into my house — the one in Arizona, where the feds put us to be safe? Sent them in dressed like Charlie Manson and they murdered my wife. They butchered my wife, Mr. Accardo."

Tony swallowed slowly. "I . . . Michael, I *didn't* know. I'm sorry, Michael . . . truly sorry. The feds must've put a lid on it, and Giancana sure as hell didn't come to me for the okay." The gangster leaned forward. "You *have* to know I wouldn't sanction *that.*"

"That's why you're not dead, Mr. Accardo." Satariano leaned forward, too, turning the snout of the .45 toward the ganglord. "But you do understand that I could have killed you? And that I may be one man, but I won't be easy for your people to kill; I'm my father's son, and if they try and fail, I won't have any trouble repeating tonight's little lesson . . . with the slight difference that you'll be among the dead in the sum total."

Tony lifted his palms up, as if in provisional surrender. "I do understand. But I'm not sure I understand why you wanted to talk to me."

Satariano sighed. "Mr. Accardo, I owe the government nothing. They promised me safety for my family and they did not deliver. So all they have from me is a couple of weeks of interviews. Nothing they can use in court. I'm not saying what I told them won't help them; but I am saying . . . I am pledging you, giving my word as a man . . . as a *made* man . . . that I will *not* testify for those people."

"I'm glad to hear that, Michael."

"Do you believe me?"

"Yeah. Yeah, I do."

"Good. . . . I'm going to kill Sam Giancana. Do you have a problem with that?"

Tony smiled. "None at all. Help yourself. We owe you that one."

Satariano studied the gangster, then said, "I have an idea I might be helping you, taking Mooney out."

Tony shrugged. "I won't lie to you. You would be doing us a favor, yes."

A nod. Then: "When this is over, Mr. Accardo, I intend to disappear."

"Good idea."

"I don't need money. I'm just going to take my daughter and drop off the edge of the earth."

"Which is what I would do, your shoes."

Satariano leaned forward again. "Mr. Accardo, you'll be pressured to do something about me. You may feel, as Al Capone felt, as Frank Nitti felt about my father, that letting me live would cause you to lose face."

"Let me worry about that, Michael."

"No, I prefer to do my own worrying."

Tony thought for a moment. "You'll settle for my word, son?"

"I will, sir."

"Then you got it."

Satariano sucked in a breath, cocked his head. "Anything you can do, clear a path for me, with Giancana would be helpful. Starting with . . . where *is* the bastard?"

Tony chuckled. "Right at the first place you'd look: that crummy house of his in Oak Park."

Satariano's eyes tightened. "With the steel door in the basement?"

"Yeah. But maybe that could be unlocked, by accident; Sam goes out to tend his garden and sometimes forgets to lock up proper, when he comes back in."

A single humorless laugh. "I can see how that could happen, Mr. Accardo."

Now Tony's head cocked. "Michael, I could give you a phone number . . . so we can stay in touch."

"Why don't you do that, Mr. Accardo?"

"Want me to write it down?"

"Just tell me."

Tony did.

Then Tony Accardo stuck his hand out.

And Michael O'Sullivan, Jr., shook it.

Finally the slender figure with the World War II rifle slung over his shoulder, and the World War I automatic in his fist, trotted off the patio, heading around the side of the house, going for the gate.

Next to Tony, the attorney slumped. He was breathing hard; almost sobbing.

"You all right, Sid?"

"Angel . . . Angel of fucking *Death?* Who's gonna show up next? Dillinger's kid? Bonnie and Clyde's niece? *Fuck* me!"

Tony put a hand on the lawyer's shoulder. "Everything will be fine, Sid.

Why don't you go in the house and change your pants?"

The attorney, embarrassed suddenly, nodded, and almost ran inside, stealing a shuddery glance at the skinny corpse of Jimmy T.

And Tony Accardo, in his terrycloth robe, sat in the dark in the presence of the corpses of two of his men. He found a cigar and a lighter in his robe pocket and lighted up; then he sat and smoked, rocking just a little, eyes narrow, thinking about the bargain he'd made, and the word he'd given.

11

Palm Springs had an unofficial ban on the word "motel" — you could find lodges, inns, villas, manors and even the occasional "guest ranch." But the Solona Court on the outskirts of the swanky resort town consisted of a dozen modest cabins whose sole creature comfort was television with rabbit ears. With the exception of the latter, this dreary little mission-style motel with its framed bullfighter litho, pale plaster walls and featureless furnishings could have been one of a dozen such fleabags where Michael and his father stayed in 1931, on their six-month road trip to Perdition, Kansas.

In a courtyard illuminated only by the moon and the green-and-red of motel neon, Michael left the Garand rifle in the trunk of the Lincoln, but took the .45 Colt automatic with him, as he slipped inside Room 12, the cabin farthest from the highway.

He did not hit the light switch — Anna was sleeping in one of the twin beds — but the bathroom light had been left on, the door ajar. A small air conditioner chugged, making no more noise than a Volkswagen with a faulty muffler; but the girl — under the sheets in her pink nightshirt, lost in a deep, sedative-aided slumber — was past noticing or caring.

In addition to throwing the bolt and the latch, Michael wedged the back of a chair under the knob. On the nightstand between the twin beds he set the .45 next to the .38 Smith & Wesson already there, and picked up an envelope propped against the lamp.

The letter, labeled ANNA, he tucked away — for now — in his Samsonite.

In the bathroom he pissed and brushed his teeth and lifted a few handfuls of water to his face. Back at his bed, he slipped out of his crepe-sole shoes, but left on the rest of his clothing — long-sleeve T-shirt and black jeans and black socks — then lay on top of the covers, staring at the ceiling, hands locked behind his head, elbows winged out.

He would take a chance on Accardo.

The man some called Big Tuna, others called Joe Batters, was the last of the Capone crowd — the surviving Outfit leader with any sense of Old World decency. Michael in his brief mid-'40s tour of duty as

Accardo's lieutenant had never really bonded with the ganglord — not as he had with Nitti and Ricca, anyway — but he had nonetheless witnessed a boss who must have been like the old turn-of-the-century Mafia dons, fair and never hasty to act, approachable, willing to help a "family" member.

Accardo truly viewed the Outfit as an extended family, and those backyard barbecues he used to throw every summer indicated his good heart, even though it eventually got the real-life Godfather into trouble, attracting more unwanted guests than invited ones — the press hanging around taking pictures of the attendees, and the FBI showing up with their own clicking cameras.

Still, while Michael could risk his own life, trusting Accardo, he would take extra precautions where Anna was concerned. Right now the motherless girl was a wreck — a newlywed who'd lost her husband on the honeymoon — and she had wept and slept in the backseat on the way from Tahoe to Palm Springs. At the Solona Court, she'd willingly taken the sedatives to help her sleep deeper, and he had not told her he was going out.

What he had done was leave her that

sealed envelope with a letter in it. On the back, he had penned in his small cramped precise handwriting:

Anna —

If you wake up and I am not here, do not worry. I will be back soon.
If for some reason I am not back by morning, open this envelope. Please do not open this otherwise.

Dad.

And the letter inside said,

Dear Anna,

Take the briefcase from my bag. You will find half a million dollars inside, it is yours. Do not go to the police. Do not go to the FBI. Drive to DeKalb and go to your Aunt Betty's.
If you have not heard from me in a week, you must assume the worst, and start your life over.
You are not known in DeKalb but Betty and Ralph are, and that is good. You will be able to go to a bank and get a checking account. Do so. Put ten

thousand dollars in. Put the rest of the money in a safety deposit box and do NOT tell anyone about it, not even your aunt.

Replenish the checking account from the safety deposit box as need be. When you are older and have an education, you may wish to invest the balance of the money.

I cannot really tell you what to do, sweetheart. Not any more. If I am gone, I lose every right to influence you. But just the same I ask you to stay in DeKalb and attend Northern, where your mother went. The arts program is not bad, you will get the lead in every play they put on, I bet. I would very much like you to honor my request that you spend your college years in DeKalb where your aunt and uncle can provide moral support. I do not expect you to live with them and in fact think that would be a mistake, because they are much more conservative than we have ever been and would drive you nuts.

Get an apartment or maybe pledge a sorority. Sorry. Trying to live your kid's life for them is a hard habit to break, even though it never really worked in the first place.

The things I have done should not come back to haunt you. I cannot think of any reason why anyone from my world would look for you or cause you harm. But you should be careful about the money. And you should use your married name.

You are Anna Grace now. It is a good name for you. Your mom and I have always been proud of you and your talent. I hope some day you will forgive me for not stopping your brother from going to Vietnam, you were right, I was wrong.

Please know that your mother loved you more than life itself. I love you more than life itself.

Be strong. Take care.

Dad

The letter, written for tonight, would also serve later, when he went after Giancana. He'd designed it that way.

He'd called his wife's sister before heading to Accardo's estate at Indian Wells Country Club. Anna was already asleep, but he had used a telephone booth outside the restaurant next door, not wanting to risk waking the girl.

"Betty? It's Michael."

"Michael! Is something wrong?"

The response was appropriate: two months ago, Pat had made a supervised phone call, through the WITSEC switchboard, to inform her sister of their situation; to tell Betty that the family had been relocated by the Witness Protection program, but not giving her their location or new names. He and Pat had the right and ability to make other such WITSEC-routed calls to Betty, their only close living relative, but hadn't chosen to.

Betty's husband Ralph was a nice guy but a Born Again preacher of some kind, spun off from the Baptists, who were just not Holy Roller enough. Pat and Betty had rarely talked in recent years, because their conversations always deteriorated into political arguments. Nonetheless, the O'Hara sisters had grown up together and had been close for decades, until wild girl Betty suddenly got saved, after her second divorce, and grew a stick up her ass.

Carefully, he said, "You haven't heard anything?"

"Haven't heard what? Michael, what is this *about?*"

She sounded irritated, which was typical, but also frightened.

"Betty, I have bad news."

". . . oh no. What is it? Should I sit down, Mike? I should be sitting down, shouldn't I? . . . It's Patsy Ann, isn't it? Is she sick?"

"We lost her, Betty."

Silence.

"Do you understand, Betty?"

The voice returned, with a tremor in it. "What . . . Mike, what happened?"

"She was killed, Betty. Our house was attacked by the people I'm supposed to testify against, and they killed her."

"Oh my God. . . . Oh dear Jesus." She wasn't swearing; but she wasn't exactly praying, either. "Anna! What about Anna?"

He told his wife's sister in almost no detail that Pat had been murdered in her sleep. That neither he nor Anna had been harmed, but that his daughter and he were on the road, and in danger.

"*You* did this to her! *You* did this to her! You and those gangsters you work for. Gambling and drinking and debauchery . . . *you* did this!"

He sighed. It would be unkind to point out that, in her time, Betty had indulged in far more gambling and drinking and debauchery than either Michael or Patricia.

Then her voice changed. ". . . Michael, I'm sorry. Forgive me. I'm so sorry that I . . ."

"Blame me if you like, Betty," he said without rancor. "I really don't mind. If it helps you, blame me."

"What *good* would it do? Nothing will bring her back. Was she . . . *right* with the Lord, Michael?"

"She loved Jesus very much, Betty," he lied. "We were talking about it just the night before she died."

"Thank God. Praise Jesus. What can I do to help, Michael? What can Ralph and I do?"

"I need you to do right by your sister."

"How?"

"I'm going to give you a phone number and a name."

"I'll get something to write with . . ." Ten seconds later, she said, "Ready."

He gave her the number and said, "Talk to Harold Shore, he's the associate director of the OCRS — the government agency we were dealing with."

"*Were* dealing with . . . ? You're not anymore?"

"No. For obvious reasons, I don't have a high opinion of their ability to protect me and what's left of my family."

"Does that . . . include us?"

"You and Ralph are in no danger. Anna won't be, either, when I'm out of the picture."

"What does that mean, 'out of the picture'?"

"It means people are trying to kill me, and they may well succeed. But in the meantime, you call Director Shore and tell him you want to claim your sister's body."

A sudden intake of breath leapt from the receiver. "Oh, Michael . . . I hadn't even thought it through that far. . . ."

"I'm sure the government can have Pat's body sent to your local mortuary. I know they'll do that much for us."

"Michael, oh . . . oh, Patsy. . . ."

"I won't be able to attend the funeral. Neither will Anna. That would be a high-risk proposition, our being there . . . but not for anyone else. Pat had a life in DeKalb. Friends. History. I'd like her to be buried next to her parents in the cemetery there."

"All right, Michael. All right."

"I'll send you money for —"

"I'd like you to let Ralph and me handle that, Michael."

"Well, actually, that's generous. Kind. Loving, but I need you to buy a plot for me, too. I'll want to be buried next to my wife — when the time comes."

"Oh, Michael . . ." She was crying. ". . . forgive me for being so . . . so darn terrible."

Yes, "darn" terrible. Betty wasn't allowed to be "goddamn" terrible, anymore. . . .

"There's one other thing, Betty. . . . There's a chance Anna may turn up on your doorstep one of these days."

"We'd love to have her," she said, in a painfully forced upbeat way. "Sheila's only two years younger than Anna, and they could be like . . . like sisters."

Betty was crying again. He heard a male voice, Ralph's, saying, "What is it, honey? What's wrong?"

Michael let her deal with her husband, then when she returned, told her, "I'm hoping, if something happens to me, that Anna will go to college there in DeKalb, and have you folks to fall back on. So she's not . . . alone in the world. Would that be agreeable?"

"Of course it would, Michael."

"She'll have her own money."

"Well, Ralph and I would be glad —"

"No. She's a young woman, and she will be self-sufficient. What you don't know, Betty, is that Anna was married recently."

"Married! At her age! Michael, that's —"

"Her young husband was murdered yesterday. He caught a bullet meant for me."

"Ooooh. . . . oh God . . ."

Fear in her voice now. Finally. Good.

"Betty, these are deep, dark waters. And treacherous. If she comes to you, treat Anna like a grown-up, because she is one, or anyway will need to be. And she won't have time *for* . . . or, knowing her . . . patience *with* any sanctimonious bullshit. You just be a good, loving aunt to her. I don't mean to be unkind, but am I clear on that?"

"You are," she said, nothing irritated in her voice at all now. "I promise you that, Michael."

"Thank you, Betty," he said, and hung up.

In the morning, Anna woke before him. She had already showered and was in bell-bottom jeans and wedge sandals and a dark blue scoop-neck tank top, all that brown hair cascading down her back. She was brushing her teeth when he approached, still in his commando black.

"What's," she said, and spit out toothpaste into the sink, "with the get-up?"

"Oh. I slipped out for a little while last night, after you went to sleep."

"Ninja convention in town?"

337

"There's a powerful man I had to see."

"What . . . one of your gangster friends?"

"Sort of. I needed to make sure where we stood with him."

She rinsed; spat. "Where *do* we stand, Daddy?"

"He's with us. I think."

"Oh. Well, gee, that's comforting. But other people still want us dead?"

"Yes."

She shook her head, smirked humorlessly, said, "Bathroom's yours," and brushed past him.

He shat, showered, shaved, changed into a fresh Banlon, rust-color, and tan trousers. He was brushing his teeth when Anna popped up in the bathroom doorway, as he had done with her.

"What's the plan?"

"The plan," he said, and spat into the sink, "is to keep us both alive."

"Okay. But with Mom dead, and Gary, being alive doesn't quite have the . . . appeal like it used to, huh?" Her eyes were filled with tears that belied her flip manner. She'd had twelve hours of sleep to replenish her tear ducts.

"Ask yourself if Mom would want us to give up," he said. "Ask yourself if Gary would want anything to happen to you."

She nodded, numbly, and shuffled off.

When he emerged from the bathroom, she was sitting on the edge of her bed, facing his, slumped, legs apart, hands laced together hanging between her knees. Staring at the floor. Her handbag — an off-white crocheted jute shoulder affair — was next to her.

From the nightstand, he removed the .38 and handed it toward her.

"I want you to carry that in your purse."

She didn't argue. She took the gun and unsnapped the bag and slid the big weapon in among cosmetics and Kleenex.

"Guess all those gun club years are finally comin' in handy, huh, Pop?"

He sat across from her. "Couple details. Couple realities . . . not any fun, I'm afraid."

She looked up with an eyebrow raised. "Oh — is the fun over already?"

"Gary's parents will've been called back from their Caribbean trip by now."

She hung her head again, shaking it. "Those poor people . . . poor, poor people. . . ."

"I'm assuming they knew nothing about the marriage?"

"Not any more than you and Mom did."

". . . Is there anything in the house —

marriage license, photos, anything that might come in the mail, that would tell them about you two . . . ?"

"Getting hitched?" she said archly. "No. I don't think so." She frowned at him, confused. "Why?"

"I'm thinking . . . there's no reason for them to know about it. I'm thinking it would just complicate things. All they know right now, from talking to people who were there, is that you sneaked back to go to the prom with Gary. And that he was an innocent bystander in some kind of gangland violence that broke out in the parking lot of a casino with that kind of history."

She was thinking. "Maybe . . . maybe it *would* be better this way. Just be harder on them, knowing . . . and they'd just be . . . madder at us."

"I guess that's right."

"D'you suppose his funeral's today?"

He nodded. "Or tomorrow."

His father had led him to the bed where his mother's body lay, where Papa had tucked her in. "Bid her Godspeed now, Michael — there'll be no attending the services for us . . . no wake . . . no graveside goodbyes."

He said, "We could have flowers wired.

Would you like that?"

Looking at the floor, she swallowed. Sighed. Nodded. "What . . . what about Mom?"

"I called Aunt Betty. They're handling it."

"We won't be going to her funeral, either, will we?"

He shook his head.

She grimaced. Then her face softened into a blank pretty mask. "Daddy, what *is* the plan?"

"A safe place and a fresh start for both of us, but, first . . . I have to do something back in Chicago."

"What kind of something?"

"Do you want me to tell you?"

Her dark eyes flashed up from the floor. "I'm fucking asking, aren't I?"

He held those eyes with his. "The monster who did this to us — who caused your mother's death, and your . . . your husband's. He has to die."

"You have to kill him."

"Yes."

"You're going to Chicago to kill him."

"Yes."

She nodded. Shrugged. Said, "Can I help?"

At a Denny's across from the motel, they

both ate modest breakfasts, but at least they were able to eat. Michael checked the Los Angeles newspapers to see how much coverage the Cal-Neva incident was getting.

Much as he'd outlined it to Anna, the papers reported that at Lake Tahoe, the Cal-Neva "which had attracted headlines in the days when singer Frank Sinatra was an owner" had been the scene of "mob-style" violence. Gary Grace, eighteen, had taken a bullet intended for the unidentified male target of two mob assassins who had been killed by said target. The names of the dead men were being withheld by federal authorities, although an unnamed source linked them to "notorious" Chicago gangster Sam Giancana, "recently returned from Mexico and said to be contemplating a comeback in organized crime circles."

No mention of Michael by name or even description, though the cops would surely know about the Lincoln. A small mention of Anna: "The young victim had been attending the prom with a teenaged girl who had moved away recently and returned for the event." His daughter's name — and that she'd got in the car with the "unidentified target" prior to the bystander teenager's killing — was not mentioned.

Had the feds withheld that info, or

didn't they know? Maybe the eyewitnesses hadn't seen Gary open the car door for Anna, and her get in, their attention not attracted until the gunfire began. In the midst of weapons blazing in the night, and the Lincoln screeching out of the Cal-Neva lot, perhaps no one noticed the girl in the front seat. Of course, she *had* been screaming. . . .

They drove down a commercial strip toward Palm Springs and stopped at a florist, sending flowers to the funeral home in Incline Village for Gary. Then Michael trawled for just the right used-car lot, found it, and traded his Lincoln in on a three-year-earlier model Eldorado, a deep blue vinyl-top number with sixty-thousand miles, paying the guy eight thousand cash. In reality, the used-car salesman should have been paying Michael a couple grand, but this was a no-paperwork, off-the-books transaction.

Father and daughter transferred their possessions to the big boat of a Caddy — everything from the rifle to their suitcases to the four-track tapes — and soon were heading up North 95 to connect with Interstate 40, east.

As they sat in air-conditioned comfort, listening to Bobby Darin sing "The Good

Life," his daughter said, "These aren't the most inconspicuous wheels I ever saw, Daddy."

"They're less conspicuous," he said, "than that Lincoln, considering I got it from the government . . . and we were seen in it at the Cal-Neva."

"Ah. But, still . . ."

"Baby, I hardly have the heart to tell you, but —"

"Oh, *bad* news now?"

He sighed. "We have three days of driving ahead of us, ten or twelve hours a day."

She frowned. "If we're going that far, and were getting rid of our car, anyway, why didn't we just fly? Or take the train or something?"

"The G-men may be watching the airports and train stations for us."

She laughed. "Did you just say 'G-men'?"

He smiled, embarrassed. "I guess I did. Kinda dates me, huh?"

"Only to around the turn of the century."

The first day took them home, in a way — Arizona, the turnpike cutting through endless stretches of mesas and buttes dotted with yucca and sagebrush. Heat and clouds conspired to turn the desert shades of yellow, pink, brown and gray, overseen by ragged barren mountains.

They didn't talk much in the morning, Anna catching naps, the depression breaking through a few times, and she'd cry softly into Kleenex, though neither would comment.

At a gas-station greasy spoon on the Seligman turn-off, they had delicious cheeseburgers and french fries and Cokes, and Anna offered to take the wheel a while.

"Let me help out," she said. "I'm used to it."

She was referring, obliquely, to the driving she'd done when she'd gone with Cindy Parham to meet Gary in Vegas, and then on with Gary to Tahoe.

"That'd be good," he said.

The start of the afternoon took them into a forest preserve, the world green suddenly, pines and firs and oaks and spruce and piñon.

"What's the rest of the plan?" Anna asked. Behind the wheel, now.

"After Chicago, you mean."

"Yes, after Chicago."

"Assuming all goes well, I'm thinking Vancouver."

She flashed him a surprised look. "Really? Why?"

"Money won't go as far there as in Mexico, but we'll fit in better, be an easier . . . transition. You can go to college up there, pursue your theater. I can find work."

Her eyes, on the road again, tensed; she was thinking.

Some while later, they'd run out of forest, in fact run out of Arizona — this was New Mexico now — and he was driving again, when she said, with quiet bitterness, "Canada, huh?"

"Hmmm? Yeah. Canada."

"Kinda funny, isn't it?"

"What?"

"That's where Mike'd be. If I'd had *my* way, anyway."

She looked out the window, and he could see her reflection in it — she was crying again, chin crinkled; she dried her eyes with the knuckles of a fist.

They had supper at a diner in Gallup, New Mexico, and outside Albuquerque found a motel not unlike the Solona, arriving about ten o'clock. Very little conversation preceded bedtime, although they did watch Johnny Carson (which jarred Michael, remembering the last time he'd heard Ed McMahon summon the host with, "Hiiii-yo!"). Neither laughed at anything, though they did smile occasionally.

The following morning, with Michael behind the wheel, the rolling plains of New Mexico encouraged boredom so severe that the daughter actually initiated a conversation.

"Daddy?"

"Yes?"

"Can I ask you something?"

He let out a laugh. "What, and take me away from this fascinating scenery?"

She smiled politely, then said, "Who were your real parents? What did you mean when you said that you'd . . . sat where *I* sat? Was your mother . . . my real grandmother, was she . . . murdered, too?"

He'd forgotten he'd blurted that to her, at the prom; and her words punched him in the belly. He glanced at her, his mouth open but no words finding their way out.

"And your father, not Gran'pa Satariano, but your *real* father, who-he-was has something to do with why you got in with those . . . those Mafia people . . . doesn't it?"

He was still searching for words.

She went on: "Hey, I know you provided for us well and everything, and we had really nice lives, really great lives, till, uh . . . recently. But why'd you choose that road to go down? Or did it choose you?"

He glanced at her, hard. "You really . . . really want to know all this?"

"I would, yes."

"It's a long story."

"Daddy — it's a long drive."

"I'm not much for talking, sweetie."

"Hmmm. Must've been some other father lecturing me and Mike all those years."

He grinned a little. "All right. Only . . . if you get bored, or tired of it or anything . . . just say so, okay?"

She did not get bored.

For almost two hours, until his throat was as dry as New Mexico itself, he told her, the words tumbling out, the story of the Michael O'Sullivan family in Rock Island, Illinois. How his father worked for John Looney, the patriarch of the Irish mob in the Tri-Cities, and how Mr. Looney had been wonderful to the O'Sullivans. How he and his brother Peter wondered exactly what their father did for Mr. Looney, and how Michael had stowed away in the back of a Ford and wound up witnessing a murder committed by Mr. Looney's crazy son, Connor, and also saw a machine-gun massacre, with Michael O'Sullivan — his father, her grandfather — wielding the tommy.

And how John Looney's son Connor had killed Peter — thinking the younger boy was murder-witness Michael — and his mother, Annie.

That had been one of a handful of times the girl interrupted: "Annie . . . ? My real grandmother was named Annie? I was named for her?"

"Yes."

"But Mom never lived in Rock Island or anything . . ."

"No, I didn't meet your mother till I was in DeKalb, a year or so later. But she knew everything about me, including that I'd lost my mother. It was her idea to name you, more or less, after your late grandmother."

Anna smirked. "But *I* couldn't ever know, right?"

"You know now."

She blew air out, shook her head, said, "So what happened after my grandmother was murdered? What did your dad *do?*"

And so he told his daughter about the eventful road trip he and his father had taken in 1931 — how he'd been an underage getaway driver. This, and various exploits he related, earned a number of exclamations from Anna, all pretty much the same: "Wicked" or sometimes "Wicked cool" or the ultimate: "Wicked awesome."

She was appropriately somber, however, when he came to the end of his tale — the death of his father at the hands of an assassin in a farmhouse outside Perdition.

"And *you* . . . you killed the guy?"

"Yes."

"How old were you, anyway?"

"Twelve."

"That is out there. That is way the fuck out there."

"Anna . . ."

"Oh, the kid getaway driver wanted in six states thinks his daughter's language is too salty? Sorry!"

She had him, and he laughed.

"And what's . . ." She did a silly impression of cornball Paul Harvey from the radio. ". . . the *rest* of the story?"

"Why don't we save that for later. I'm getting hoarse from all this. Aren't you hungry yet?"

In a roadhouse-type diner outside Amarillo, Texas, they sat in a booth by a window and shared one order of Texas fried steak the size of a hubcap, with country swing on the jukebox that wasn't half bad.

"You and your father . . . my *grandfather* . . . were you kind of, like — famous?"

"In a way."

"I think I saw an old movie about you on TV."

"There were a couple, actually."

"Who played you?"

"Jimmy Lydon in the '40s one. Bobby Driscoll in the '50s."

"Never heard of them."

"Well, your grandfather fared better — Alan Ladd and Robert Mitchum."

"Cool!"

He promised her the second half of the story on tomorrow's drive, and let her tool the Caddy across the rest of the Texas panhandle.

In Oklahoma, the red earth and the rolling plains sparking memories, he said, "We traveled through here, your grandfather and I. No turnpikes, then."

"Like in that movie — *Bonnie and Clyde*?"

"Right."

Then, as they left 40 and headed north on 35, he found himself telling her about the time he caught scarlet fever, and he and his father had to stay put in one place for a while; and how bounty hunters had caught up to them, and how they'd gotten away. Over supper in Wichita, he told her about the shoot-out in the country church, and when they stopped for the night, at a motel outside Kansas City, shared with her the time his father had robbed a police station of the week's bag money — right here in K.C., the very town they were staying in!

In the dark, after *The Tonight Show*, she said, "Daddy? Is it terrible that we . . . had a kind of a good time, today?"

"I don't think so, sweetheart."

"Mom . . . Gary . . . Your life with Mom is over . . . and mine with Gary never really got . . . got started; and we're laughing and talking and eating and . . . are we evil?"

"No. We're just . . . I don't know."

"Dealing with it?"

"In our way, yes."

This was the first night she hadn't cried herself to sleep, and Michael felt more alive than he had since losing Pat. He and his daughter were closer now; they'd always been close, but finally she knew him. Knew who he was. Knew who he'd been.

And didn't hate him for it.

That day, they angled up 35 through Nebraska — "Great," Anna said, "Oklahoma again, minus the interesting red dirt" — into Iowa, which seemed rich and green and varied, compared to what they'd endured. They shared the driving evenly, and he told her "the rest of the story."

Anna already knew about her father's life growing up in DeKalb with the Satarianos, and going steady with her mother in high school. And the heroic service on Bataan, and coming home and getting married.

But she did not know that he'd gone to work for the Chicago Syndicate in order to take revenge on Al Capone and Frank Nitti. The ins and outs of that were complicated, and the tale made today's trip a more somber one, with not a single "wicked," much less "wicked cool," though the girl listened in awestruck attention.

On Interstate 80, he said, "Short side trip," and took 61 down into the Quad Cities. Anna said nothing; she seemed to know what he was up to, if not where exactly he was headed, which turned out to be downtown Davenport and across a black ancient-looking government bridge over to Illinois.

In Rock Island, in Chippiannock cemetery, father and daughter stood with bowed heads, paying silent respect at small simple gravestones honoring Michael O'Sullivan, Sr., Anne Louise O'Sullivan and Peter David O'Sullivan. The afternoon was cool for June and a breeze ruffled the many trees on the sloping grounds. Alone together in the vast graveyard, surrounded by stone cherubs and crosses — "City of the Dead," the cemetery's Indian name meant — they held hands and Michael was surprised to find himself praying, silently.

After a while, Anna said, "You didn't go to your mother's funeral, either, did you?"

"No. And I'm afraid, for us . . . for all our sorrow right now . . . this will have to do."

Her hand slipped from his and she knelt at her grandmother's gravestone and touched the carved name there. Looking up at him, she said, "O'Sullivan. . . . Is that who I am, really, Daddy? Annie O'Sullivan?"

He reached out to her, helped her back up, slipped an arm around her shoulder and said, "No, sweetheart. You're Anna Grace."

She sucked in a breath. "I am, aren't I? I am."

"Lovely name. For my lovely girl."

She hugged him and they made their way out of the cemetery.

In twenty minutes, they were back on Interstate 80. A quick supper at a truck stop would mark their last meal on the road.

By mid-evening they would be in Chicago.

12

At the turn of the century, Oak Park had been dubbed Saints' Rest, due to its many churches, and perhaps because the idyllic, largely white village was so quiet, and quietly affluent.

But on this June night, Chicago's nearest neighbor to the west suffered under a hellish humidity, heat lightning streaking the sky, wind rustling the leaves of the suburb's many sizable trees in an unsettling, ceaseless whisper.

Just before ten, walking easily up Lexington Street, Michael — in a black sportcoat over black Banlon with black slacks and matching loafers and socks — might have been a priest but for the lack of white collar. Despite the thick-aired swelter, and the ominous atmosphere, the neighborhood seemed peaceful; a dog barked, crickets chirped, window air conditioners thrummed. Houses here dated to the 1920s, substantial bungalows blessed with generous yards, while countless shade trees — mostly namesake oaks — stood sentry.

He and Anna had arrived in Oak Park less than two hours ago. This represented something of a homecoming, as the Satarianos had called the village home until about ten years ago. But Anna had just been in first grade, and her memories were hazy, while Michael had maintained no friendships here. No real risk being seen.

Though the suburb boasted a few gangster residents, it wasn't nearly as dangerous for them as that nearby Outfit enclave, River Forest (where Tony Accardo lived, when he wasn't in Palm Springs). The downtown might have been a theme-park replication of a typical quaint shopping district of the 1950s, before shopping-mall casualties. At the south edge, they sought out the Oak Arms, a four-story tan-brick residential hotel whose specialty was being nondescript.

In a featureless lobby, Michael paid the desk clerk seventy-five dollars and eighty-five cents, cash — the weekly rate — for a "suite" on the second floor. What father and daughter got was a small apartment consisting of a bedroom, living room with "sleeper" couch and a kitchenette — everything brown, tan or dark green, and not because any long-ago decorator had been thinking "earth tones." They were on the alley, which was fine with Michael, the fire escape access next door, sharing space with Coke- and candy-vending machines.

They sat on the uncomfortable nubby couch, pregnant with fold-out bed; he was in a light blue sportshirt and tan chinos, she in an orange tank top and brown bell-bottom jeans — what they'd worn driving today. The glow of a streetlight bounced off a brick wall in the alley and filtered in through a gauzy secondary layer of curtain; a small lamp on an end table provided the only other illumination, a parchment-style shade creating a yellow cast.

He told her, "I think you should get some rest — maybe take a couple of Mom's sedatives again."

She eyed him with frank suspicion. "Why? I'm not having any trouble sleeping, anymore."

"It's just . . . tomorrow's a big day."

"What's big about it?"

He shrugged a little; they were eyeing each other sideways. "Tomorrow's when we're taking care of the problem."

"The 'problem.' That man, you mean . . . Giancana. *That* problem."

He sucked in air, nodded, let it out.

"I thought you respected me," she said, chin crinkling.

"I do, sweetheart."

"Then don't yank on my ying yang."

"Huh?"

"Don't *lie* to me. You wanna dope me up, like you did in Palm Springs, so you can go play Charles Bronson again! Well, I won't put up with it — *I'm* part of this, too, you know."

He patted the air with a palm. "Baby — really. It's better I do this alone."

She crossed her arms; her jaw was set. "No fucking way."

"I can't involve you in this — if we got caught, or, or . . ."

"Killed?" Her eyebrows hiked. "What if I was Mike? What about that . . . *Daddy?*"

"I, uh . . . don't know what you mean, honey."

She swung around, and sat on her legs Indian-style, so she could face him, confrontationally. "If it was Mike, with Mom murdered, you'd hand him a goddamn gun and say, 'Come on, son.' Man's gotta do what a man's gotta do. Tell me I'm not right!"

"You're *not* right."

"You're lying."

And he was.

Then he said, "Baby, this is no time for some kind of . . . what, feminist stand. I want you to stay here, *right* here, while —"

"You want to knock me out with sedatives, I-am-woman-hear-me-snore, while you go off and maybe get killed, maybe because you didn't have, what, *back-up* when you needed it."

He was shaking his head. "Don't be absurd."

She played pattycake with the air. "Wait a minute, wait a minute — aren't I talking to the eleven-year-old baby-face bank robber? Wanted in six or seven states?"

". . . That's beside the point."

"*Hell* it is! It's *right* to the point — *your* father took *you* along, made you his *partner,* trusted you to drive the damn *getaway* car. Me? I'm supposed to take my medicine like a good little girl and zonk out, and maybe wake up an orphan. No way. No *fucking* way, Daddy."

He just looked at her — she seemed so young and yet much older than when this trip had started. Did he have any right to leave her behind? Giancana was responsible for her mother's death — and her husband's death — and had created the utter shambles that was now both their lives. . . .

Of course he had the right: he was her father. When Michael O'Sullivan, Sr., had gone for the final showdown with Connor Looney, Michael O'Sullivan, Jr., had been left behind in a residential hotel not unlike this one, in Prophet's Town, Illinois. . . . What had it been called? Could it have been . . . the Paradise Hotel?

And Papa had left him a letter, like the one he had ready to leave Anna, and . . . how had he felt about it? Frightened, alone, and a little betrayed. He'd promised his father he would not open that envelope, and he had stared at it long and hard, wondering what was inside, terrified of what was written in there, and that his father would never return.

What an awful, endless night that had been. . . .

"All right," he said. "You can drive."

"All *right!*" she said, and swung a tiny fist. "And I'll have my gun along? I'll be armed and dangerous, won't I?"

"Bet your life," he said.

But he left his eighteen-year-old getaway girl in the Caddy, parked on Lexington, and walked a block before turning right and walking another three to Wenonah Avenue, where he turned right again. Two blocks later he could see the house on the corner of Wenonah and Fillmore, a distinctive red-tile-roofed yellow-brick bungalow, one-and-a-half stories with arched windows — solid, spacious, unassuming, perfect digs for the gangster who wants comfort without calling undue attention to himself.

Earlier, from a phone booth at the Interstate 80 truck stop, Michael had called the number Accardo gave him, and Accardo himself called back in two minutes — better service than the WITSEC panic button.

"Edgar's kids've been watching the place," Accardo's rough baritone had informed him, meaning the FBI had an ongoing surveillance of Giancana's residence. "Kind of trading off with the neighborhood kids."

Indicating the Chicago P.D.'s organized crime unit was also keeping an eye on the house. Though using a supposedly "secure" line, the ganglord was speaking somewhat elliptically, so Michael followed suit.

"Hmmm," Michael said. "Well, I might make some noise."

"When you thinking?"

"Tonight."

"Any special time?"

"Around Johnny Carson."

". . . okay. You been to the guy's house before?"

Meaning Giancana.

"Couple times," Michael said. "Wasn't exactly on a recon, though."

"A garage back there, on the alley. You'll see some garbage cans. People throw the damnedest things away these days. Perfectly good items."

"Yeah, it's a real waste."

"Backyard's fenced in — I hear there's been trouble with the lock on the gate in the fence, lately."

"Too bad. Risky with all the vandalism."

"Sure is. Garden back there, head of the house likes to putter, but never at night. Sometimes he forgets and leaves the house open in back."

"Isn't that the door we spoke about?"

The steel door with the Joe-sent-me peephole. Joe Batters, in this case.

"Yeah," Accardo said. "That door."

"Okay. Will he have any friends over?"

Bodyguards or security staff?

"No. I have on good authority, a couple guys who usually keep him company won't be around. They work hard. Deserve a night off."

"What about his housekeeper and his wife?"

That was the DiPersios, Giancana's longtime, seventy-something caretaker and his housekeeper wife, who were live-in.

"Their apartment's upstairs, on the second floor. They go to bed early."

"Probably early risers, too, then," Michael said. "Do they set the alarm, d'you suppose?"

Giancana was known to have an electric-eye burglar alarm.

"Not tonight," Accardo said darkly. ". . . Anything else I can help you with, son?"

"No, sir. Thank you."

But now as Michael strolled down the tree-lined street toward the alley beside the bungalow, he noted with surprise no suspicious cars. Several vehicles were parked along nearby curbs, but not the unimaginative standard-issue black sedans both the feds and Chicago P.D. were noted for — in fact, right across from 1147 South Wenonah were a red Mustang convertible and a white Pontiac Trans Am with a blue racing stripe.

No surveillance here, not at this moment — of course, the feds and cops liked to eat, and everybody had to piss now and then.

In the alley he found the garbage cans, three of them, nestled next to the yellow-brick garage. The first lid he lifted revealed a .22 target pistol perched cherry-on-the-sundae atop a fat, filled garbage bag.

With a black-leather-gloved hand, Michael lifted the target pistol out — a High-Standard Duromatic whose four-inch barrel had been tooled down to receive a six-inch homemade noise suppressor, a threaded tube drilled diagonally with countless holes. Fairly standard Outfit whack weapon, these days — a .22, not unlike the ones the two DeStefano hitters brought to the Cal-Neva, before Michael killed them. He checked the clip — full. The ammo looked fine.

If Accardo's people had left him a sabotaged gun, he still had his .45 in a shoulder holster. But with the chance of cops or feds returning, within easy hearing range of a gunfire, this silenced .22 would do the trick nicely. He stuck the somewhat bulky weapon in the waistband of his slacks, leaving his sportcoat unbuttoned.

As promised, the gate in the stockade-type fence was unlocked. Michael opened and closed it with little sound, entering a backyard with no security lights, though the moon gave an ivory glow to this immaculately tended little world of putting green, clipped hedges and colorful flower beds. A circular stone patio hugged the house, but Michael's crepe soles made no sound as he crossed to descend the cement steps to the steel door, which stood slightly ajar. A pleasant, spicy cooking odor wafted out.

That was not surprising. Michael had been at the Giancana home several times, and had been in the elaborately "finished" basement, with the spacious paneled den where the little gangster loved to spend his private time, and sometimes hold court. What lay beyond the steel door was a fully equipped modern kitchen.

One hand on the butt of the .22 target pistol in his belt, Michael pushed the door open — it creaked just a little, but the voice of Frank Sinatra covered for him: "Softly, As I Leave You" was playing, not loud, just background music, a nearby radio or distant hi-fi. Michael recognized the album — it was one of the four-tracks he'd tossed in Walker Lake.

He stepped inside to air-conditioned coolness, shutting the door behind him, as the pleasant cooking smell tweaked his nostrils. The counters and appliances were white, the paneling and cupboards a blond oak, the overhead lighting fluorescent. At the stove a swarthy, skinny little man — bald but for a friar's fringe of gray — in a blue-and-white-checked untucked sportshirt, baggy brown slacks and slippers with socks was tending two pans, frying sausage in olive oil in one and boiling up spinach and *ceci* beans in the other.

Both Mama and Papa Satariano had been magicians in the kitchen, so Michael knew exactly what the basement chef was up to — the sausage would be removed, and the spinach (or was that escarole?) and beans would eventually be transferred to the other pan to saute in the sausage grease, with pinches of garlic no doubt, while the sausage would be added back in, for a killer of an Old Country snack.

The man at the frying pan sensed the presence of another, and before turning, said, "Butch — is that you? Forget something?"

"No," Michael said, and withdrew the .22.

Sam Giancana — deep melancholy grooves in his stubble-bearded face, his nose a lumpy knob, his eyes at sad slants, an effect echoed by white, bushy eyebrows — looked at the gun first. Then up at Michael.

"So it's a Saint they send." Giancana laughed hollowly. He nodded toward the sizzling pans. "You want some of this?"

"Step away from the stove, Momo. I don't want grease in my face."

Giancana — looking a decade older than

just a few months ago, when he'd slipped into Michael's Cal-Neva office and started all this — shrugged and did as he was told. He even held his hands away from himself, a little, and up. "Those need to cook a while, anyway. You want some wine? Beer? Wait . . . Coca fucking Cola, right? You're the Saint, after all."

"No thanks. Nothing for me."

Giancana sighed, nodded, offered a chagrined grin. "Guess we kinda underestimated each other, didn't we, Mike?"

"I guess."

Giancana's head tilted to one side. "Why didn't you shoot me, standing at the stove? Wanted to see my face, first?"

"Frankly, Momo, your face doesn't do jack shit for me."

The little gangster frowned, more confused than angry. "Then why ain't you *shot* my ass? Ain't that why Joe Batters sent you around?" He sneered. "Funny! I ask you to knock off that head job Mad Sam, and you go all righteous on me. But Accardo you play torpedo for, no problem . . . I told you, Mike, told you you're the same bad-ass today who shot Frank Abatte back in —"

"Shut up."

Giancana sneered. "Then *shoot,* Saint."

Shrugged. "Didn't I always say, 'Live by the sword, die by the sword?' So my string ran out, finally. It was a good ride. I fucked men over and fucked women silly — who could ask for more?"

Michael's finger began to tighten on the trigger.

Giancana braced himself . . .

. . . but the diminutive don had said it before: *why wasn't Michael shooting?*

"Or maybe," Giancana said, smiling just a little, the sideways slitted eyes narrowing even further, deep creases in the forehead signaling thought, "maybe you know that when you kill me, certain questions go un-answered — maybe forever. Questions like — how did I know you were in Arizona? Tucson? In Paradise the fuck Estates?"

Michael's eyes tightened. "How *did* you know, Momo?"

A smile blossomed on the stubbly, wrinkled face; he looked very small, chest sunken, even frail. Of course, the man was in his late sixties, and recovering from gall bladder surgery.

Mooney's voice was soothing now, almost charming. "Saint, why don't we talk . . ."

The gangster gestured past the adjacent dining area through the open doorway into the den, where the large, rectangular dark oak table and ten high-backed chairs had been home to many an inner-circle Outfit meeting, back when Giancana was boss.

Michael knew he should just shoot this son of a bitch; but Giancana was right: when Mooney died, information would die with him.

"You first, Momo."

Slowly, hands half-raised, Giancana led Michael into a spacious, light-oak-paneled room cluttered with armchairs, a sofa, and endless bric-a-brac: porcelain ashtrays, beer steins, sterling silver pieces, glassware and bowls, some filling a Gothic hutch, others decorating tables; oil paintings, lighted from beneath, ran to Sicilian landscapes, and from a low-slung stereo cabinet, Sinatra was singing "Talk to Me, Baby" next to a fully stocked liquor cabinet.

One area of the den was devoted to golf, including a golf-bag wastebasket and a framed golfing clown print. Half the pipes in Chicago were displayed on a rack, and on a Louis XV desk a cigar humidor was initialed G.

But the vast conference table was dominant, and Giancana and Michael sat across from each other at the near end, closer to the scent of sizzling sausage.

Michael of course had checked for

hidden weapons, alarm buttons, and patted down the scrawny gangster, who seemed vaguely amused. But the shark's eyes had a glimmer Michael recognized: fear.

"Let me tell you why you shouldn't kill me, Saint," Giancana said, hands flat on the tabletop.

"Why don't you."

"You're a smart man. You recognize power when you see it. You see the possibilities." Another shrug. "Aiuppa doesn't have the brains to run an organization like ours, with its national and international interests. And Accardo is an old man who just wants to retire and clip coupons. You know, I spent the afternoon talking with Butch Blasi and Chuckie English. Planning."

"Don't they work for Aiuppa now?"

Giancana snorted a laugh. "*Aiuppa* thinks they do. They go back with me, for . . . for fuckin' ever. I got friends in the Outfit, from the old days, who remember what it was like having a *real* leader. The new turks, they heard of me, they heard the stories, the legend. Whispers about Jack Kennedy and Marilyn and Bobby. And how I fucking killed all three."

"This is quite an argument you're making."

He raised a withered palm. "Just providing a . . . whaddyacallit, context for all of this. First thing you need to know is, I didn't authorize what happened at your house. In Arizona."

"Really."

"I ain't gonna tell you I was not in favor of shutting you up, permanent. We both know the kind of things you could yak about on the witness stand."

"That's funny, Momo. Lot of people feel the same about you."

Giancana paused. "I did not tell Inoglia and them guys to do that terrible thing to your family. I would not do that. I got kids, too. I lost a wife who I still love to this day. . . . Don't look at me like that. It's the truth."

"Who *did* tell them to do it?"

"Thing is . . ." He twitched a nervous smile. ". . . I don't know exactly. I only know what went down in your place 'cause . . . well. You probably heard I picked up, over the years, certain . . . contacts in government. These contacts are concerned about, you know . . . what you said. Me testifying."

"CIA. I heard the rumors. But you don't remind me at all of James Bond, Momo."

His slash of mouth tightened. "I am *not*

shitting you, Saint. I was dealing with a voice on the phone. This voice said, don't give us up to the committee . . . Senate committee, you know . . . and we'll protect you. We'll give you Michael Satariano."

"I'm not a fool, Momo . . ."

"Hell, *I* know you aren't! But think about it, Mike — *think!* How could I know you headed back to Tahoe, to pick up that prom queen daughter of yours? *How could I know that?*"

His gloved hand tight on the pistol grip, Michael said, "Anna and her boyfriend kept in touch."

"How?"

"By phone."

"Who taps phones, Mike? Do I tap phones? Does the Outfit tap fucking phones? Who the hell does *that* sound like — the fuckin' G, and that don't-the-fuck stand for Giancana, does it?"

The truth of it sizzled inside Michael's brain like that damn sausage on the stove.

"A leak," Michael said. "In WITSEC."

"Has to be," Giancana said, and pounded the table in emphasis. "*Has* to be — working with the spooks, one government agency leaning on another."

"*Who?*"

He threw his hands up. "Hey, you got *me* by the balls." His hands came down and folded, prayerfully, respectfully. "But you come over to my side, Mike, you be my right-hand man . . . like you were Frank Nitti's? And when I retire —"

"All this will be mine?" Michael grunted a mirthless laugh. "I'm not into ashtrays and beer steins, Momo."

Giancana swallowed, sat forward, urgency in his voice. "You take my offer, you ride back to the top with me, Mike, and I promise you, I will play those government cocksuckers like a ten-cent kazoo, and we will find out who ratted you out! We'll find the WITSEC leak and you will plug the bastard. Personally!"

Michael stared at the little shell of the once powerful mob boss, in whom desperation had replaced charisma.

"Inoglia, Nappi, Caruso — they were your men, Momo, before I sent them to hell."

"Who said they weren't?"

"You say what happened in Paradise Estates wasn't your doing. That some faceless voice on the phone, representing the CIA skeletons in your closet, gave me up to you as a favor . . ."

"Yeah! What don't you get, Saint? I let it

be known I was unhappy about my 'company' pals not protecting me from those fuckin' Mexicans! I had tens of goddamn millions in the bank down there . . . and Uncle Sam can't do anything about it? And now I gotta testify, and make Accardo and every paranoid asshole in the Outfit think I might spill the secrets, like that prick Valachi?"

"They couldn't get your money for you, and they couldn't put the brakes on the Senate committee . . . but they *could* give me up."

"Fucking exactly!"

"Fine. Who 'exactly' is 'they'?"

An elaborate shrug. "I met dozens of these spooks over the years, gray assholes in gray suits, and I could give you names, but you think they're *real* names? You think I got an address book so I can send you and your vengeance hard-on to the homes of every government spy in Washington? Get real, Saint."

"Maybe. But you sent those three Outfit *goombahs* to my house, Momo. And Inoglia murdered my wife. Explain that away — I'm listening."

"Wait, wait, wait the fuck! I was in the goddamn hospital, in Houston, getting my gall bladder filleted! I gave that . . . that *voice* Inoglia's name and contact crap. Do you think I woulda had them dress up like hippies? If I was gonna kill you, Saint, I'd want the world to know. You'da been an example. Whose fucking interests did it serve havin' that hit look like Charlie Manson?"

Very softly Michael said, "The Witness Protection Program."

Giancana was nodding. "Right, Mike, right. If it's some whacko drugged-out flower people who butchered an innocent family, the government's not to blame. But an Outfit hit, on a protected witness and his family? They'd be over. Done. WITSEC'd never have another player for their new-name-fresh-start game show."

Sinatra was singing "The Look of Love."

Feeling a little numb, Michael asked, "Who killed Mad Sam DeStefano?"

A small shrug, this time. "Just who you think — the Ant and Mario, Mad Sam's own damn brother. Hey, I don't deny framing you for that. Shit runs downhill — I gave you a direct order, and you thumbed your nose at me. What did you fucking expect me to do? Who twisted your arm to be part of Our Thing? Did you or did you not go down this road of your own free will?"

"I did," Michael admitted.

"Well, then. I rest my fucking case." He stood, scooching his chair back, making a tiny chalk-on-the-blackboard screech. "My offer is sincere. Why don't you and your daughter just . . . take a vacation for a while. Mexico went south on me, so to speak, but I still have friends in very nice places — Bahamas, Jamaica — where you and your kid can relax. . . . Let me get my house in order, recuperate a little from this damn surgery — and I'll deal with this Senate thing, and in the meantime, Butch and Chuckie and me'll gather my forces, and if it means taking Aiuppa out, so be it."

"You mean, just watch from afar," Michael said, "and you'll call me in, when the time is right."

A big grin split Giancana's grooved, dark face. "Works for me! . . . I better get back to my sausage and beans. Be a goddamn shame to waste ingredients like them. . . . My daughter Francine brought 'em over today."

Sinatra had stopped singing; the album over.

Some cockiness in his step now, Giancana headed through the dining room and back into the kitchen, Michael right behind him, the .22 at his side.

Giancana returned to the two pans and began stirring the sausage. "A little too brown on the one side, but it's still gonna be nice. . . . You know, Michael, what our problem is? We're too much alike, you and I. Pity we got off to such a bad start."

"It really is," Michael said, and shot him in the back of the head, the silenced pistol's report like a cough.

Giancana jerked, then crumpled to the floor, sprawling on his back. Life flickered in the dark shark-eyes and he was still breathing, so Michael stuck the snout of the silenced weapon in the man's mouth and the pistol coughed again.

No more life in the eyes now, but Michael, lips peeled back over his teeth in something that was not at all a smile, shoved the gun under the gangster's chin and fired again and again and again and again and again.

Giancana, quite dead now, lay on his back with his ankles crossed, right arm crooked at his side, his left hand above his head as if doing a native folk dance. Dark red streamed from the gaping throat wounds, and trails trickled from his nostrils and began to pool beside him on the linoleum.

Michael turned off the stove and slipped out into the garden, shutting the door behind him. He stood under a sky that flashed with heat lightning while the moon painted pale ivory the lovely landscaping, muting the color-splashes of flowers.

He should have fled quickly, but he froze there, a voice in his mind — belonging to, of all people, his wife's sister Betty — saying, *What good would it do? Nothing will bring her back.*

Sam Giancana, the man responsible for Patricia's death, was dead. And nothing had changed. Michael felt only an emptiness. No satisfaction. *What had his father felt, when Connor Looney died?* Heat lightning flashed, as if a coded answer, daring him to figure it out, and he suddenly sensed something.

He looked up at wispy gray clouds and spasms of lightning and a strangely accusatory moon, and he could feel God watching.

And in Sam Giancana's garden, with the dead gangster still bleeding onto a kitchen floor but a few yards away, Michael O'Sullivan, Jr., knelt on the stone patio and prayed, clasping gloved hands, one of which still held the murder gun.

"Forgive me, Father," he said quietly,

but out loud, head unbowed, beseeching the electricity-pulsating sky, "for I have sinned."

Confession over, he got to his feet, and the hell out of there.

And he didn't even realize he was crying until he was back to the car and his daughter said something.

"Are you all right, Daddy?"

"Fine, sweetheart. Fine. Drive. Normal speed."

She drove them through the shady lanes of the residential suburb. The pistol was not in the car with them — he had tossed it in the sewer walking back.

"You're crying, Daddy. Why?"

"Just . . . your mother. Thinking of your mother."

". . . Is he dead, Daddy? The man . . . the man who killed Mom?"

"He is. I killed him, baby."

She was about a block from the residential hotel when she asked, "Do you feel better about it? With him dead? . . . Should *I* feel better?"

That was when he noticed she was crying, too.

13

At first glance, the stone-gray monolith —
somehow simultaneously squat and towering — might have been a government
building, an art deco courthouse from New
Deal days, perhaps. On closer look, the
wildly contradictory geometric overhangs
and vaguely Egyptian columns of the
washed-pebble, poured-concrete study in
cubism suggested something more ethereal
than tax money might buy, even under the
WPA.

This was Unity Temple, the most famous of Oak Park's many churches, Frank
Lloyd Wright's 1906 study in cantilevered
concrete, built to replace the former
temple, which had been hit by lightning in
1905 and burned to the ground, a heavenly
hint the church leaders hadn't taken. Perhaps that explained the lack of a spire,
though Wright claimed to be avoiding
cliché when lightning rod was more like it.

An architectural landmark and tourist
attraction, the cement church at Lake
Street and Kenilworth gave daily informal

tours — nothing too structured from a denomination that defined itself as nondenominational. The last one, on this sunny afternoon in June, had ended at five p.m., fifteen minutes ago — Michael had instructed Associate Director Harold Shore of the Organized Crime and Racketeering Section to take that final tour.

On returning last night from Giancana's house, Michael had called the panic-button number, and said he was ready to come in from the cold — and wanted to meet with Shore, ASAP.

"Where?"

"Chicago."

"Can you be a little more specific, Michael?"

"I will be, after you arrive."

"Then I'll fly out tomorrow — first thing."

"I'll only talk to you and Hughes. Nobody new. Understand, Harry? I spot any backup, I'm vapor."

"Understood."

"Do you have a regular hotel?"

"Usually the Drake. Give me a second, Michael — let me check the plane schedule . . ."

"If you're trying to trace this call, Harry, I'll be annoyed."

"No, no, no. . . . Assuming no airline delays, I'll be at the Drake no later than two-thirty p.m."

"I'll call you there at that time."

And Michael had, giving Shore detailed instructions about meeting him at Unity Temple, including attending the final tour of the day, and lagging behind in the sanctuary.

Now the last visitor had trailed out — actually *around,* because the entrance was behind the structure, which had no doors on the street, another stated avoidance of cliché by the architect, probably in reality an effort to evade nearby El noise.

Across the way, Michael waited and watched another ten minutes, tucked behind some trees next to a church as Gothic as the Wright structure was modern. His post provided him a necessary catercorner view, since that rear entrance could be approached from either side.

As he jaywalked over to the Temple, Michael — in a brown sportjacket, yellow pullover and lighter brown slacks — might have been another tourist, albeit not one with a camera, rather a .45 Colt automatic in a shoulder holster. He followed the sidewalk back to a bank of wood and stained-glass doors — adorned with Wright's usual geometric designs — that joined the two wings of the modernistic monument. He unbuttoned his sportjacket, for easier access to the weapon, as he entered beneath the bold bronze words:

FOR THE WORSHIP OF GOD
AND THE SERVICE OF MAN.

Michael had already thoroughly scoped the building out, and arranged for the use of the auditorium. He'd said (truthfully, as far as it went) that he needed to talk to some gentlemen from the government about the welfare of his daughter, and wished to do so in the privacy of this spiritual, sacred space. Michael's sincerity — and a one-hundred-dollar contribution — convinced the reverend, who would be off having his supper with his family in the parish house.

The low-ceilinged, almost dreary foyer, with typical Prairie-style highbacked wooden chairs, did not provide direct access to the inner church — corridors at left and right led around it, to various entrances . . . apparently Frank Lloyd Wright didn't want worshipers in search of something meaningful finding it too easily. Michael chose left, continuing on a journey that —

from street to sanctuary — took seven turns and a walk equal to twice the building's length.

A short flight of dimly-lit steps rose into the brightness of the sanctuary, a mode of entrance designed to allow latecomers a discreet arrival — not a bad thing for Michael, under the present circumstances. He emerged at the rear of the worship area, a sort of glorified box of cool pastel planes with dark horizontal and vertical wood trim, with room enough for hundreds yet as intimate as a tea room, double tiers of balcony on three sides, and a front-and-center pulpit facing a handful of central pews, four rows divided by an aisle.

In the second pew from the back, seated as per Michael's instructions, were Shore and Hughes, the two feds staring up in awe at the ceiling's grid of wooden beams with countless inset squares of stained-glass skylight. Even in late afternoon, sunshine streamed down, turned amber by the leaded windows, whose geometric shadows made their presence known as well.

Michael slid in behind them. "Gentlemen."

Shore and Hughes slid left and right, respectively, and turned toward their host. Against the brown suit with brown/rust/yellow paisley tie on a tan shirt, bald Shore looked puffy, pale and annoyed, his eyes slitted behind the big heavy frames and buggy lenses. Hughes, on the other hand — in a dark blue suit with blue-and-white polka dot tie against pale blue shirt — seemed detached, the Apache-cheeked, light blue-eyed marshal still taking in the unique architectural surroundings.

His tone both soft and tight, Shore said, "Before we begin, Michael, tell me you didn't hit Sam Giancana last night."

"I did not," Michael said. Lies had been told in churches before. Offhandedly he added, "But I did go see him and talk to him."

Now Michael had Hughes's arched-eyebrow attention, too. "And you *didn't* whack the son of a bitch?" Then the marshal winced, remembering where he was, whispering to Shore, "Sorry."

"I talked to him," Michael said, matter of fact. "Got some interesting information. But I didn't kill him."

Shore sighed heavily, eyes rolling behind the magnifying lenses. "We can't do business if you did. You do understand that, don't you, Michael?"

Their voices echoed somewhat, in the resonant room.

"I understand. But I saw the papers, the

TV, like everybody else — so I know what went down there last night, after I left. You tell me, Harry — would I have shot Mooney with some kind of half-assed silenced weapon . . . what did they find again?"

Hughes said, "A Duromatic .22."

"What," Michael said, "a target pistol?"

Shore nodded. "With a silencer out of shops class. Admittedly not your style."

"That was a *mob* hit," Michael said, with a dismissive shrug. "Would I have shot him, how many times?"

"Six," Shore said, eyes glued to Michael.

"Back of the head, then five times in the jaw, to rip his tongue apart? Outfit symbolism for a squealer, right? What would *I* have done, Harry?"

"Once in the head," Shore said, locking eyes with Michael. "Looking right at him."

"Using what?"

Hughes half-smirked and said, "That .45 of yours."

Michael smiled genially. "Fellas, we see eye to eye on this."

Hughes said, "Giancana's old buddy Butch Blasi was seen in the neighborhood, not long before that caretaker upstairs found the body. Chicago P.D. and FBI both like him for it."

"Butch works for Aiuppa now," Michael said, "but Giancana would've still trusted him. Makes sense."

Shore made a face as if tasting something sour; his usual smiles were nowhere to be seen. "This has Accardo written all over it."

"No argument," Michael said.

Hughes was still taking in the multileveled but simple sanctuary with its tinted glass, natural colors, abstract designs. "Why *this* place?"

"I wanted someplace public," Michael said, "where we could talk in private."

Hughes frowned as he looked around. "Yeah, but what's the deal with this crazyhouse, anyway? What the hell kind of church is this?"

Shore frowned, too — but at Hughes. "Be respectful."

But Michael answered him: "As I understand it, they believe in peace, respect and justice. Hey, you're Justice Department guys. What better place?"

Vaguely irritated with this line of chitchat, Shore said, "It's sort of . . . nondenominational."

"I've made a contribution to the church," Michael said, "so that we can talk without interruption — for at least an hour."

Shore said, "Our business won't take that long. You've convinced me that you had nothing to do with Giancana's murder. And the Outfit scum you encountered at your house in Paradise Estates, and the other two lowlifes at the Cal-Neva parking lot, prom night . . . well, that was clearly self-defense. So WITSEC feels it can welcome you back into the fold, Michael, open arms."

Hughes said, "We're looking at maybe a half a dozen major organized crime trials in the next three years — you'll be valuable to the process. Welcome home."

"And," Shore said, "there'll be no slip-ups, you have my word. You and your daughter will be safe in your new lives. . . . Where is Anna, Michael?"

"She's safe." He let the sarcasm show as he said, "Not as safe as if she were in the protective arms of WITSEC, of course — you guys being so expert at protecting people and all."

Shore's sigh was weight-of-the-world. "I understand your bitterness, Michael. But you are making the right decision, and —"

"You may not like my terms, gents."

Hughes grunted a laugh. "Why? What kind of 'terms' do you have in mind?"

"Well," Michael said, leaning back in the

pew, putting his arms along the back of the bench, enjoying the way the two feds had to twist around to talk to him, "while you *will* be relocating Anna and me, in new lives of our choice . . . I *won't* be testifying."

Shore said, *"What?"*

Hughes laughed harshly and said, "Then why the hell would we want your ass back? If you're not gonna play the game."

"I'll play the game, fellas. But my rules. My conditions."

Shore's eyes were half-lidded behind the glasses. "Which are?"

"You relocate us. Set us up, the full WITSEC boat, to my specs. I don't testify."

"Don't *testify!*" Hughes said, forehead taut.

"Don't testify. But I also don't go public."

Shore frowned, but said nothing; he didn't have to — he got it at once.

But Hughes asked, "Public, what the hell, public?"

"Public about how WITSEC got my wife killed. About how I had to go on the road with my daughter and protect her myself because you people didn't. Or couldn't."

Shore swung around in the seat, facing the empty pulpit, his back to Michael, now. The man lowered his head, covering his face with a hand, an elbow on a knee; but he was not praying.

Hughes, sideways in the pew and still looking back at their recalcitrant witness, said, "Who's gonna believe *you?* You don't think the government isn't capable of denying everything? You haven't heard of disinformation, dipshit?"

Shore looked at Hughes. "Don, shut up." Then he craned back around in the seat and said to Michael, "You have a deal."

Hughes blurted, "Are you *crazy,* Shore? You're gonna let this asshole —"

"Please, Don," Michael said. "It's church, remember? Voice down. Little respect. Please."

Shore in a gravel whisper said to the marshal, "WITSEC won't *last* a 'sec' if what happened to the Satarianos gets in the media. The program will be over. No one will trust us to testify. We'd be the Watergate of law enforcement. Mr. Satariano will . . . I should say Mr. *Smith* will —"

"Actually," Michael said, "I'll be using O'Sullivan."

Unaware of the name's significance, Shore waved that off. "Fine, fine, that's the least of our problems. . . . So are you and Anna prepared to pack your bags and come with us, then?"

"Let's not get ahead of ourselves," Michael said. "You haven't heard the rest of my terms."

Hughes's eyes showed white all around. *"Rest* of your terms? *Jesus!"*

The word echoed in the sanctuary.

Quietly, patiently, resignedly, Shore said, "What else do you want, Michael?"

"First, I need to tell you something, something that you may not believe. It's one reason why I thought a church would be appropriate for this meeting. Anyway. See, I've had what's sometimes called an epiphany."

Hughes frowned. "A what?"

Shore's eyes were closed.

"Something happened, recently — something personal, private, that I don't feel like sharing with you." Because that would have involved telling the truth about killing Sam Giancana. "But let's keep it simple, and just say I'm turning over a new leaf."

Shore shook his head, sighed yet again. As if in pain, he said, "What kind of 'new leaf' would that be, Michael?"

"A long time ago I chose a path . . . a road. Where it led was violence and revenge. And, looking back, I don't think that ever worked out all that well — for me, or anybody. Right here in this sacred place, gentlemen, I'm telling you that I am no longer seeking revenge. I hope never to have to perform another violent act in my life."

Hughes, bitterly amused, said, "Well, glory hallelujah, and goodie for you."

Shore, relieved, flashed Hughes a dark look, then brightened and said, "Well, that's a 'condition' I'm pleased to embrace, Michael. In fact, I'd insist upon it."

"Understand," Michael said, and raised a gently lecturing finger, "I have no moral barrier against self-defense, or protecting my daughter."

"Fine," Shore said, and smiled, more strained than usual. "Who can argue with that? So. Are we done?"

"Almost. Harold, I just need you to take Don here into custody."

Shore started to smile, but then noticed the stricken expression on his marshal's face.

Michael's eyes locked with those haunting sky-blue eyes bookended by Apache cheekbones, and said, "You may not know what 'epiphany' means, Don . . . but you're fucking lucky I had one. Or you'd already be dead."

Hughes swallowed thickly. "What the

fuck are you babbling about? What are you, high?" He swiveled to Shore. "Harry, the guy's fucking nuts, or coked to the gills or some shit — he's talkin' out of his ass!"

Calmly Michael said, "Giancana told me last night that the CIA made a gesture of goodwill to him, partially paying him back for various inconveniences, by giving me up to him. And they did that through somebody in WITSEC, Harry. Some security breach. But really, only you two were in on my family's relocation every step of the way — the program is set up on a 'need to know' basis, right, Don? Very tight. Controlled."

Hughes was shaking his head, smiling, but a sick smile. "Harry, you can't be buying any of this shit. I don't know what he's up to, why's he's doin' this, maybe he believes it, and is so upset by his wife's death that —"

Michael slapped Hughes. Hard. It rang in the high-ceilinged chamber.

"Don't *ever* mention her," Michael said.

Hughes, his cheek blazing red, was trembling — with fear, with rage.

"The tap on Gary Grace's phone," Michael said, calm again, "that's federal; Outfit doesn't tap phones. Telling Giancana's assassins to disguise the hit on my home as a mass murder by mad hippies, who would do that? Someone protecting the Witness Protection Program. Someone inside. Actually, Harry, I thought it might have been you. . . ."

"Only it wasn't me," Shore said quietly, and his eyes were on Hughes, blazing.

"I don't know whether Marshal Hughes was acting out of patriotism," Michael said, "helping out the government's Intel boys, or if an investigation into his finances will reveal recent windfalls. Of course, knowing the CIA, we might be talking Swiss accounts. Even so, an upswing in Don's lifestyle might be apparent if —"

Hughes leaned toward Shore and said, words tumbling, "Come on, Harry, you can't believe this fractured fairy tale, come *on,* man! How long have we worked together?"

Michael said to Shore, "Harry, we can wrap this up, quick . . . with a simple question about Don, here — where does Marshal Hughes work out of?"

"You know the answer to that, Michael," Shore said. "Washington, D.C. We both do."

Michael's gaze moved back to Hughes, whose brow was beaded with sweat, though the sanctuary was cool. "Don, maybe I'm wrong about you."

"I'm telling you, Satariano, you *are* wrong!"

"It's O'Sullivan. Just answer one question. If you work out of D.C., why were you in Tucson the night my wife was murdered? Why were you at the airport, waiting for me?"

The nine millimeter Browning was in Hughes's hand — snatched off his belt holster — in less than a second.

"Don't bother, Don," Michael said. "You're already covered."

And Michael nodded behind and up, to the balcony where Anna pointed the Garand rifle right at the marshal.

"You may remember from the night you helped us move, Don," Michael said, "all those first-place ribbons from the Tahoe Gun Club . . . ?"

The girl held the gun with confidence, sighting down the barrel.

"And if you're thinking," Michael said, "she's just a kid . . . well, you're right. A kid whose mother you killed. And the Grace boy? Her prom date? They got married in Vegas, the night before your Outfit trash murdered him."

Nostrils flaring, cords standing out in his neck, Hughes jumped to his feet, grabbed Shore with his free hand, and thrust the plump, shorter fed in front of him as a shield, nine mil's nose in Shore's neck. The marshal's eyes were moving very fast. Michael could almost read the man's thoughts: *if everyone died here but him, he could find a story, he could find a story the world would* buy. . . .

Michael said evenly, "Don, just put the gun down. I'm sure your buddy Harry, here, will have a nice warm spot in WITSEC for you . . . because I'd rather you lived . . . really, truly. I'd rather you testified and brought down the faceless 'company' assholes whose lackey you are. The people really responsible for Pat's death, cold-blooded CIA renegades in bed with gangsters, self-serving traitors who need to be exposed."

"You don't know the kind of people you're dealing with," Hughes said, with hollow laughter; he was trembling, the nine mil's snout stuffed deep in the fleshy folds of the other fed's neck. "Petty little dago dogshit like you, what do you know? . . . Those boys are the big leagues, and you're outa yours, you stupid son of a bitch. . . ."

"Anna!" Michael said. "I warned you, honey, it might come to this. Sweetheart — got to be a head shot. You can do it. It'll shut off his motor skills like a light switch."

"Okay, Daddy," she called down, and it echoed.

Past a terrified Shore, Hughes looked up with a little fear but mostly arrogance at the teenage girl pointing the rifle at him from the higher of two rear balconies. "You really think I believe —"

The shot sounded like a thunderclap.

Director Shore's eyes and mouth were open wide, as just behind the human shield, Marshal Don Hughes froze for a particle of a moment, just long enough for Michael to see the blankness in the eyes in a skull cracked like an egg by the bullet that had pierced it between, and just above, the sky-blue eyes.

Then Hughes dropped out of sight between pews, hitting the floor noisily, like a bag of door knobs, punctuated by his nine mil clunking to the wooden floor, leaving a stunned Shore just standing there, saved in church.

Michael got to his feet. "You're going to have to deal with the reverend, Harry — Anna and I will be in touch."

Shore's eyes pleaded as he reached out and said, "Michael!"

The director was getting a crash course in the violent realities behind the abstraction of his program.

"You'll be fine, Harry. But I can't be here when the cops come. You've cleaned up crime scenes before. Cheer up — didn't we repair your security breach?"

And Michael slipped out of the sanctuary, where the sunlight was fading, creating an indoor dusk. An ashen Anna was coming down the stairs in a tank top and jeans with the rifle in her hands, clearly shaken.

"I killed him, Daddy," she said.

He took the Garand from her, and wrapped it in his sportcoat (they'd brought the rifle in, field-stripped in a gym bag, and he'd assembled it for her in the balcony).

"Only because you had to, sweetheart. Only because you had to."

Not revenge, he thought. *Justice.*

Weapon tucked under one arm, he slipped the other around her, and they moved quickly down the long corridor.

Her face was white. "I . . . I feel weird."

"Can you hold it in?"

She nodded.

"Good girl," he said, and they were to the car, parked right along the Temple on Kenilworth, before she puked.

14

In their suite at the Oak Arms, Michael and Anna sat at the small '50s-era Formica table in the kitchenette and, over a Coke and a Tab, talked. The night was sultry, humid with rain that desperately wanted to happen, the window open, two layers of drapes fluttering — the bedroom had an air conditioner, which was on and chugging mightily, but its efforts never made their way into the tiny living room/kitchenette.

"You're going to be okay," he told her gently.

She sat slumped, staring at the gray speckles of the table top. "I know I am. But I feel . . . guilty . . ."

"That's to be expected."

". . . about *not* feeling guilty." She looked up at him. "I could hear everything in that church, Daddy. I heard what you said to them about that . . . that Giancana . . ."

"I had to lie, sugar. We need Director Shore and what he can do for us through WITSEC. My only other option is to go back to work for the Outfit."

Her brow tightened. "They'd *take* you back?"

He nodded. "I did a big favor for Tony Accardo, removing Mooney Giancana. And Accardo knows we were victims in this thing, from the start. He's like Frank Nitti — best man in a bad world." He shook his head. "But, honey, that's not what I want for us."

"You did kill that man, though — Giancana. You shot him over and over, the papers say. Was that . . . to make it look like some . . . Mafia thing?"

He could have lied to her; but instead he said, "No. I used that to convince Shore I hadn't done it, but no, baby. I was over the edge — way over, thinking of what they did to Mom. It was pure rage. Normally, I'm . . . cool. That's how it is in war. But not last night, not killing that creature. The expression — seeing red? I saw it. Nothing but red. Blood red."

Her eyes were on him, now. She nodded and sipped the glass of Tab on ice (he was drinking from a can), and stared at the gray table flecks again. "I killed him as much as you did."

"No."

"Wouldn't the law think so?"

"Yes."

"I don't care. I'm glad he's dead. I don't think I could have done what you did, but . . . maybe I could. But I was . . . like you said? Cool, cold. In the church? I just aimed at that marshal, that fucking bastard, and . . ." She covered her face; her eyes were shut. She was not crying.

He reached for her left hand, took it, squeezed it, then held it. "That was not murder, sweetheart. I saw that animal's eyes — he was about to kill me, and Director Shore, and if the reverend of that church had come running in, followed by a class of Sunday school kids, Hughes would've shot them, too. Feeling a lot less than you're feeling."

"So what I did . . . it was like, self-defense?"

"Survival."

"Anyway, I'm glad he's dead, too. Gary died because of that fucker. Mom, too. I could do it again."

He squeezed her hand. "But you won't. Honey, my father did not want me to go down his road. He wanted more than anything in this world that I would not turn out like him — but I did."

"*Because* of him?"

He shrugged. "Well, sure . . . on some level. But *I* made the choice. We have to choose where we're headed, baby, and carefully."

She formed a half-smile, fully wry. "It's not like we have a lot of options."

"No." He smiled, just a little. "But Director Shore will help. You want to go back to school, don't you? Get back in theater?"

Her laugh was short yet hollow. "I don't know. It seems so . . . abstract now. I feel removed from it, distant, detached. . . . Have I gone dead inside?"

Patting her hand, he said, "No, baby, you're just protecting yourself. . . . Hey, it's over; we've woken from the nightmare."

Her eyes and forehead were tight. "Are you sure, Daddy?"

"We'll always have to be careful in a way most people aren't. What I'm asking you to do is join up with your life again, your goals, your dreams."

Her eyes looked past him, at nothing. "My dreams had Gary in them."

"I know. And my dreams had your mother in them. But we have to go on, anyway. I know you don't want to hear this, but you're wrong — you will fall in love again."

She shook her head, her expression blank. "But I won't."

"You won't stop loving Gary, ever — but

you will find someone else."

She didn't argue. Her expression turned quizzical. "What about you, Daddy? Think you'll find someone else?"

". . . No. No, sweetheart, your mother was the only woman I ever really loved. That's a road I won't go down again. I had many wonderful years with her, and with my family, and that part of me is . . . satisfied." He shifted in the chair. "And that's one thing I wanted to talk to you about, darling . . . it's something I've been thinking about, a lot, but I'm afraid I'm just being foolish. Or maybe gone crazy."

Now she squeezed his hand. "What, Daddy?"

What the hell. He just said it: "How would you feel about going back to school — together?"

The immediate response was amusement, but she caught herself, and said, "You want to go to college?"

He couldn't look at her. "Well . . . actually, that's a string I need pulled for me, but Director Shore has managed bigger miracles. See, I took junior-college night classes, oh, twenty years ago, getting a two-year business degree."

She regarded him with one eyebrow arched. "And you want to finish?"

"No . . . no. I'm going to ask Shore to turn Michael O'Sullivan, Jr., into a college graduate. So that I can go on to seminary."

Her expression froze. ". . . Seminary."

"Yeah."

"You want to be a . . . priest?"

He shrugged, still couldn't look at her. "A lot of priests were married, once. Widowers who wanted to take another path."

She leaned toward him, smiling gently. "You want to go from bullets to Eucharists? You're joking, right? . . . You're *not* joking, are you?"

"No." Now, finally, he committed his eyes to hers. "I haven't had some mystical experience, honey; Jesus didn't come talking to me in the night or anything. But I was raised in the Catholic Church, it's a tradition that comforts me. And it's a world where I can make up for . . . things I've done. I can find some kind of redemption, and I can help others."

She wasn't smiling now. "Do you even believe in God?"

"I do. Your mother didn't. But I do."

Again she smirked. "Well, I sure as hell don't. Not anymore."

"I can't blame you. But, just the same, I'm asking you to respect my decision."

"I don't know, Daddy. . . ."

"Will you try? Will you at least try?"

She swallowed. Her brow tightened.

"What I'm hoping is," he said, trying not to sound desperate, "we can find some college somewhere, some university, where you can study in the arts while I'm taking the seminary. Small apartment, live together. Maybe not a college girl's dream, but —"

Her smile was back. "But for the next few years, Father O'Sullivan, the fighting priest, wants to make sure no Mafiosi come out of the closet to kill his baby's butt. Or his own holy heinie?"

". . . Does it sound so very absurd to you?"

Nodding, she said, "Frankly, Daddy, yes, it does."

"But will you try to accept it?"

She sighed.

Thought for a while.

Finally said, "If you don't come to your senses, in the days and weeks and months ahead? Sure. I can learn to stop calling you 'Daddy' and start calling you 'Father.' If I really, really have to."

He leaned over and kissed her cheek. "You'll always be my best girl."

"Don't tell the Virgin Mary."

They would leave the next morning.

Michael had in mind flying to Hawaii and spending a couple of weeks on the beach, giving Anna some genuine vacation time, really getting away while Director Shore put their house in order. His daughter certainly had no objection to that, and they went across the street for Chinese, then returned to watch a little television. Early on in Johnny Carson, Anna got sleepy, kissed her father's forehead, padded into the bedroom yawning, leaving the uncomfortable couch all to him

He didn't make it through Carson, either, and stripped to his underwear and pulled out the bed and climbed between the sheets; he was so exhausted, physically, mentally and emotionally, that even the paper-thin mattress and cruel springs did not keep him from dropping off almost instantly.

He dreamed of his son. Mike was in full battle gear, but he was sitting at that kitchenette table with them, listening to Anna and Michael conduct a somewhat garbled version of their real conversation. Mike just listened politely, his helmet on the Formica table; then finally he said, "Dad — sis! I'm here. I'm still here — why don't you *talk* to me?*"*

Then Mike said, "Wake up, you cocksucker," a harsh whisper, but it wasn't

Mike, and something cold was in his neck.

The snout of a gun, a revolver's nose.

His eyes shot open and his right hand made a break for the end table where the .45 was, or rather had been, because his fingers found nothing but wood for his nails to scrape, and the voice whispered, "It isn't there, asshole."

The intruder, keeping the gun in Michael's neck, sat on the edge of the sleeper, making the springs creak and whine, and, still sotto voce, said, "Just be quiet. I don't want to have to do sleeping beauty, too, in the other room. She don't deserve what you're gonna get, you fucking prick."

The curtains were back to let air in the open window, so streetlamps bouncing off alley brick sent in enough illumination for Michael to take stock of his guest. This was a young man — probably around his son Mike's age — who Michael did not recognize, though he made him as an Italian kid, from the dark complexion and eyes, the dark curly hair worn shoulder-length, and a Roman nose too big for his young Dino-ish face. The black leather jacket and black jeans fit the profile, too, as did the gold chain around the neck.

"Then fucking kill me," Michael whispered, "and go."

The kid shook his head; he was grinning and cocky, but it was a front — this boy was nervous, and his dark eyes were glistening. If that .38 nose weren't buried in his neck, Michael could have easily done something about this. . . .

"You don't get off so fuckin' easy, old man. It ain't enough for you to just fucking die."

"Sure it is. Squeeze the trigger and run."

He shook his head and drops of sweat traveled. "No, no, no — you gotta know, you gotta *know* who did this to your evil ass. Why he . . . *I* . . . did this!"

The kid was getting tripped up in his own melodrama.

"Okay, son, I'll bite — who are you?"

Teeth were bared in the almost-handsome face like a wolf getting ready for a meal. With exaggerated, stupid deliberation, he said, "You are looking at Sam DeStef-*ano*."

Michael frowned. "The hell . . ."

Kid smacked his chest with a fist made from his free hand. "Antonio DeStefano — Little Sam, they call me. Sam was my *uncle*. And you fucking killed him, you rat fuck bastard . . ."

"Step away!"

Goddamnit! Just what Michael feared. . . .

The door had swung open without either him or Little Sam seeing, and framed there in a pink-and-blue floral nightshirt that ended at her knees, nipples perking the cotton accusingly, hair an endless dark tangle, stood tight-jawed Anna with the long-barreled .38 in her two clutching, aiming hands — the Smith & Wesson that Michael had plucked from the belt of Inoglia, her mother's murderer, back in Arizona.

If the kid had known what the hell he was doing, he would have fired the gun in Michael's neck, then swung it around and used the shock of the moment to blow the girl away, too.

But the kid was, well, a kid, inexperienced, afraid, in way too deep here, and reflexively jerked away, scrambling to his feet, lurching from the bed to thrust the gun toward Anna.

Thank God neither fired!

The two children weren't three feet away from each other, now — the weapons aimed at each other's young faces.

"Back away, bitch," Little Sam snapped. "This isn't your fight!"

"Not yours, either," she said coldly.

Michael eased out of bed and positioned himself alongside them, a referee trying to break up a fight on a basketball court. He was so close to them both he could hear Anna's slow steady breathing and the boy's heavy, ragged variation; but these kids were facing each other and to throw himself between them risked a stray bullet finding Anna, even making its way through her father's body into hers.

"Anna," Michael said, "don't do anything. Antonio, you have to listen to me."

Through clenched teeth, the wild-eyed kid said, "*Fuck* I do!," the mane of curly black hair catching the alley light in a shimmer, a side effect of how bad the boy was shaking.

"Son . . ."

"Don't *call* me that!"

Michael raised two surrendering palms. "Mr. DeStefano, I know all about family loyalty. And can give chapter and verse on revenge. I could tell you it's a dead end and you'd never believe me . . ."

"Shut the fuck *up!*"

". . . but you need to know a couple of things before you take this any further, starting with I didn't kill your uncle. Sam Giancana did."

The kid shook his head and sweat flecks flew. "You're a liar! You're a goddamn *liar!*"

His voice as calm as young Sam's wasn't, Michael said, "You are looking at the two people who killed Giancana, just last night — because my daughter lost her husband, and she and I lost her mother, when Giancana framed me for killing your uncle, and the DeStefano crew came looking for us."

He shook his head, a dozen spastic times. "You're *not* telling the *truth!* Why should I *listen* to this shit . . . ?"

"Because you're about to lose your life, or maybe take a life or two, for the *wrong* reason. The man who killed Mad Sam DeStefano was Spilotro — the Ant? I'm sure you know that charmer, and he did it for himself and for Giancana."

". . . the fuck, you say."

"I can prove it."

"*Fuck* you can!"

"You followed us here from the Temple, right?"

"What if I did!"

"Because a bent marshal dropped the dime. Guy named Hughes . . . only he's dead now."

The boy's eyes somehow got wilder. "Who says he's dead! And so *what* if he told me!"

Patting the air, just a little, Michael said

reasonably, "I knew that, only because I also knew this same bent cop sicced your DeStefano guys — and some Giancana crew, too — on me and my family. It was part of the same damn frame."

Spittle flitted. "Talk till you're fuckin' *blue,* you still killed my uncle!"

"Are you Mario's boy?"

"No! He's my *other* uncle . . ."

"Mario was in it with Spilotro."

Little Sam seemed about to cry, the gun trembling in his hand, but still pointed right at Anna's face. ". . . why should I believe *you?* You wanna send me off to kill somebody *else?* What kinda putz do you *take* me for?"

Anna said, "Is that a trick question?"

"Shut-up, bitch!"

"Anna . . . please. . . . Antonio, I am not suggesting you go after your uncle and that crazy asshole Spilotro . . . you'll *really* get yourself killed, then. But you need to know who you're defending. Your father was Angelo, right?"

His chin quivered; his eyes were moving side to side. "What, what are you bringing up that ancient hist—"

"You never really knew him, though. Your father. He's been gone a long time."

Little Sam's voice seemed small, now,

though the gun remained big enough. "What does that have to do with shit?"

"Did you know he was a drug addict?"

The voice grew large, again. "What the fuck *business* is that of *yours!* You are *so* going down. . . ."

"You must have been told that your father was murdered."

". . . that, that, that's the kind of business we're *in,* Satariano. You know that!"

"What you don't know is, your beloved Uncle Sam? The man everybody but *you* called 'Mad Sam'? . . . killed your father. And everybody but you knows it."

Little Sam's face whitened and his eyes grew big. But the voice was back to small. ". . . you're lying. That's crazy. You're lyin', that's crazy horseshit . . ."

"Everybody knows Sam was ashamed of Angelo — considered him an embarrassment, a burden. Mad Sam stabbed your father to death, in a car, and then he took him somewhere and washed him clean. Your uncle bragged about it. Told people he wanted to make sure his brother went to heaven with a clean soul. That's why your father was found the way he was — naked . . . dead . . . freshly bathed. In the trunk of a car, right?"

Little Sam was shaking, head to foot, in-

cluding the .38 in his grasp. ". . . my uncle
. . . my uncle wouldn't . . ."

"How well did you know your uncle,
son? Did you ever see his private workshop? With the ice picks? What kind of life
advice did he give you? Do unto others?
Fuck them before they can fuck you,
maybe?"

The boy swallowed; he was breathing
very hard now, tears streaming down his
face in glistening ribbons. He began to
hunch over, the revolver limp in his hand.

"I'm going to take that, son," Michael
said, stepping forward, holding his hand
out for the gun.

"You'll . . . you'll shoot me . . . you'll . . .
shoot my ass . . ."

But the boy allowed Michael to take the
revolver from him, and Michael said, "No,
Antonio, I won't shoot you. Anna, put that
gun down. Get our guest a glass of water,
would you?"

She looked at her father as if he were
crazy, but the unspoken "Huh?" did not
come out.

"Anna? Please?"

Into the kitchenette she went, smirking
and shaking her head, but obviously relieved, though her definition of putting the
gun "down" was aiming it at the floor, and

not setting it anywhere. She switched a light on.

The boy dropped to his knees. Hung his head. He was crying.

"Forgive me," Antonio said. "Forgive me."

Michael put his hand on the boy's shoulder, then he knelt beside him.

"Only God can do that, son."

"I'm sorry . . . I'm sorry . . . God forgive me."

"He will," Michael said. "Pray to Him . . . right now, pray to Him. And ask. Just ask."

Antonio snuffled snot and nodded, black locks of hair shimmering in the dim light, and clasped his hands and began to pray, silently, while Michael squeezed the boy's shoulder, his own head bowed, too.

Knowing that this time, finally, he'd made the right choice.

ROAD TIPS

This novel follows *Road to Purgatory* (2004), the prose sequel to my graphic novel, *Road to Perdition* (1998), on which the Sam Mendes film of 2002 was based, starring Tom Hanks, Paul Newman, Jude Law, Tyler Hoechlin and Stanley Tucci. To coincide with the release of that film, I also wrote a novel version of *Road to Perdition* based on my original work as illustrated by Richard Piers Rayner (and David Self's screenplay adaptation); unfortunately, the book was published in severely truncated form, and my hope remains that the full text will eventually be published.

Nevertheless, this completes the "Road" trilogy, although sharp-eyed readers will note certain loose ends that may some day lead to another novel. A second graphic novel, *Road to Perdition 2: On the Road* (2004), indicates my continuing interest in these characters, and the O'Sullivan family saga as it intertwines with organized crime in twentiethth-century America.

Despite extensive speculation, supposition and fabrication, this novel does have a basis in history. Many real-life figures appear under their own names, including crime figures Sam Giancana, Tony Accardo and Sam DeStefano. Other characters are either wholly fictional — despite his real uncle, Little Sam DeStefano is an imagined character, as is Marshal Donald Hughes — or fictional ones with real-life counterparts, such as lawyer Sidney Horshak and WITSEC Associate Director Harold Shore.

The major liberty taken here is time compression, with events that took place between April 1973 and June 1975 telescoped into a few months. As much as I pride myself on accuracy, the play remains the thing, and I make no apology for the "1973" of this novel containing elements of all three years, including pop culture and sociological references.

My first two novels, written while I was still attending the Writers Workshop at the University of Iowa, were published in 1973; they had to do with a fifty-year-old bank robber on the run from his former mob bosses (so much for progress). Having written twenty-five or more historical crime novels, I found it sobering to be writing "historical" fiction set within my own career; also, had I known I'd be writing about the mid-'70s, I'd have paid more attention. Among the works that helped refresh my memory were the extensive booklet included with *Have a Nice Decade: The '70s Pop Culture Box* (Rhino Records); *Stuck in the Seventies* (1995), Scott Matthews, Jay Kerness, Tamara Nikuradse, Jay Steele and Greg White; and *Rolling Stone: The Seventies* (1998), edited by Ashley Kahn, Holly George-Warren and Shawn Dahl. Homes depicted herein were influenced by the massive, lavishly illustrated (and dead serious) *The House Book* (1974), Terence Conran; and the hysterically funny *Interior Desecrations* (2004), James Lileks.

Joining in this effort in reluctant nostalgia was my longtime research partner, George Hagenauer. George focused on Chicago crime, as usual, and was especially helpful on the Witness Protection Program, leading me to two key books: *The Alias Program* (1977), Fred Graham; and *WITSEC: Inside the Federal Witness Protection Program* (2002), Peter Earley and Gerald Shur (WITSEC founder). I also consulted *On the Run: A Mafia Childhood* (2004), Gregg and Gina Hill.

Cal-Neva is of course a real casino and

resort, and the backstory comes from research, though Michael Satariano's tenure is heavily fictionalized and is in no way meant to negatively reflect on this landmark slice of Americana, still going strong. Books consulted on Cal-Neva and Lake Tahoe included: *Tales of Tahoe* (1969), David J. Stollery, Jr.; *Wood Chips to Game Chips: Casinos and People at North Lake Tahoe* (1985; 1999), Bethel Holmes Van Tassel; and *The Last Good Time* (2003), Jonathan Van Meter, the story of Skinny D'Amato, who ran gambling at Cal-Neva in the Sinatra '60s.

Although Frank Sinatra is not an on-stage character in this novel, his stormy history with Cal-Neva made it inevitable that much about the resort would be found in such books as: *All or Nothing at All: A Life of Frank Sinatra* (1997), Donald Clarke; *Frank Sinatra: My Father* (1985), Nancy Sinatra; *His Way: The Unauthorized Biography of Frank Sinatra* (1986), Kitty Kelley; *Mr. S: My Life with Frank Sinatra* (2003), George Jacobs and William Stadiem; and *Rat Pack Confidential* (1998), Shawn Levy. I thank all of these authors, and apologize to Nancy for listing her with Kitty.

Though the John Looney aspect of this

novel is minor compared to the previous *Road* trips, I would again like to acknowledge Rock Island historian BJ Elsner for both her invaluable book *Rock Island: Yesterday, Today & Tomorrow* (1988), and her friendship. Also, my *CSI* associate Matthew V. Clemens helped me on Vegas questions.

Several books by the late FBI agent William F. Roemer, Jr., were key, including *Accardo: the Genuine Godfather* (1995); *The Enforcer — Spilotro: The Chicago Mob's Man Over Las Vegas* (1994); and *Roemer: Man Against the Mob* (1989).

Gus Russo's *The Outfit* (2001) is an excellent, detailed overview of the Chicago mob, and helped bring me out of the Capone/Nitti years, with which I'm so familiar, into the latter half of the twentieth century. The best book on Sam Giancana remains *The Don: The Life and Death of Sam Giancana* (1977), William Brashler, and I'm indebted. But helpful, too, were *Double Cross* (1992), Sam and Chuck Giancana; and *Mafia Princess: Growing Up in Sam Giancana's Family* (1984), Antoinette Giancana and Thomas C. Renner. Richard Lindberg's *Return to the Scene of the Crime* (1999) and *Return Again to the Scene of the Crime* (1999) are essential

Chicago illustrated criminal histories, the Giancana and DeStefano entries critical to this novel. Key to understanding the interworkings of the mob-influenced gambling business was *Casino: Love and Honor in Las Vegas* (1995), Nicolas Pileggi. Other useful organized-crime books included *The Last Mafioso* (1981), Ovid DeMaris; and *The Mafia Encyclopedia* (1987), Carl Sifakis.

Chicago references consulted included *Chicago on Foot: Walking Tours of Chicago's Architecture* (1977), Ira J. Bach; and *Architecture 3: Frank Lloyd Wright* (1998), Robert McCarter (Unity Temple section only). The updated '60s and '70s editions of the WPA guides for California, Arizona and Illinois were also helpful, as was the picture book *Arizona* (1978), David Muench and Barry Goldwater.

The handling of notification of an M.I.A during Vietnam was derived chiefly from the excellent *Vietnam: Angel of Death* (2002), Harry Spiller.

Various Internet sites provided vintage Tahoe photographs, details on criminals, geography, Vietnam, buildings, school colors, the 1970s and even Sam Giancana's final recipe; thank you to scores of cyber scholars and enthusiasts.

I would like especially to thank and acknowledge my editor, Sarah Durand, not just for her intelligent and helpful editing, but her understanding and support when real life intruded on the writing of this book. Also, I would again like to thank Trish Lande Grader, who saw potential in my proposal for prose sequels to *Road to Perdition*.

I am, as always, grateful to my friend and agent, Dominick Abel, who recognized movie potential in *Road to Perdition*; and to entertainment lawyer Ken Levin.

Right to the end of the road, my co-pilot Barbara Collins — wife, friend, collaborator — was with me for every twist and turn. More than any novel I've ever written, this one benefitted from Barb's suggestions and her ability to know when to be sounding board, and when to be editor; also, she attended college in Tucson in the late '60s, and shared memories of the campus and the town. My son, Nathan, and my late father, Max Allan Collins, Sr., inspired this trilogy, and my love and thanks to them both.

ABOUT THE AUTHOR

MAX ALLAN COLLINS was hailed in 2004 by *Publishers Weekly* as "a new breed of writer." A frequent Mystery Writers of America "Edgar" nominee, he has earned an unprecedented fourteen Private Eye Writers of America Shamus nominations for his historical thrillers, winning for his Nathan Heller novels *True Detective* (1983) and *Stolen Away* (1991).

His graphic novel *Road to Perdition* is the basis of the Academy Award–winning film starring Tom Hanks, directed by Sam Mendes. His many comics credits include *Dick Tracy*; his own *Ms. Tree*; *Batman*; and *CSI: Crime Scene Investigation*, based on the hit TV series for which he has also written video games, jigsaw puzzles, and a *USA Today* bestselling series of novels.

An independent filmmaker in the Midwest, he wrote and directed the Lifetime movie *Mommy* (1996) and a 1997 sequel, *Mommy's Day*. He wrote *The Expert*, a 1995 HBO World Premiere, and wrote and directed the innovative made-for-DVD feature *Real Time: Siege at Lucas Street Market* (2000). *Shades of Noir* (2004), an anthology of his short films, includes his award-winning documentary *Mike Hammer's Mickey Spillane*.

His other credits include film criticism, short fiction, songwriting, trading-card sets and movie/TV tie-in novels, including the *New York Times* bestseller *Saving Private Ryan*.

Collins lives in Muscatine, Iowa, with his wife, writer Barbara Collins; their son, Nathan, graduated with honors in 2005 with majors in computer science and Japanese at the University of Iowa in nearby Iowa City.

PN